BLESSED WITH LOVE

The Sisters of Rosefield Book 6

EMMA EASTER

Blessed With Love
by Emma Easter

Paperback Edition

CKN Christian Publishing
An Imprint of Wolfpack Publishing

6032 Wheat Penny Avenue
Las Vegas, NV 89122

This book is a work of fiction. Any references to historical events, real people or real places are used fictitiously. Other names, characters, places and events are products of the author's imagination, and any resemblance to actual events, places or persons, living or dead, is entirely coincidental.

Paperback ISBN:978-1-64734-173-2
Ebook ISBN: 978-1-64119-885-1
Library of Congress Control Number: 2020936942

BLESSED WITH LOVE

The Sisters of Rosefield Book 6

To my devoted readers who made this book series a reality.

ONE

Trisha stooped down and kissed Molly on her chubby cheeks. She straightened again and smiled tenderly at her younger daughter. Molly looked just like her older sister, Ruby, and acted like her too. They had both been a handful today. Trisha loved how they were always exuberant and full of life. They had played hard, but, thankfully, were finally asleep.

Ruby, gregarious and mischievous, had been the first one to pass out from gleeful exhaustion. Molly, who followed her sister about and copied everything she did, had fallen asleep soon after. Frank had put her to bed and read her a bedtime story.

Trisha smiled with relief as she looked at Molly. Finally, after a long day, she could climb into bed beside Frank and they could cuddle together before they both fell asleep.

She switched Molly's bedroom light off and headed toward the room she shared with Frank. Just before she opened the door to their bedroom, the doorbell rang.

Trisha frowned. She glanced at her wristwatch and saw it was some minutes past ten o'clock. Who could be visiting at this time without calling first?

She sighed wearily and turned around. Quickly making her way to the living room, she opened the front door. And then her eyes grew wide with astonishment. She screamed and gathered Sienna into a tight hug. She pulled back from Sienna and stared at her sister in disbelief.

Chuckling, she asked, "What on earth are you doing here?" She looked behind Sienna and saw Bryan with Ethan in his arms. Shaking her head in surprise, she hugged Bryan and kissed Ethan on his cheeks. She stepped back again, looked at Bryan, and giggled. "What are you both doing here? Shouldn't you still be in Peru?"

Sienna laughed and said, "Shouldn't you be letting us into the house, Trish? It's late."

Trisha looked down at their travelling bags on the ground. She picked up one of the bags with her left hand and lifted Ethan out of Frank's arms with her right. Carrying the bag and Ethan into the living room, she smiled at her little nephew.

Sienna and Bryan followed her in.

She sat on the couch and settled Ethan, who was half-asleep, onto her lap. Sienna came and sat next to her while Bryan sat on the sofa facing them. Trisha looked at them and grinned, still in disbelief. How had they kept their coming to America a secret? She looked down at Ethan and ran her fingers gently through his hair. He'd gotten so big. She couldn't hold back her surprise anymore and said, "You guys, you didn't tell me, or anyone for that matter, that you were coming. How did you keep it a secret?"

Sienna chuckled and Bryan smiled.

"We wanted to surprise everyone, so we simply told no one that we were coming," Sienna said.

A sliver of worry ran through Trisha. Was something wrong with their ministry in Peru?

She shared her concern with both of them, but Bryan shook his head quickly. "Everything is fine," he said. "Though we both have news to share with everyone."

Trisha studied their faces and her worry increased. "There is something wrong, isn't there?"

"Nothing is wrong, Trish," Sienna said. "It's just that we have some news to share."

"What news?" Trisha asked curiously.

"We will tell everyone once Audrey and Ken come to Rosefield," Bryan answered.

"By the way, when will that be?" Sienna asked.

"They will probably be here before the end of the week," Trisha said. She reached out and hugged Sienna again, thrilled that she was here. She hadn't seen Sienna in over a year. She had spoken to her and Bryan, and even baby Ethan, on the phone and chatted with them on video calls numerous times, but she had yearned to physically see them; to hug her sister and hold her nephew. She drew back from Sienna and said, "I'm so glad you guys are here. I am glad I've finally met Ethan." She gently caressed Ethan's cheek.

Sienna said, "I've been thinking about something."

"What is it?" Trisha asked.

"You know it will be Mom and Dad's fortieth wedding anniversary soon. I've been thinking we should do something special for them. I am not yet sure what, though."

Trisha raised her brows. "I've been thinking about bringing up the idea of doing something for their anniversary as well, but because we are all in different places, and knowing how emotional it will make us, I wasn't sure when or if I should even bring up the idea. But since you are here now and Audrey will soon arrive in Rosefield, maybe we can think of something really special to mark the occasion." She smiled widely and said, "Do you have any ideas about what we should do? I haven't been able to come up with anything yet."

"I haven't, either," Sienna answered. "But since Bryan and I have a long leave of absence and a long vacation this time, we will be here. Hopefully, when Audrey arrives, we can all put our heads together and come up with something to mark their fortieth anniversary."

"It has to be something really special and meaningful," Trisha told her.

"Yes, it definitely has to be," Sienna replied.

Trisha nodded and changed the subject. They talked about Bryan and Sienna's ministry in Peru; about the orphanage and the new church they had planted there. Bryan told Trisha about the unique challenges they were facing running an orphanage, pastoring a church, and also traveling to different parts of Peru, holding evangelistic outreaches and programs. "It is hard, but quite rewarding," he said.

Soon, they switched topics again.

"I can't wait to see Esther again," Sienna said and smiled down at Ethan still sleeping in Trisha's arms. "It's been a year and a half since Audrey and Ken adopted her and I miss that girl."

Trisha beamed. "Esther is precious. She has won the hearts of everyone in Rosefield."

Sienna smiled. "I'm so glad the adoption process went smoothly and Audrey and Ken were able to adopt her in just a few months."

Trisha sighed and said, "Audrey and Ken love that girl, but they want another child. They have been trying to get pregnant but haven't been able to. Audrey has wanted a baby since she and Ken got married. The fact that they still don't have one has been very hard for them, especially Audrey. Because of that, she has been feeling really gloomy these days. I don't know if she has told you how she feels."

"Whenever we talk on the phone, she does tell me how discouraged she is," Sienna said. "I think we might need to go on another trip to get her out of her funk so she isn't constantly thinking about her inability to have a baby now."

Trisha perked up. "I think that will be a good idea. Maybe we can also use that trip to mark Mom and Dad's anniversary. What better way to celebrate their fortieth than a family trip? You know how they always dreamt of taking us all on vacations abroad but were never able to."

"I know," Sienna said. "Of course, Dad could have used his inheritance if he hadn't abhorred it and his father so much."

Trisha smiled sadly. "That is true."

"Anyway, it has to be not just a luxury vacation, but a trip that will be truly meaningful," Sienna said. She turned to look at Bryan and Trisha's eyes went to him as well. He had been quiet for some time now. His head was against the sofa and his eyes were closed. He was already asleep.

Sienna yawned and said, "Trish, I think I will go to bed now. I'm really tired after the long trip and both my boys are already sleeping."

Trisha nodded and stood up with Ethan in her arms.

Sienna walked over to Bryan, slowly ran her fingers through his hair to wake him up, and then smiled when he opened his eyes. "Let's go to bed, baby," she said to him.

As they walked to one of the guest rooms with Trisha leading the way, she talked to Sienna about Faizan and the last time she had spoken to him. "You know Zainah is pregnant now," Trisha said.

"I know," Sienna said with an expression of longing on her face. "Audrey told me. I wish I could speak to Faizan on the phone again. I cannot remember the last time I did. At least you and Audrey get to speak with him whenever Ken is able to reach him."

"You know it is very hard to reach him. Actually, I also haven't spoken to him in months."

"I wish we could go and see him and Zainah," Sienna said wistfully.

They reached the end of the hallway and Trisha opened the door to the guest room. She remembered clearly the last time the guest room had been used — by Sienna and Bryan, actually. They had arrived days before Faizan and Zainah were supposed to get married; before Zainah left for Africa and Faizan went after her fully knowing he would not be able to come back to the United States if he did.

Trisha switched on the light and Sienna and Bryan walked into the room. "Let me go and get the cot Ruby used when she was about Ethan's age," she said. She handed Ethan to Sienna and left the room quickly. She went upstairs into the small storeroom where knick-knacks and lots of small discarded furniture were kept. She carried the cot out to Sienna and Bryan's room and placed it beside the king-sized bed Sienna and Bryan would be sleeping on.

Bryan was already stretched out on the bed with his eyes closed, while Sienna slowly walked around the room holding Ethan and singing softly. Trisha left the room again to get clean sheets for the cot. She got one from her bedroom and quickly went back to Sienna and Bryan's. After making Ethan's bed, Sienna gently laid him in it and then bent down to plant a kiss on his cheek.

Trisha said, "You guys really surprised me. Frank will be astonished when he wakes up tomorrow and sees you and Bryan here. I won't tell him anything. I'll just let him walk in to you guys." Trisha chuckled. "So, Audrey doesn't know that you and Bryan are here?"

"No, she doesn't. We spoke on the phone a few days ago, but I didn't tell her." Sienna began to shed her jeans and top. She put on a peach lacy nightgown, reached out and hugged Trisha again. Stepping back, she said, "I've missed you so much, Trish, and I have missed Rosefield. I'm so glad I'm here."

Trisha squeezed her hand and said, "I am glad you are here, too." She smiled once more and said, "Let me let you guys sleep. We will catch up some more tomorrow." She stepped out of the room and slowly closed the door behind her. Walking to the living room, she sat on the sofa and smiled. But soon she frowned as she remembered what Sienna had said about having some news to share. Sienna had said it was not bad news, but Trisha was slightly worried. So much had happened in the past year and the last thing she needed was bad news. However, she was excited about the prospect of marking their parents' anniversary with a family trip. She was excited, but slightly somber.

She stood up once more and walked to her bedroom. As she climbed into bed beside Frank, she smiled again. The most important thing was that they were all going to be together soon ... well, except for Faizan. She had not seen Audrey in months now. Since Audrey adopted Esther, her older sister had understandably reduced the amount of times she came to Rosefield.

"I miss you so much, Mom and Dad," she whispered, her heart flooding with sadness. She sighed and finally brushed away her gloominess. Their upcoming anniversary was a time to celebrate, not mourn. She soon fell fast asleep, her dreams filled with exciting ideas for the trip.

*****

Ken bent down in front of Esther and searched his daughter's eyes. His heart burned. She looked so sad. He took her hand. Since they'd adopted her from Peru and brought her to America about a year and a half ago, he and Audrey had never been away from her. Once Audrey had quit her job to concentrate on raising Esther and try to get pregnant about a year ago, they'd mostly stopped going to Rosefield, choosing to stay in Miami so Esther could attend school regularly. They had only been to Rosefield twice since she was adopted and that was only for a few days.

Ken smiled sadly at Esther. Now that he had a long vacation, he and Audrey planned to go to Rosefield and surprise her sisters and their spouses with the good news they had for them. Unfortunately, Esther could not come along as school was still in session and they were planning to go on vacation to somewhere Esther couldn't go.

Esther hugged Ken fiercely, drew back again, and held Audrey's hand. "Why can't I go with you?" she asked in English. She usually spoke both English and Spanish to them now. She had been learning English in school since she'd arrived in the United States. Ken and Audrey also spoke English to her at home. Now, she spoke English almost as fluently as Spanish.

Audrey hugged her. When Esther began to cry, tears ran down Audrey's cheeks.

Ken pressed his lips together and said, "You won't be able to come with us to where we are going." He looked up at his mother, who had come to Miami a few days ago to take Esther to Boise with her. "Grandma will take good care of you, I promise."

Esther nodded and wiped her tears away, and Ken sighed in relief. She had spent some time with his parents when they went to visit them months ago. He wished with all his heart he could stay with her, but Audrey and her sisters needed this trip and Audrey would not be able to be apart from him right now. He had to go. And so did Audrey.

Audrey drew back from Esther and he hugged the little girl again. He clearly remembered how much he had been against adopting her. Now he couldn't imagine his life without her. At the time they went to Peru to see Bryan and Sienna, his mind had been so far from adopting a child. He had butted heads with Audrey about that, which had led to many fights, adding to the ones they were already having because of his refusal to have a baby. He had come away from it all with a deep sense of repentance and regret for his stubbornness and an equal sense of gratitude. His mind traveled back to the day he'd finally agreed to adopt Esther. It had been the very day they'd left Peru for the States.

Just before they'd gone to bed the night before, Audrey had been almost inconsolable when she finally realized that he would not budge and that she might never see Esther again. He had turned away from her in order to go to sleep as they had an early flight the next day, but he could not sleep. Before bed, they'd had another fight about the adoption and his decision not to have a baby. He'd instinctively known it was the final straw for Audrey and that he might lose her.

He'd spent the night praying and asking the Lord what he should do. He knew there was no place for a child in their lives... at least, so he had thought. They were still so busy with their jobs and shuffling constantly between Miami and Rosefield. But Audrey didn't seem to care. They quarreled all the time because of that. He couldn't allow his marriage to continue like that and eventually disintegrate. There had to be a solution.

He'd started in fear when he'd heard an audible voice say, "There is a solution, and you know what it is."

His eyes had flown open. Had he just heard the voice of God?

Throughout the years he'd spent talking with God, he'd never heard His voice. He'd hardly even heard it in his heart. Bryan was the one who heard God's voice clearly and regularly. But for the first time, he had heard the Lord speak to him, and in an audible voice for that matter. Hearing the words brought him to tears. He looked at Audrey.

She was sleeping soundly. He whispered, "Lord, we can't adopt that little girl. I haven't even agreed for us to have our own baby, not to talk of adopting a child." He waited to hear what the Lord would say again, but he heard nothing.

Ken sighed. The Lord had said he knew what to do. Did he? But if the Lord had said it, that meant he did. He looked over at his wife and sighed again. Was the Lord asking him to give in to Audrey's demands and adopt a seven-year-old girl or agree to try for a baby now?

For a long time, he wrestled with the idea. Finally, after hours of resisting, he asked the Lord what he should do. If he wanted to keep hearing God's voice and save his marriage, he had to obey.

"Okay, Lord, I give in. We can have a baby. That is the best I can do." As for adopting a child, that he could not do. Hopefully changing his mind about having a baby now would be enough for the Lord and his wife.

He shut his eyes to go to sleep, but knew that it would not be enough. He was surprised when he heard a clear whisper in his heart; "What time is it?"

Picking up his phone from the bedside table, he stared at it and saw it was almost six o'clock in the morning. That meant he had not slept a wink.

The still small voice whispered in his heart again, "Go to the orphanage now. Go and see Esther."

He blinked in surprise. He had to go to the orphanage now? He sighed wearily and climbed out of bed. He had no choice but to obey the Lord.

He went to the bathroom, showered, and tiptoed around the room using his phone as a flashlight so as not to wake Audrey up. He dressed quickly, grabbed his wallet from the dresser, and soundlessly left the house.

He found a taxi in front of the house, which was a surprise to him as he'd hardly found taxis passing by this way since they'd come to Peru. He got into the taxi after he told the driver where he was going and muttered to himself, "What are you doing, Ken? You should be preparing for the flight right now instead of going to the orphanage."

But he knew he was doing the right thing. He was being obedient to God even though he didn't want to.

As it was early, there was no traffic on the road yet and he reached the orphanage quickly. He paid the driver and got out of the cab. He went through the gate and headed straight for the hostel. Getting there, he stood for a long time in front of the building, reluctant to enter. The children would probably still be asleep.

His eyes widened in surprise as children began to pour out of the building. Glancing at his wristwatch, he saw it was already seven o'clock. And then he realized it was a school day.

His eyes grew wider as Esther came out of the hostel, her shoulders sagging and tears streaming down her face. He had actually only seen her twice. The first time he had seen her, Audrey had brought her to him so he could meet her and he had stubbornly refused to. The second time was when Audrey was going around the orphanage grounds with her. He and Bryan had been standing near the car, talking, but his attention had been divided. He had watched Esther with Audrey. She had seemed like a happy girl, skipping beside Audrey rather than walking, a smile planted on her face. But now, she was crying. Audrey must have told her that they would be leaving Peru for the United States today. Was that why she looked so sad?

He watched her for some time as she followed the other children to another building not far from the hostel. Bryan had told him that the building, smaller than the hostel, was the children's school. He started when someone spoke from behind him, "Mr. Baylor. I did not know you were coming here today."

He turned around and saw one of the teachers he had met on the first day he came here, as well as several times after. He smiled at the woman and said, "My visit here was actually unplanned." He turned around again but did not see Esther. Facing the teacher, he asked, "The little girl my wife is really fond of... Esther... can I speak to her before classes begin?"

"Of course," the teacher said.

The woman led the way into the school building. Ken followed her into a small classroom and saw about ten children seated in it. His eyes immediately found Esther and her eyes grew round as she looked up at him. A big smile appeared on her face and his heart raced.

What a sweet girl, he thought. He had always avoided her whenever he came to the orphanage and yet she was smiling sweetly at him. It was probably because she thought of him in connection to Audrey. And she clearly loved Audrey.

The teacher walked over to Esther and said something to the little girl.

Esther stood up and hurried toward him. He blinked in surprise when she took his hand. She looked at him with her beautiful big brown eyes and huge smile, and his heart melted. He immediately understood why Audrey had fallen in love with her.

She held on to his hand as they walked out of the classroom together. He was amazed and filled with joy at the fact that, without question, she'd left the classroom with him, fully trusting him because she trusted Audrey. And yet he did not deserve her trust. He was the one standing in the way of her having a mother who loved her.

His heart suddenly burned with guilt. They walked some distance away from the school building, and then he stopped and looked down at her. When she smiled widely at him again, he couldn't take it anymore. He crouched before her, searched her eyes, and said in broken Spanish, "How would you like for me and Audrey to adopt you as our child?"

She grinned and flung her arms around him, hugging him tightly.

He felt overwhelmed with emotions as he held her. He laughed with joy and said, "I guess that is a yes." He held her away and said, "Do you want to speak with Audrey on the phone so we can share the good news with her?"

Esther nodded eagerly and Ken brought out his phone from his pocket and dialed Audrey's number. He had still not forgotten the joy in Audrey's voice on the phone that morning. The adoption process had been easy, but he knew it was the favor of God.

Ken sighed now as he watched Audrey and Esther hugging again. They were so close, these two. Just like him, Audrey did not want to leave, but he knew she recognized they would not be given the opportunity for this upcoming trip again. And Audrey was eager to share the news with her sisters and go on the trip with them.

After he hugged Esther again, he promised to call her every day. He and Audrey waved to Esther and left the house together.

They drove to the airport in silence and he knew Audrey was slightly sad. But when they got on the plane, she smiled. "I am going to miss Esther, but I can't wait to tell Trisha and Sienna the good news."

Ken nodded. "I just hope Sienna and Bryan will be able to make the trip."

Audrey smiled. "They will."

Ken frowned slightly and said, "How do you know?"

Audrey smiled again. "Sienna cannot hide a secret to save her life... at least, not from me.
She and Bryan are planning a trip to Rosefield. I am very sure of it. When we facetimed some days ago and I told her were going to Rosefield soon, I immediately knew she was planning a surprise trip there as well from the way she looked at me."

Ken said, "Well, I hope you are right."

"I won't be surprised if they are already in Rosefield."

Ken smiled and shook his head. "This was partly why I married you, Audrey."

Audrey lifted her brows and stared at him.

He said, "You are one of the most perceptive people I know." When she rolled her eyes, he added, "But not just perceptive. You are smart, and beautiful, and the best wife a man could ever hope for."

She gave him a heartwarming smile and leaned in to kiss him. She drew back and said, "I just wish I could give you a baby."

His heart squeezed at the sadness on her face. He wove his fingers through hers and said softly, "You've given me everything I could ever want. I have you and our beautiful daughter. That is enough for me." He gave her a kiss that he hoped would show her how much she meant to him. When he drew back, he frowned. She still looked worried. He was worried as well. He had gone from not wanting a baby to yearning for one in the space of two years. They loved Esther with all their hearts, but they wanted a baby desperately. Still, he had to be strong for Audrey and help her to see that even if they never had a baby of their own, they had each other, and they had Esther. And that had to be enough.

TWO

Audrey smiled as she and Ken stood in front of Trisha's house. They had already gone to their own house, dropped their bags off, and freshened up. Now, about to surprise Trisha and Frank, and maybe Sienna and Bryan if her guess was right, Audrey felt her heart racing with excitement. Not only would she get to see Trisha, and maybe Sienna, she would get to share the good news with them. She couldn't wait.

She reached out and rang the doorbell. Taking Ken's hand, she grinned at him.

Seconds later, the door opened and Trisha peered at them. "Audrey!" she exclaimed. "I thought you guys were coming at the end of the week!" She hugged Audrey tightly and then hugged Ken.

Audrey followed Trisha into the house, Ken behind her. She braced herself as Sienna came running into the living room screaming. She threw her arms around Audrey and said, "I have missed you so much!" Audrey grinned and stepped back slightly to study Sienna. "You didn't tell me you were coming to America, Sienna."

"And yet you don't look surprised to see me here." Sienna laughed.

"You are very bad at hiding anything," she said to Sienna. "I guessed you and Bryan were going to come."

"Of course you did, Audrey," Sienna said.

Audrey grinned.

"Where are Bryan and Frank?" Ken asked Trisha.

"They are both at the park with the kids."

"Okay," Ken said. "I'll go and surprise them there."

After Ken left, Audrey sat on the couch, in between her sisters. Trisha turned to Audrey and said, "Sienna nearly gave me a heart attack when she arrived at my doorstep with Bryan and Ethan. I was so surprised… but it was a good surprise."

Sienna giggled and threw her hand around Audrey's shoulders. "You look like you are bursting to tell us something. Yes?"

Audrey nodded and beamed. "I have great news to share. Actually, Ken is the one who is supposed to share it. Maybe I should wait for him to come back."

"No!" Sienna and Trisha screeched. "Tell us now!"

Audrey gave Trisha and Sienna a teasing smile. "Guess what it is."

Sienna's eyes grew big and she covered her mouth with her hand. "You're pregnant, Audrey!"

Audrey's heart sank and her excitement evaporated. She shook her head slowly and said, "No. Unfortunately, I am not pregnant."

Trisha pursed her lips and said, "Sienna, why did you bring that up? You know Audrey is sensitive about it."

Sienna bit her lip, looking mortified. "I'm so sorry, Audrey," she said.

Audrey gave her a sad smile. "Sienna, there's no

need to apologize."

Trisha reached out and rubbed Audrey's back soothingly while Sienna smiled cautiously at her. Audrey brushed aside her sadness and injected excitement into her voice again. "Let's forget about all that for now and focus on the good news I have to share," she said.

Sienna said, "Okay, Audrey, tell us the good news. The suspense is killing me."

Audrey smiled and Trisha exclaimed, "Out with it!"

"Okay, okay! I'll tell you guys now." Audrey chuckled as she looked at the eager expressions on her sisters' faces. "So, the government still won't let Faizan back into the country, but they have finally decided that Faizan isn't such a security risk anymore. They have agreed for us to go and see him… but only within the next two months."

Sienna squealed and wrapped her arms around Audrey while Trisha beamed and began to clap.

"Finally!" Trisha said happily. "I've missed Faizan so much." She looked at Audrey and added, "Just this morning, Sienna and I were talking about how much we miss him. Now we will get to see him soon."

Sienna said, "Audrey, we were also talking about Mom and Dad's anniversary. We think it will be a good idea if we all did something special to mark their upcoming fortieth anniversary. We were even talking about going on a trip but we didn't know where. Now we do! Taking a trip together to that women's camp will be perfect. We can also take some things we will donate to the women and children there."

Audrey nodded. "That's a great idea."

"So, we agree to go and see Faizan and use that trip to mark Mom and Dad's fortieth wedding anniversary?" Trisha asked.

"We do," Audrey and Sienna said together.

Trisha said, "It's in only three weeks. I hope

Frank will be able to go by then. The restaurant has been so busy these past few months."

Sienna said, "Bryan will definitely be ready to go. We've taken a long break from our ministry." She looked at Audrey. "And speaking about that, I told Trisha that Bryan and I have news to share with everyone."

Audrey stared quizzically at Sienna. "What news?"

"Oh well, I might as well tell both of you now," Sienna said. "Bryan and I are moving out of Peru."

Audrey yelped with joy. "That means you're coming back to the United States!"

Sienna bit her lip and shook her head. "We're not coming back."

"Then where are you moving to?" Trisha asked, her voice tinged with worry.

"We're not sure yet," Sienna answered. "Dr. Lincoln said he has another job for us somewhere else. He just told us a week ago."

Audrey pursed her lips. "Does that mean you guys don't know when you will return to the States at all?"

"No," Sienna looked down at the floor. "We don't. All we know is that it won't be anytime soon."

Audrey's heart sank.

Trisha shut her eyes and opened them. She said in a sad voice, "I really thought you would stay in Peru for about two or three years and then move back to Rosefield. Now, I don't even know when or if you will move back here. Meanwhile, Audrey hardly comes to Rosefield anymore."

Sienna leaned over Audrey and gave Trisha a hug. "Don't look so sad. We will call each other as regularly as we always have. Nothing will really change."

"What if you move somewhere remote where we can't video chat or even talk on the phone?"

"I have thought about that but I'm hoping and

praying that isn't so."

"Can't you guys just come back here and start a ministry or something?" Audrey asked.

"We can't just go anywhere we want to. We have to follow the Lord."

Audrey sighed again, but Sienna took her hand and said, "We all have reasons to be unhappy now, but let's forget about all that and focus on the happy news. We will get to see Faizan soon and also have what I know will be an amazing vacation together. I can't wait to see Faizan and Zainah."

Audrey nodded, becoming excited again. "I remember when Zainah told us about her daily life at that women's camp. It all sounded so exotic and wonderfully strange. I've actually been dreaming of going there and experiencing the desert life for myself."

Audrey looked up as the door opened. The men came into the house, laughing, and Audrey smiled. She said to Ken, "Have you told Bryan and Frank about the open door to go see Faizan?"

"I have," Ken said.

She began to tell the men about their idea to use the trip as a way to celebrate and mark their parents' fortieth wedding anniversary.

Trisha said, "We have to go soon." She looked at Frank. "Baby, will you be able to leave the restaurant and travel with me? We might stay there for quite some time."

Frank looked up thoughtfully and said, "This period has been very busy at the restaurant, but I definitely want to go. I don't want to stay here without you, Trisha. I guess I will have to get Nick to come and help with the running of the restaurant while I am away."

"And Bryan... Sienna said you would have no problem going away on vacation for a few weeks."

"Yeah! It all sounds really exciting. I am already looking forward to going."

"So it is all settled," Audrey said and looked at Ken. "We are all going?"

Ken nodded and everyone said they were in.

Audrey breathed a sigh of relief and said, "Good! Now we have to start planning the trip as soon as possible."

*****

Faizan bent down and put his hand on Zainah's huge belly. They were outside their tent at the camp, just talking and enjoying each other's company. He kissed her belly and then smiled up at her. "The baby is growing, my darling. Soon, we will have a beautiful baby who looks just like you," he told her.

She beamed at him and said, "No, Faizan. Our baby will look like you."

Faizan chuckled. "Okay. Let's agree that if our baby is a girl, she will look like you, but if he's a boy, he will look like his papa."

"'Kay," she said. "I like that we don't know our baby's gender. It will be a surprise. Either way, we will love this baby dearly." She rubbed her stomach and looked up at the clear skies. It was a beautiful day.

Faizan couldn't take his eyes off her. She looked so beautiful as she gazed up at the sky. He had never been as happy in his life as he'd been since he married Zainah. He loved her dearly, and he loved the life they had made for themselves in this place. It was just like heaven on earth. The camp was simple compared to the life he had made in America, but he wouldn't give it up for anything. He still missed his sisters, but the few times he had gotten to speak to them on the phone had been very precious and he prayed every day that he would be able to physically see them soon. But for now, he was completely content.

"What are you thinking about?"

He lifted his brows and focused his attention completely on Zainah. "I was just thinking about how happy I am to be married to you and to live here." He reached out and pulled Zainah into his arms. "I was also thinking about my sisters. I miss them terribly. I don't think I would ever want to move back to America again, but I wouldn't mind seeing them and hugging them again. I miss that."

Zainah ran her fingers through his hair and said, "I know, Faizan. I wish there was a way you could go and visit them or they could come here."

Faizan sighed. "The US government won't let that happen."

Zainah smiled sadly. "I feel as though I am to blame for what happened. If I had not gone back to Mali, you would still be in America with your sisters."

He shook his head. "And have to live without you? Never! Besides, you had no choice. You had to return to Mali when you did. And I have never been as happy in my life as I am right now with you. I miss my sisters, but I cannot live without you." He smiled as he put his hand on her stomach again and then leaned in to kiss her on the lips.

Zainah smiled when he pulled away. "I love you with all my heart, Faizan," she said.

He grinned and kissed her again, and then took her hand and said, "Let's go for a walk."

Zainah chuckled. She looked around the camp and waved her hand, "Where are we going in this vast, crazy desert?"

Faizan looked back at the tents near theirs. Women milled around the camp. Some were weaving colorful rugs on their looms, others doing various chores, while some stood in front of their tents, chatting and laughing. A few young children played together in the sand. He looked at Zainah again and said, "Who knows, we might discover something we have never seen before." He laughed.

"We could discover some hidden treasure."

She laughed along with him. "The only thing we will discover is more sand."

He wrapped his arm around her waist and she threw her arm around his. They walked away from the camp, talking and laughing as they usually did when they were together. They walked for a long time, chatting about random things, and then Zainah suddenly stopped. "Let's go back, Faizan," she said. "If we keep walking on, we might get lost."

Faizan said, "We are not going to get lost, Zainah. I have lived in the desert for years. I think I can trace our way back to the camp easily."

Zainah said, "It's not just that. I promised Leila that I would spend some time with her this evening. Yesterday, she told me she misses me. Imagine that."

Faizan raised his brows. "How can she miss you when you both live in the same place?"

Zainah stopped walking and said, "Since she came back to the camp two years ago, after she and Malik broke up, she hasn't been herself really. She seems really skeptical about everything and she complains constantly that I don't spend enough time with her the way I used to before I got married. I just want to reassure her that I still love her and that she's still my best friend."

"I thought I was your best friend," Faizan said, pretending to sulk.

"Okay, she's my second-best friend."

"That's better," Faizan said, grinning.

"I am serious, Faizan. Leila needs me."

Faizan stopped smiling and nodded. "I understand."

Zainah dug a hole in the sand with her sandals. "I feel so sorry for Leila. She still refuses to tell me everything that happened after she went to see Malik at the farm."

"I know I might sound slightly insensitive," Faizan said, "but I really think it's time Leila got over it all. It has been two years. She needs to move on."

Zainah smiled sadly and said, "Move on to where or who, Faizan? Do you see any other men around here except for you? Leila's dream was always to get married and have a family. She even wanted it for herself more than I did. I think she is a little resentful of me because I found you and she doesn't have anyone. Her dream of getting married and starting a family is lost now, so you can't really blame her for how she feels."

Faizan pressed his lips together and then said, "I shouldn't have said what I did. I guess I don't understand what Leila is going through. I wish there were more men here, but at the same time, the camp is a wonderful place and the women are the nicest people on Earth. She has you and she has other friends, too. It's not the same thing as having a loving spouse, but it still comes close."

"Does it, Faizan? I love the women at the camp, but the love I have for you is so different and so deep. You are a part of me. I don't think the way I feel about any of the women… even Leila, comes close to how I feel about you."

Faizan gazed at her, feeling too overwhelmed to speak. Finally, with a voice choked with emotion, he said, "I feel the same way about you, Zainah." He took her hand and kissed each of her fingers. "I guess you are right and now I feel really bad for Leila."

Zainah sighed. "Besides, she wants children and she needs a husband for that."

Faizan nodded.

They continued to walk and Faizan told Zainah how much happiness being married to her had brought him. After that, they talked about Rosefield, reminiscing about the small American town. After a while, Faizan looked up and said, "The sun is beginning to set, Zainah. You're right. We should start heading back."

He started to turn around, but Zainah said, "Wait. Let's stay and watch the sunset."

They held on tightly to each other while looking up as the sun gradually disappeared from the sky. After that, they started to turn around again, but Faizan frowned as something caught his eye. "Look, Zainah!" He pointed at what looked like flames some distance away from where they were. "Is that a fire I see in the distance?"

Zainah craned her neck and then blinked. "Let's turn back. It might be dangerous for us to go there."

"What if it's a plane crash or something like that? If you had not come to rescue me when you did, I would be dead now."

Zainah didn't speak for a long moment and then nodded. "Okay, let's go and see what it is."

They began to walk toward the fire. The closer they got, the more certain they were that it was not a crash. Soon, they found it was fire from a stack of wood on which sat a massive smoky pot. Clearly, someone was around somewhere cooking whatever was inside this pot.

Faizan said, "Someone lives here."

Zainah shook her head. "Not someone. Some people. This pot is huge. The food being cooked in it is not for just for one person."

They continued to walk toward the pot on the fire and immediately stopped when they saw men dressed in white tunics and pants milling around various tents, tents similar to the ones at the women's camp.

Zainah gasped. "Faizan, a men's camp!"

Faizan looked around the camp. Zainah was right. As far as he could see, there were only men here. There were about two dozen tents and men came in and out of them. The camp was not as large as the women's camp, but there were still quite a few people here.

Zainah grabbed Faizan's hand and whispered, "Let's leave before they see us!"

One of the men suddenly turned in their direction and it seemed like that prompted all of them to do that.

"Oh no! They have seen us," Zainah whispered harshly, still clutching Faizan's hand. "Let's go now, Faizan!"

"Wait, Zainah," Faizan said. "I know dangerous men when I see them and these men don't look like they are dangerous." Still, he knew he had to be careful. Looks could be deceiving.

All the men were looking at them now. The expressions on their faces varied from surprise to curiosity. A few even looked fearful. One of them, a man who looked around fifty, walked toward them, a look of curiosity on his face. The man carried himself with authority and humility at the same time. He seemed as though he was the leader of these men.

Faizan held tightly to Zainah's hand and stood his ground.

"Are you friend or foe?" the man asked, looking at him.

Faizan narrowed his eyes and said in a grim voice, "Neither. It depends on you. If you are a friend, then I am. But if you are not, then you will live to regret ever meeting me."

Zainah squeezed his hand. He was surprised when she said in a sweet voice, "We are friends. Can you tell us who you are?"

The man glanced briefly at her and then looked at Faizan again. "We call ourselves 'the friends of Christ' and arrived here about a week ago." He turned around and waved his hand around his camp. "As you can see, none of us pose any threat to you or your loved ones."

Faizan stared at him for a full minute and then

nodded. In these parts, it could sometimes be dangerous to refer to oneself as "Christ's friend" the way the man had. They were most definitely genuine. He gave the man a small smile and said, "Anyone who is a friend of Christ is my friend."

The man's uncertain demeanor suddenly changed. Faizan's eyes widened in surprise when the man came forward and gave him a bear hug. The older man glanced at Zainah again but quickly averted his gaze as though she were just a fixture at his side. When Faizan turned to look at Zainah, she seemed slightly put off.

The man said to Faizan, "I am so glad to know you are a friend of Christ. I would invite you into the camp but unfortunately I can't because of her." He did not look at Zainah.

Faizan said, "I can't come into the camp because of my wife?"

The man said in a kind but firm voice, "I'm sorry. I hope you aren't offended. We left the world and everything in it, especially women, so we can fully focus on our faith and our relationship with God."

Faizan looked at Zainah again. She still had a smile on her face, but he knew her. The smile was just a camouflage for her true feelings. He asked the man cautiously, "May I come and visit you again tomorrow? Alone?" He did not dare look at Zainah again.

The man smiled widely. "Yes! We would love that!"

Faizan smiled once more at the man and said, "Thank you. I guess my wife and I have to go now."

"Do you live around here?" the man asked.

Faizan considered his question for a few seconds and decided to conceal the truth, as he wasn't totally sure he could fully trust any of the men in this camp yet. Plus, he was certain it wasn't a good idea to let the men here know there was a camp full of women not far away. He answered simply, "We both live somewhere far from here."

After the men said goodbye, Faizan turned around and walked away from the camp with Zainah. He said nothing to her, afraid of what she was going to say. But after a while, he could not take the silence anymore. "Can you believe there's a camp not far from ours? And a men's camp, for that matter. Best of all, they are followers of Christ as well."

Zainah nodded, the expression on her face thoughtful.

Wondering what was on her mind, he asked slowly, "Do you mind if I go and see them tomorrow without you?" He sighed. "You know what, I won't go since they don't want you there."

Zainah stopped walking and turned to him. "No, you should go. I understand why they don't want me to come into their camp. Our camp is a women's camp and though not as strict as theirs, men are not exactly allowed to live there."

"But I live there," he said.

She gave him a tired smile. "Yes, my love. You are different... but we don't make a habit of letting men stay in the camp."

He wanted to go to the men's camp but if she was uncomfortable in any way about it, he would not go. He told her so.

"I understand their reason for not wanting women at their camp," Zainah said. "Women might be a distraction to them, just like men would be at our camp."

"But I am not a distraction," he said.

"Yes you are, Faizan. I see the way many of the women at the camp look at you."

He winked at her and chuckled. "So you're jealous?"

"I'm not," she answered. "They know you belong to me. None of them will do anything untoward.

Anyway, you can go to the men's camp without me anytime you want."

"Thank you," he said. "I don't think it's a good idea to tell anyone yet about the men's camp… even Leila. If you tell Leila, she might tell someone else, who will in turn tell another person. Soon, everyone at the camp will know. The women can be very curious. They will search out the men's camp." He grinned. "I can just imagine how those men will look when women suddenly invade their camp."

Zainah laughed. "I can see it too. It's so funny to me. The very thing they are trying to run away from infests their camp."

Faizan shook his head. "Infests? It's not funny, Zainah." But he couldn't help laughing along with her.

They got to the camp as the stars began to peek out of the sky. Miriam ran to them with worry clearly written on her face. "Where have you both been?"

"We went for a walk," Zainah said.

"I sent Leila and Halima to look for you, but they didn't find you."

"I'm sorry, Miriam," Faizan said. "I was the one who led Zainah farther away from the camp than I should have."

"You had a call," Miriam said. "From your brother-in-law, Ken. That's why I was looking for you everywhere. It was very important."

Faizan raised his brows and his heart began to drum. "What did Ken say?"

Miriam answered, "He told me to let you know that they have finally been given permission to come visit you."

Faizan's mouth fell open and he hollered in excitement. "Oh, thank you, Lord!" He turned and hugged Zainah.

"There's more," Miriam said. "Ken said they would all be coming soon. Maybe even next week."

Faizan's jaw dropped. "Next week! Wow! Okay then. We have to prepare for their arrival."

Miriam said, "About that, Faizan. It won't be possible for all of them to stay here."

Faizan frowned. "Why not?"

"Because this is a women's camp, Faizan. Even though you are a man, you became a part of the camp ever since we rescued you from that plane crash and you married our Zainah." She smiled.

Faizan put his hand on his head and thought how ironic and strange it was that he and Zainah had just encountered almost the exact same thing back at the men's camp. Maybe he'd entered an alternate universe.

"I'm sorry," Miriam said.

Faizan rubbed his head and said, "Did you tell Ken they couldn't come here?"

"No," Miriam answered. "I'm leaving that to you." A wry smile appeared on her face and she left before he could say anything.

"Thanks a lot, Miriam," he said under his breath.

Zainah took his hand and said, "Wow! This is just strange. Miriam just repeated almost the same thing that man at the men's camp told us."

Faizan said, "Maybe the Lord is trying to say something… but I don't know what."

Zainah put her hands around him, kissed him, and said, "I'll see you at dinner, honey. Let me go and see Leila now."

"Do you have to go?" he muttered, holding on to her. "I know something else we can do right before dinner."

She shook her head and giggled. "No, Faizan. Not now." She tried to extricate herself from him. "You see what I told you earlier. You are such a distraction."

He chuckled. "Okay, but I am a good distraction."

She finally escaped his grasp and said, "Yes, you are. But a distraction still."

"And you are a distraction, too," he said as she walked away. He laughed as she began to sway her hips in an exaggerated way. He shook his head after she disappeared from sight and then his stomach bubbled up with excitement. Finally, his sisters could come and visit him. He would finally get to see them in person and hug them. He would be able to share his idyllic life at the camp with them. Unfortunately, their husbands would not be able to come. Thanks to Miriam, he had the unsavory job of telling them that. He would have to wait until Ken called again before he could tell him.

THREE

Leila looked up as Zainah walked into the tent she shared with Halima and Binta. Her tent was at the edge of the camp and, being very pregnant, it must have taken Zainah some time to get here. She smiled as Zainah waved at the other women in greeting and then walked toward her corner of the tent. "Should I sing a song of thanksgiving to God?" Leila asked as Zainah reached her. "I'm surprised you actually came."

"Of course I came," Zainah said. "Why wouldn't I come, Leila? I promised you I would."

Leila shrugged as Zainah slowly lowered herself onto one of the rugs on the floor. Two big kerosene lanterns stood at both ends of the tent, illuminating Zainah's pretty face. "I wasn't sure you would come," Leila said. "You and Faizan are joined at the hip. You never leave each other's side."

Zainah raised her brows. "That is because we are married, Leila. It's what sometimes happens when you are happily married."

Leila winced inwardly as she felt a slice of pain go through her. Zainah had exactly what she wanted but could never have; what she had dreamed about all her life. Now, she had given up on everything regarding love and marriage and having kids of her own.

Still, Zainah's marriage to Faizan and their intense love for each other was hard to watch. It reminded her of Malik and what they had shared, which was now lost forever. Her marriage to Dauda had been dissolved more than a year ago and she had known she would never get married again. Not living at this camp.

"I'm sorry, Leila," Zainah said. "I shouldn't have said that, knowing how much you are still struggling."

Leila shrugged and pretended she was okay. "It's nothing."

Zainah smiled at Leila. "I have something to tell you, but it's a secret. You have to promise not to tell anyone." She looked toward Halima and Binta who were on the other side of the tent, and then looked at Leila. "Faizan would kill me for telling you."

Leila sat down beside Zainah, her curiosity rising at the excited look on Zainah's face.

"What is it, Zainah?"

"Shhh," Zainah put her index finger to her lips. "Nobody must know what I am about to tell you."

Leila's eyes widened as she stared at Zainah. "Wow! Tell me. What is it?"

Zainah lowered her voice and said, "This afternoon, Faizan and I decided to go for a walk."

Leila fought the urge to roll her eyes. As much as she hated the envy that settled in her heart every time Zainah talked about her and Faizan's constant expressions of love, like taking a walk in the backdrop of a sunset, she wished Zainah would stop telling her about it.

She said nothing and Zainah continued. "We started walking away from the camp while we talked. After a while, I told Faizan it was time to turn back so we would not get lost, but he assured me we wouldn't. He wanted to explore some more.

"At a point, Faizan decided that we needed to go back, but just before we turned around, we spotted a fire some distance away. We went to investigate and you will not believe what we found."

Leila's heart began to beat fast as she recalled vividly the day they had rescued Faizan from a plane crash. She wondered if it was another crash. "I heard nothing at the camp," she said. The day they had found Faizan, they had all heard the loud, awful sound of the plane crashing to the ground. With trepidation, she asked Zainah if it was another crash, praying it wasn't. The sight she'd seen that day at the crash site was one she prayed she would never see again.

"It wasn't a crash," Zainah said. "It was a camp full of men."

"What?" Leila's mouth dropped open as she stared at Zainah in astonishment. "Did you say a camp full of men is somewhere near our women's camp?"

Zainah nodded.

"Are you serious?"

"Yes. They were all dressed in white or black tunics and pants. And they are all Christians like us."

Leila stood up and then began to pace the ground in front of Zainah.

"Sit, Leila!" Zainah said.

Leila sat beside Zainah again. She said, "I can't believe it. Who would have thought there was a camp near here? Not to talk of a men's camp!"

"We spoke to one of them... or rather, Faizan did. They just arrived in the desert last week."

Leila was mystified by it all. She listened as Zainah told her everything the man had said.

"How come there are only men there?"

Zainah answered, "They wanted to escape the many distractions of the world. The man we spoke to said women were the major distractions. He wouldn't even speak to me directly. He mostly spoke to Faizan. He said he would have invited us into the camp but women were not allowed in.

Faizan asked him if he could go back to the camp alone tomorrow and he said yes."

"So, it's a little like our own camp."

"Except theirs seemed stricter."

Suddenly, for the first time since she broke up with Malik, hope rose in Leila's heart. And then she blinked and scolded herself. She stuffed the hope back deep into her heart. She said, "I'm glad they don't let women into their camp and we won't let them into ours, either. I just wish they were not here. One of the women is bound to discover their camp and tell everyone about it. If that happens, this place will not be the same again."

Zainah stared at her and said, "I thought you would be a bit more excited than this. When I found out about them, I felt the same way as you. But now that I have thought about it some more, I actually think it would be a good idea if we could mix with them. Maybe we could get them to open up more. Wouldn't it be lovely if some love matches were made? I mean, it's time that..."

"Stop it! Stop it, Zainah! This talk about love matches and mixing with the men all needs to stop. Those men are right about the distractions that the opposite sex can bring. The women in this camp need to stay away from those men so we can be totally holy to the Lord."

"How can you say that, Leila? Not too long ago you were talking about getting married and having children, and now you don't want any of the women here to even have a chance for that? I know you're heartbroken because of Malik, but that doesn't mean you can't move on and find someone else. I want you and the other women here to have what I and Faizan share."

"First of all," Leila said, irritated, "it wasn't 'not too long ago.' It's almost two years now since Malik broke up with me. Secondly, I and the women in this camp are better off without men and their fickle love."

"You can't be serious, Leila. Don't you want the women here to find love?"

Leila turned away and said, "If the Lord wanted me or any of the women here to be married, He would not have led us to this place." She turned back to Zainah and said, "Or He would have caused men to drop from the sky for all of us when we arrived here."

Zainah shook her head.

Leila said, "Did Faizan not literally drop from the sky for you?"

"I guess he did," Zainah said in a cold voice. "And you won't let me forget it."

Zainah sounded really hurt, and Leila sighed ruefully. "I'm sorry," she said. "It's just that most people are not as lucky in love as you and Faizan are. Romantic love is mostly a lie. All you can trust is God's love and we have it here. Why should we look for something else?"

"It's not true," Zainah said. "The Bible is full of examples of romantic love. If it wasn't for us, then why do we have examples of it in the Bible? Besides, my relationship with Faizan shows that there is a place for that here, and I know some of the women here want what Faizan and I have. And I want it for them, too."

"I think you should let it go," Leila said. "The camp is okay the way it is."

"Leila, just because you don't want love in your life anymore doesn't mean other women here don't deserve..."

"No, Zainah. Nobody deserves anything except what the Lord gives. He has given Himself and that is enough." She opened her mouth to say something more, but the bell signifying dinnertime began to ring.

Zainah stood up slowly with her hand on her belly, and lovingly rubbed it.

A dull ache went through Leila, and resentment rose within her. Her past dreams of carrying her own child one day would never happen. She took a deep breath and let the resentment go. She quietly repeated the words she said constantly to herself these days, "I am satisfied with Christ and I have enough. I have no need of anything or anyone else."

She left the tent with Zainah and they walked toward the large dinner tent together. Miriam had come up with the idea of everyone having dinner together about a year ago. They had breakfast and lunch separately, but every evening, they all gathered together in the large tent and ate and fellowshipped together. Miriam called it a time to break bread together just like in the Bible, even though they never ate bread in the evenings.

They entered the tent and Leila sighed as Zainah left her side and made a beeline for Faizan, who was already seated in the middle of the tent. As a man, and a handsome one at that, he stuck out clearly in the sea of women.

Leila thought of what Zainah had told her about the men's camp and the implications of it being discovered by the women here. That could not be allowed to happen. She went and sat on the left side of the dinner tent, in the middle of a long row of women.

She looked around her at all the women here. She personally knew some who had the same dream she'd had in the past of getting married and having children. Maybe Zainah was right. Maybe the women in the camp who really wanted to have husbands and children needed to know about the men's camp.

She pressed her lips tightly together. No, she was still sure it wasn't a good idea. She'd had love and then lost it. It was beautiful when you had it, but heart-wrenching when you lost it. She wouldn't wish it on anyone. She hadn't known how easy it was to lose what she thought was true love until Malik had broken up with her… just like that. She had known she could not marry him if he did not convert to her faith, but she had been sure that he loved her enough to do that. Apparently, he had not.

She felt a hand on her shoulder and looked up. It was Miriam smiling down at her. "Pray for the food, Leila," Miriam said.

Every evening at dinnertime, Miriam chose someone to pray. Apparently, it was her turn today. Leila stood up and went to the front of the tent. The whole place was buzzing as women chatted with each other. When she looked over at everyone in the tent, the noise died down and everyone focused on her.

"Lord," she began, "thank you for the food we are about to eat. Thank you for providing it for us, but most of all, thank you for providing this place for us. A place where we as women can come apart and be totally dedicated to you. Help us to present our bodies and minds daily as living sacrifices unto you. Keep us holy and keep our minds only on you."

As she continued to pray, she began to feel as though she was letting some bitterness from her past experiences seep into her prayer. But then she chided herself. She wasn't letting bitterness seep in. The Lord had taught her lessons from her past experiences so she could know how to pray for others, especially at a time like this. She asked the Lord to draw them close to Him and to keep away everything that would be a distraction.

She finished praying and went back to her seat.

Soon, some of the women entered with pots of steaming food. The delicious aroma immediately hit Leila's nostrils and her stomach rumbled. She remembered she hadn't eaten lunch that afternoon, which was why she was so hungry. She couldn't wait to dig into the food.

As the women whose turn it was to cook dinner began to dish out the food and pass it around the tent, Leila's eyes traveled to Zainah and Faizan and she held back a groan as a wave of envy hit her again. Faizan and Zainah had already been served their food and Faizan was feeding Zainah as though she could not feed herself. It reminded Leila of the days she had spent in Dogon, eating and laughing with Malik. Sometimes, he had fed her while she gazed into his eyes, her heart brimming with love for him.

She blinked away the painful memory. Looking away from Faizan and Zainah, she thanked the woman who handed her a plate of steaming chicken and wheat porridge.

Leila told herself to stop with the envy. It was constant now. She would have to find a way to move on from these painful memories of Malik and trust the Lord with all her heart. Yes, she would stay single forever, but that wasn't so bad. Or at least, it didn't have to be. She had the Lord and she had friends in the camp.

She continued to eat and then moaned inwardly when Malik's face appeared again in her mind. Would she ever forget him? They broke up two years ago. Why couldn't she just let go?

She pursed her lips and then forcefully pressed his image from her mind. No matter how long it took, she was determined to forget him completely. Thankfully, she would never again have to go through the pain of being dumped by someone whom she loved dearly. And she would make sure no woman in this camp ever had to go through what she went through. It was imperative that none of them find out about the men's camp.

*****

Audrey held Ken's hand as they left Doctor Reed's office. The doctor was about sixty-five years old. He was their family doctor, and had been since before her parents had died. As usual, he had tested her and Ken, and he had come to the conclusion that there was nothing wrong with either of them, fertility-wise.

Audrey was angry again. He had told her on a previous visit that her eggs were getting old and she needed to start having babies now. He had also told them the same thing he'd said just now—that they needed to stop worrying and in due time they would get pregnant.

But when was that? Was it when her eggs were finally too old and useless, which, according to him, was very soon?

Audrey got into the car and buckled her seatbelt. Ken got into the driver's seat beside her. "I'm so tired of this, Ken," she said.

Ken said, "We won't stop trying. You heard what Doctor Reed said. We need to stop worrying about it and in due time it will happen for us."

Audrey looked out of the window and bit her lip. Whispering a prayer to the Lord, she said, "Please, Lord, please give us a baby now." A few people had told her she should be satisfied with Esther. She and Ken loved Esther with their whole hearts, but she wanted a baby. A baby that would grow in her belly, created from the love she and Ken shared. And she wanted a sibling for Esther as well. She had grown up with sisters and she could not imagine her life without them.

She felt Ken's hand on her shoulder and turned to him. "Stop worrying, Audrey. We won't give up until we get our baby. And it will be soon. I am sure of it."

"How are you sure?" she asked, frustration rising up within her.

"I just am."

She studied him as he drove, his eyes on the road. All his words were meant to reassure her and to comfort her. But she knew him. He was as worried as she was but he probably felt he had to be strong for her. She felt a deep sadness weighing heavily on her and decided to change the subject. "I can't wait for us to go to that women's camp to see Faizan and Zainah. It will be a good break for us."

"I can't wait, either. So far, though, I'm enjoying our vacation here in Rosefield. Even though I miss Esther, it's nice getting this time off and getting to spend time with Bryan and Frank. Faizan was a great addition to our clique of brothers when he was in Rosefield. It will be great to have him back in it."

Audrey laughed. "I am sure it will be. What I am looking forward to the most when we go to that camp is experiencing the daily life there. I am really glad that you're coming with me though, Ken. I hope they have private rooms for couples."

Ken chuckled. "I doubt they do. I think I heard Faizan say when he still lived here in Rosefield that they mostly live in tents. So what you should be praying for is for them to have private tents."

"Okay, private tents," Audrey said. "We still need to keep trying to have a baby there."

"That might be a little awkward at first," Ken replied. "But I am sure they can set up new tents for us."

Audrey giggled. "It will be such fun."

They kept talking about their trip to North Africa and specifically the women's camp until they got home.

"Ken," Audrey said as they both sat on the couch. "Yes?"

"Why don't you call that lady, Miriam, so we can speak to Faizan and ask if they have and can set up extra tents for us couples? It would be a bummer if we arrived there and they didn't have any. If we tell Faizan now, he can make preparations to set up new tents before we all arrive."

Ken looked at her. "You know it's hard to get through to Miriam. A lot of times her phone is off. Getting her on the phone is a matter of luck. And even if I got her, Faizan might not be around. You know the last time I called her so I could speak to Faizan and tell him we were coming, he and Zainah were not at the camp."

"That's why we should try calling again. We need to be sure that Faizan has gotten the message that we are coming in less than a week so he can make preparations for us. Imagine if he hasn't even been told and we arrive there?"

"Well, it wouldn't be so bad. It would be a pleasant surprise. But you are right. I should call again." He brought out his phone from his pocket and dialed Miriam's number. When he put the phone to his ear, Audrey leaned forward so she could see his face clearly. His eyes suddenly lit up and she knew he had gotten through. He put them on speakerphone and said, "Hello, is this Miriam? This is Ken, Faizan's brother in-law. And his sister, Audrey, is also here."

"Oh, Ken! I am surprised you called so soon since you just called yesterday. You are lucky. My phone battery is still high since I charged it when I went to town a few days ago. I will go and get Faizan and Zainah for you. I think they are in their tent."

"That would be great, thank you," Ken said.

Miriam didn't speak again and Audrey whispered, "Imagine staying in a place without electricity for weeks, Ken. It will be so exciting!"

Ken shook his head. "That excites you?"

"Yes, it does! We will be truly off the grid. No internet, no calls, no TV or distractions like that.

Just nature, the desert, and interesting people from what Faizan and Zainah told me."

"Well, I guess that..." Ken stopped talking as Faizan's voice came on the line.

"Ken!" Faizan said.

"Faizan!" Ken exclaimed. "It is so good to hear from you, bro! Your sister is here with me."

"Audrey!" Faizan hollered. "I have missed you. How are you?"

"I have missed you too, Faizan. It's been months since we last talked. I am fine. How is Zainah? Is she there?"

"No. It's her turn to cook the camp dinner so she is in the kitchen tent preparing the food with the other women."

"How is her pregnancy coming along?" Audrey asked. She felt a dull ache in her heart as she asked that, considering her own inability to get pregnant. She quickly brushed aside the pain she felt.

"She is as fit as a fiddle," Faizan answered, "and as beautiful as ever."

"I am glad to hear that," Audrey said. Faizan sounded so happy and she was truly pleased for him as well.

"So, I heard the good news," Faizan said. "You can come here. And you are coming next week?"

"Yes," Ken answered. "That's why we called, actually. We wanted to know if there are extra tents there for us couples. You know we need our privacy."

There was silence on the other end of the line and Audrey's heart sank. Was the phone battery dead? She called out, "Faizan! Are you still there?"

"I am. I am sorry."

"What are you sorry for, Faizan?" Audrey asked.

He sighed loudly. "Miriam just told me that it will not be possible for you guys — Ken, Frank and Bryan — to come along. She said only women can stay at the camp, and that means only you, Audrey, and Trisha and Sienna can come here."

"Oh, no!" Audrey said, shaking her head. "Why?"

"You know it's a women's camp. The idea of the camp is a place where women can separate themselves from the world and be devoted to Christ. Many of them desire to get married, but I doubt they will feel comfortable having so many men in their midst. I am truly sorry."

Ken sighed. "That is unfortunate. I was looking forward to the trip. I guess the men and I will remain in Rosefield while the girls go."

Audrey shook her head. "There is no way I am going without you, Ken. No way!"

"But you have no choice, Audrey. Not unless you want to forfeit the trip."

"I will if you can't go."

"You have to go, Audrey. Don't you want to see Faizan? And you have been looking forward to this trip. I can't let you not go."

"I am not going without you," Audrey repeated. "If you can't go, then I am not going. And besides," she looked at him and whispered, "getting pregnant now is more important to me than this trip, even though I would love to see Faizan."

"You have to go, Audrey!"

"No, I am..."

"Stop, both of you!" Faizan said. "I have an idea, but it will probably not work. If it does, however, I will let you know. I would really love for you both to come, but if Ken can't, I hope you will decide to come anyway, Audrey."

"I hope your idea works out, Faizan," Audrey said. "I would really love to go and I want to see you again, but right now there are reasons why I don't want to go on a long trip without Ken, apart from the fact that I don't want to experience that place without him by my side."

"I understand," Faizan said. "I will try out my idea tomorrow. Call me tomorrow evening... our time."

"What if Miriam's battery dies before then?" Audrey asked.

"I hope it won't because that would be a problem."

They changed the subject and talked about Sienna and Bryan, and then Trisha and Frank.

"I am sure Bryan will be really disappointed when he hears we can't go with the girls," Ken said. "You know how fascinated he is by the idea of different cultures and the way they practice church and their Christianity."

Audrey laughed. "I won't be surprised if he is already planning on how to plant a church there."

Faizan laughed along with her. "He can't plant a church here. This whole camp is like a huge church already. Most people here are dedicated Christians, including the children, and we have fellowship twice a day, excluding the private prayer gatherings many have in their tents with friends also."

"I know," Audrey said. "Zainah told me about that. It's one of the things I am looking forward to."

"You see," Ken said to her. "You have to go even if I can't."

She shook her head again. "I have told you that…"

"Yes, you won't go unless I can," Ken finished her sentence. "You need to think about that."

"Like I said, I will try to find a solution," Faizan said.

They talked some more and then Ken ended the call.

Audrey sat back on the couch and looked at him. "That is a bummer," she said. "I hope Faizan's idea works, whatever it is."

"I hope it does, too." He drew Audrey close and held her in his arms. "I certainly won't want to be away from you for weeks." He ran his hand down her arm and smiled mischievously. "Maybe we should put in all the time we have now to try to make a baby before you go."

"You know I am serious, Ken. I won't go without you."

"I won't try to force you," he said. "I know how stubborn you are."

She hit him playfully on the arm and he laughed. "Well, what do you say about that baby making idea?" he said, not a hint of a smile on his face.

She laughed out loud, the look on his face hilarious to her. A knock sounded on the door, and she grinned. She looked at him as she stood up to answer the door. "Well, that's your answer. It will have to wait."

She went to the door and opened it. Sienna was standing there with a huge smile, Ethan in her arms.

For a minute, envy tore at Audrey's heart as she looked at the little boy. He was a painful reminder of what she yearned for but didn't have. And then she forcefully brushed the negative feeling away, reached out, gave her sister a hug, and ushered her into the house.

FOUR

Sienna sat up on the bed and bit her lip. The room was dark and she could hear Bryan snoring softly beside her. She felt for her phone on the bedside table, found it, and picked it up. Glancing at it, she saw the time was just four o'clock in the morning. She had not been able to sleep since she and Bryan went to bed at midnight. But it was typical. For the past few months, she'd had trouble sleeping. She hadn't wanted to admit the real cause of her insomnia to herself until a month ago.

She began to notice late last year that she was beginning to get mild anxiety attacks once more, but she had concluded that it was just stress from taking care of Ethan while also running the orphanage full-time. But when she started to have recurring nightmares similar to the ones she'd had before she married Bryan, she knew something was wrong. Still, she had put it at the back of her mind, as the thought that the scrupulosity was returning was too hard for her to bear. And why would it return? She was living for the Lord and not involved in anything that might stir up a guilty conscience the way her past modeling career had.

One day, after a particularly vivid and scary nightmare, she had jerked up on her bed yelling.

The sheets were soaked with sweat and her heart was racing. Bryan had woken with a start and hugged her while he asked her what was wrong. When she told him she had a nightmare, he had prayed for her, held her in his arms until her heart stopped racing, and then waited for her to fall asleep again.

She didn't have another nightmare until a few nights later, but what she did have was a familiar vague sense of guilt and condemnation hanging over her head, which gradually became stronger as weeks went by.

She couldn't understand it. Where did it come from and why? She was involved in the ministry now and her relationship with the Lord, while not as close as she would want it to be, was good. At least, it had been before the invasive guilt began. Now, she felt like she was hiding from God all the time. The constant guilt and condemnation arose from the fact that every mistake, wrong word, or real or imagined sin, was magnified until it became a reason to believe she was headed straight for hell.

She told no one about her fears, not even Bryan. Many nights, when she had a nightmare, she remained in bed, looking up at the ceiling, unable to sleep. She didn't tell anyone because she was ashamed. She was a minister's wife; someone who was supposed to have it all together. Why on earth would she be going through all this if there wasn't something deeply wrong with her spiritual life?

Today, however, she was sick and tired of keeping it all in and not telling anyone. She had to tell Bryan, if no one else. She reached over and switched the light on. Before she could reach out to wake Bryan up, he opened his eyes and looked at her. He sat up on the bed beside her and frowned.

"What is it, Sienna?" he asked.

"Bryan, I had another nightmare."

Bryan reached out, took her in his arms, and

then rubbed her back soothingly. He started to say it was just a nightmare, but she gently pulled away from him.

"Bryan, there's something I have to tell you." She clearly remembered how Bryan had been used by God to lift her out of her religious OCD before they got married. It had been a very difficult time for her and for him as well. Bryan had loved her unconditionally in spite of how she'd hurt him at the time and she was forever grateful to him. If he helped her then, maybe he could help her now.

Bryan was staring curiously at her. Because she knew him well, from the expression on his face she knew he had already guessed that the problem she had now was much more than a nightmare.

"Bryan," she said, looking deep into his eyes. "It's back."

He took her hands and searched her eyes. "The scrupulosity?"

"Yes," she said simply.

"Oh no! When did it start?" Bryan asked.

"A few months ago," Sienna answered.

Bryan frowned deeply. "Why didn't you tell me about it then, Sienna?" His expression was full of worry for her.

She sighed deeply and admitted to him that she was ashamed.

"Sienna, why would you be ashamed to tell me? Before we got married, remember you confided in me about everything you were going through. Why would you hide it from me now that we are married?"

Sienna looked down. Bryan didn't understand that things were different now. At that time, she had been a model, and even though she had a relationship with the Lord, she hadn't been a spiritual role model, or someone anyone really looked up to. Now she was a minister's wife and in a ministry. Everyone seemed to think she had to be hyper spiritual. She loved the idea of drawing closer to God every day. But the pressure of being a role model when she had this debilitating condition was not something she was equipped to deal with.

Bryan put his finger under her chin and lifted her face up so she was looking directly into his eyes. She pressed her lips tightly together as he studied her. In his eyes, she could see worry and deep love for her, as well as hope. "Sienna, we will get through it the way we did years ago, okay? Let's start by praying about it now."

For the next few minutes, Bryan prayed for her and asked the Lord to give them a solution to their problem.

She felt touched beyond words by his prayer and his love for her. He said the words "our problem" rather than "her" problem, as though he was suffering as deeply as she was. And she guessed he was. That was how deeply he loved her. In spite of herself, she smiled as she remembered when she was pregnant. He'd had many of the symptoms she did during the first few months of her pregnancy, which their doctor called "Couvade syndrome." She had teased him then because of it and they still laughed about it to this day.

After Bryan finished praying, a small sense of peace settled over her. However, she knew the anxiety, guilt, and condemnation would come back soon enough.

Bryan said, "Can you remember how it started again?"

"Not really," Sienna answered. "It started way before I actually began to pay attention to it. At first, I thought it was stress. I ignored it even though it was bothering me at the time."

He nodded and said, "We will find the root cause of it." He reached out and took his Bible from the bedside table; the one he usually preached his sermons from when he went to various church programs. He opened it and began to read several scriptures to her about God's grace and faithfulness. She listened carefully, meditating on the scriptures he read to her.

Finally, when he finished, he smiled and said to her, "I think you'll feel better if we talk about more fun topics now. I'm sure you're looking forward to your trip to North Africa to see Faizan."

She shook her head. "Bryan, I didn't want to tell you before now, but I cannot go without you." She had come back from Audrey's earlier in the day with the news that men were not allowed in the camp. Just as he usually did, Bryan had taken it in stride, even though she knew he had been looking forward to the trip with her.

He put his arm around her shoulders and said, "You have to go, Sienna. If you're worried about Ethan, you know I will take care of him."

"I'm not worried about Ethan," she said. "I know he'll be in good hands with his dad."

"Then what is it?" he asked her.

"I just don't want to go without you, and with this thing... this scrupulosity, I just don't see any way I can go without you. What if I have a serious episode like I did before we got married? Or have these nightmares I am having now?" She put her palms on his cheeks and said, "I need you, Bryan, you know that. You are my rock."

He shook his head. "No, the Lord is your rock, and you don't really need me. You have the Lord with you always."

"I know," Sienna said. "But you know what I mean." She took a deep breath and said to him, "Don't try to change my mind, Bryan. I am not going without you because I don't want to and I can't. I need you right now." She looked away from him and prayed he would not try to change her mind. She had made her decision. She had no choice. As much as she wanted to see Faizan again, there was no way she could go on that trip without Bryan.

She clearly remembered how Bryan had helped her when the scrupulosity had turned her life upside down. She didn't know what she would have done without him. When she had tried to kill herself, he had been the one who helped her out of the dark place so she never thought of doing that again. She was nowhere near all that now, but still, she needed him near.

He turned her around to face him and smiled at her. "I won't try to change your mind," he said. "You don't have to go if you don't want to."

She beamed at him. "Thank you."

He said, "It's such a shame, though, that we can't go. I would have liked to see Faizan again. Most of all, I would have liked to see that place after hearing so much about it."

Sienna smiled sadly. "So would I." She felt a deep sense of disappointment at the fact that she would not get to see Faizan. The worst part of it was that Audrey had also said that because Ken was not going, she would not go either. That left only Trisha. Would Trisha go alone without Frank or without her or Audrey? Hopefully, she would, because it would be so unfair to Faizan if none of them went. He would be very hurt by that.

She told Bryan what she was thinking, and Bryan said, "He will be hurt even if Trisha goes. The fact that you and Audrey are not going will not sit well with him at all."

Sienna shut her eyes and imagined how Faizan would feel. If she was the one, she would feel really hurt and she knew he would, too. Unfortunately, at this time, it could not be helped. The unfortunate thing was that she didn't know when next they would be given this opportunity to see Faizan. If they didn't take the chance that was given to them now, who knew when another door would be open for them to visit? She sighed. Still, she couldn't go.

Not unless Faizan's idea panned out. Audrey had told her Faizan had an idea but that it would probably not work.

"I hope Faizan's idea works out," she said to Bryan.

"What idea is that?" Bryan asked, looking quizzically at her.

"Audrey said he told her and Ken that he had an idea, but that it might not work out. He didn't tell them exactly what it was."

Bryan shrugged. "Then we shouldn't peg our hopes on that idea of his. If we can't go, then we can't go."

She smiled in spite of herself. "So typical of you, Bryan. I wish I had your attitude."

He lifted her fingers and kissed the back of her hand. "Can we go back to sleep now? We are on vacation, after all."

She lay back down on the bed and Bryan stretched out beside her. "Lord, please give Sienna a peaceful sleep, free from nightmares," he said. He drew her into his arms and held her tight, as though by doing so he could shield her from whatever nightmares she might have.

Soon, she began to drift off to sleep. There was a niggling guilt in the back of her mind. Guilt that arose from the fact that Faizan would be hurt because she and Audrey would not go and visit him. Yet, she also felt grateful that she had a loving husband to share her life with through all the difficulties she faced. Hopefully, just as Bryan had told her, the scrupulosity would soon be a thing of the past. Then she could go back to enjoying her life, her marriage, and her precious son. The Lord had blessed her abundantly, and she was determined that nothing would come in the way of that.

FIVE

Trisha looked out the car window as she and Frank drove home from church with Ruby and Molly. She turned to Frank and said, "I really want to see Faizan again, but I don't want to go without you or my sisters."

"I understand," Frank nodded. "But you know you should go. It wouldn't be fair to Faizan. He would have built up so much anticipation and it would be crushed if none of you go. It's already enough that Sienna and Audrey are not going. You need to go and represent everyone."

"I know," she sighed. "I just wish you were all coming with me. It will be so weird going alone."

"It won't be," Frank said. "Faizan and Zainah are there. You will feel super comfortable, you'll see."

She smiled, buoyed by Frank's words of encouragement. She turned around and grinned in amusement when Ruby asked how long it would take before they got home. It never took longer than ten minutes to get from church to their house, but Ruby asked the same question all the time with an impatient scowl on her face.

Molly babbled something in her unique little-girl language and Trisha said, "We will soon be home, honey. Don't you worry."

Molly grabbed Ruby's doll from her hand and Ruby yelled at her. When Ruby grabbed her doll back, Molly screamed.

"Stop it, both of you!" Trisha said, exasperated.

Molly screamed louder and Trisha sighed. "I'm sorry, sweetie."

Frank turned around briefly and then turned back to the road again. When Trisha handed Molly a keychain to play with, she stopped crying.

"Thank God," Trisha said.

They got to the house, and Trisha took Ruby and Molly into the room to change their outfits into more casual clothes. Sienna and Bryan had gone to Audrey and Ken's house to stay for the weekend with Ethan. She had called this morning to tell Trisha that she and Bryan had something they wanted to tell everyone, and Trisha had promised that she would come to the house with Frank and the girls after church.

Frank drove them to Audrey and Ken's house. When they got there, they parked right in front of the house and got the girls out of the backseat. Seconds after they rang the doorbell, the door opened and Ken beamed at them. He shook Frank's hand and hugged Trisha.

Audrey was sitting on the sofa with Ethan on her lap. She stood up as Trisha came in with Frank carrying Molly while Trisha held Ruby's hand. After hugging Trisha, Audrey kissed Molly's forehead and laughed when Ethan reached out and patted Molly on the head.

Ethan struggled to get out of Audrey's arms, and Audrey put him down. He walked over to Ruby and took his cousin's hand. Trisha watched them run over to some toys in the corner of the living room and immediately pounce on them.

"They are so cute," Audrey said, her expression both wistful and delighted at the same time.

Frank and Ken were already seated on the couch and had turned on the TV to watch a football game. Trisha asked, "Where are Sienna and Bryan?"

Audrey answered, "They are still in their room." She stood up. "Let me go get them." Just as Trisha started to walk out of the living room, Sienna and Bryan walked in. Trisha hugged both of them and then sat on the loveseat facing Ken and Frank.

Ken turned down the volume of the TV.

Trisha looked down at Molly, who had already fallen asleep in her arms. It was just like Molly. The children's teacher at church had told Trisha that Molly had been very active in the class and had played around with the other children. She usually fell asleep after she had exerted herself from a 'busy' play day.

Bryan looked around the living room and announced, "So, you know we told you all that we were soon going to be transferred somewhere else, but we didn't know where."

Trisha's heart sank. Who knew where else her sister was going to be transferred to? Hopefully, it would not be some remote place where Sienna would not be able to be contacted from the United States. Just like Faizan.

Bryan looked at Sienna and she picked up from where he stopped. "We received a call from Dr. Lincoln yesterday." A huge smile appeared on her face and Trisha knew immediately that Sienna was about to share good news. She continued. "Dr. Lincoln said we could come back to the United States anytime we wanted. He said we had stayed away from home for too long and he understood we missed our family."

Trisha squealed with joy and Audrey immediately sprung up from her seat. Audrey was the first to hug Sienna and Bryan, and then Trisha stood up, feeling overwhelmed with happiness. She laid Molly down on the part of the couch she had just vacated, and then hugged Bryan and Sienna. "I'm so happy," she whispered in Sienna's ear. "Thank God you guys are finally going to come back home."

After everyone had settled down again and the initial excitement had died down, Audrey said, "So when do both of you plan to return permanently?"

"We're not sure yet," Bryan answered. "After our vacation, I still have a few things to do in Peru and then we will hand over our small church and the orphanage to someone else. However, I am sure in a month or two, we will be back here."

"Wow! I'm so happy," Trisha could not help saying again. She was perched on the edge of the couch as Molly was lying asleep on the spot she had been sitting on. "We should celebrate," she said.

Audrey nodded. "We should."

Trisha said, "Talking about celebrating, I guess I'm the only one going to North Africa to mark Mom and Dad's anniversary. But you guys will celebrate here, won't you?"

"We will throw a small party before you leave. Don't worry about it," Sienna said. She sighed loudly. "I wish I could come with you, Trisha."

"Then come," Trisha said.

"I can't." Sienna pursed her lips.

Trisha said to Ken, "You still haven't received any news from Faizan about whether his idea worked or not?"

"No, I haven't," Ken said. "I tried to call yesterday and this morning, but I didn't get through. I'll try to call again tomorrow. Hopefully, I will be able to speak to him then."

Trisha looked over at Ruby and Ethan, who were still playing in the corner of the living room, and then turned back to listen to Sienna.

Sienna talked about how she would miss the orphanage she ran in Peru. She talked about the place with so much passion that Trisha knew it would be hard for her when she finally left.

They all stayed in the living room, chatting and laughing, and bemoaning the fact that they couldn't go see Faizan for different reasons. Trisha knew, however, that the main reason why her sisters were not going was because their men couldn't go. Audrey had told her she wasn't going to go without Ken as they were trying to get pregnant. Even though Trisha was not sure exactly why Sienna could not go, she knew it had something to do with Bryan not going. However, Trisha was sure there was something more. Trisha was worried about Sienna. She had to find out what exactly had been bothering her before she left for Africa.

Their conversation went on until Trisha casually glanced at the clock on the wall, and then shook her head in surprise. "Guys, it's ten p.m." She looked at Frank. "We've forgotten that we brought the kids along. We need to go now."

She looked over at Ruby and Ethan. She wasn't surprised that they were both asleep on the floor. Thankfully Molly was still sleeping, but then again, that might not be so good. She would probably wake up in the night.

After Trisha and Frank hugged everyone, Frank gently picked Ruby up off the floor, while Trisha lifted Molly into her arms. After they had buckled the girls into their car seats, they got in and Frank started the car.

"I can't tell you how happy I am," she said to Frank as he drove out of Audrey and Ken's driveway. "Sienna is finally coming back home."

Frank turned to her and smiled. "That is great news," he said, and then focused on the road again.

Trisha looked back and smiled at her daughters, who were still fast asleep. She reached out to smooth down Ruby's hair and tuck a stray strand behind her ear. Turning around again, she looked out the window. Frank took her hand and she turned to smile at him.

"I love you, baby," he said to her.

"I love you too, Frank," she said, beaming at him. She looked back again at her precious daughters and her heart flooded with joy. She had a beautiful marriage and two gorgeous daughters. Her life was as perfect as it could possibly be. She sighed in contentment, lifted Frank's hand, which was still clasping hers, and planted a kiss on the back of it. "Thank you for loving me and for being such a great father, Frank," she said to him.

"No, Trisha. I should be the one thanking you. I have never been as happy in my life as these past few years married to you. I get to be a father to Ruby and then Molly."

She grinned at him and said, "I can't wait until we get home so we can make out."

He laughed out loud and said, "That, my sweet wife, is a great idea. I would drive much faster now so we can get home quickly if it weren't for our precious cargo in the back."

Trisha chuckled and looked out of the window again. Peace flooded her heart and once again she thanked the Lord for her great life.

They got home about ten minutes later and put the girls to bed. After that, Frank winked at Trisha. "Are you still up for making out?" he asked her with a mischievous grin.

"Yep!" She said. She took his hand and said, "We can make out on the couch while we watch a movie."

They made their way to the living room. Just as they settled on the couch, the doorbell rang.

Trisha frowned. "Who on earth could that be?"

Frank said, "It's eleven already and we just left everyone now. So, who could possibly be at the door?" He stood up and went to the door.

Trisha sprung up from the couch when Frank yelled, "You! What are you doing here?" She went to the door to see who it was and then her eyes widened in surprise and her jaw dropped. She glared at the unwanted visitor as her surprise was replaced with rage. "Why are you here, Stan?" she asked, looking him over and hating the smug smile on his face.

He looked at her with disdain and then his eyes turned to Frank. He sneered. "I filed a custody case. I want full custody of my daughter!"

Anger boiled within Trisha, threatening to spill out at his words. He had disappeared for years again, even though she'd told him he could see Ruby whenever he wanted as long as he didn't try to take her away. Now he was back, not only wanting to see Ruby but to take her away.

Trisha laughed harshly and shook her head. "You're not serious, Stan! No court is going to grant you full custody of the daughter you abandoned for years."

"We will see about that," Stan said.

Frank, who was normally a gentle and laid-back soul, got in Stan's face. "You're not taking Ruby away! You haven't been here for her all these years and now you come back declaring you want full custody of her? It's not going to happen. I am not going to let that happen."

Stan pushed Frank back and Frank charged at him.

Trisha got between them before a fight could break out. "Please, Frank, let me handle this." She took his hand and squeezed it. "Please."

He backed away slightly and folded his arms across his chest while he glared at Stan.

Livid, Trisha said, "Stan, just go back to where you came from and don't bother us anymore!"

Stan laughed and then glowered at her. "You don't get it, do you, Trisha?" He shrugged. "Anyway, I'll see you in court."

Trisha's eyes blazed as she stared at him. "You know you won't win this battle, so I don't know why you even want to try."

He looked her up and down and said again, "We will see about that." He turned around, walked to his car, which was parked in front of the house, got in and zoomed off.

Trisha fell into Frank's arms, shaken. Just now she had been filled with so much joy as she thought about how beautiful her life was. But within just a few minutes, it had turned from beautiful to turbulent. Ruby and Molly were her world, and if anyone tried to take one of them, she would fight that person tooth and nail. And Stan was no different.

Frank rubbed her back soothingly and said, "He really has no case, Trisha."

She nodded and looked him in the eye. "No one is going to take my daughter away. No one. I won't let it happen."

"He won't take her away," Frank said. "Not on my watch."

Trisha nodded again and settled her head on Frank's chest. Even though she knew Frank was right and Stan didn't really have much of a chance of winning a custody case, she couldn't help feeling a small sense of impending doom. She whispered a prayer to God, asking that it would all go away soon and that the court would throw out Stan's request for custody.

"Everything will be alright, Trisha," Frank said, kissing the top of her head.

"I hope so," she sighed wearily. "With everything in me, I hope so."

SIX

Malik hugged his six-year-old daughter, Fanta, and smiled as he drew back from her. She clutched her doll while she looked up at him with eyes full of love and a slight worry that bothered him. He took her hand and led her to the new house he had just built. He was full of joy. He was finally out of his father's clutches. For the past two years, he had been saving money, hardly spending anything on himself except for his basic needs.

With the money his father paid him as his salary on the farm and also money he had been paid from working as a farmer on several other farms around Dogon, he had saved enough to start a small farm in a tiny village near Dogon. He had built a small house, not unlike the one he lived in on his father's farm.

Finally, he could break all ties with his father now that he had his own farm. Most of all, his daughter would be able to come and live with him in the house. That was partly due to his independence from his father, but most of all because he was soon to be wed.

They reached his house, a yet-to-be painted single bedroom bungalow, sitting on the corner of his acres of farmland. For now, he could only afford to hire two workers, but that would have to be enough.

He opened the door and entered his new house with his daughter. Yesterday, he had gone to Nira to get her from his father's house and they had only just arrived. He looked down at her and asked, "What do you think of the house?"

She scrunched up her face in her usual peculiar way and said, "It's empty, Papa."

He chuckled. "Yes, for now it's empty, but before we move in, I will get furniture for it." He led her to the small kitchen near the living room and then to the single bedroom. His plan was to furnish the house as soon as possible so that by the time he got married in a fortnight, he could move his new wife and his daughter into the house. For now, Fanta would be staying with his fiancée and her grandmother.

He led her out of the bedroom to the tiny storeroom, which he planned to convert into a bedroom for her. There wasn't a window in the room, but he would make one for her. They left the storeroom and he led Fanta to the back of the house. He said to her, "You can play here, Fanta."

She didn't say anything, but he wasn't surprised by that. She was a quiet child and very well behaved; maybe a little too well-behaved for her age. He wanted her to be a little more playful, more open; but he couldn't force her to be what she wasn't. Growing up without a mother hadn't been easy for her. It was the only reason he was getting married now. With all his heart, he wanted her to have another mother to love and take care of her. Yes, he was lonely a lot of the time, but if it was just him, he would simply continue to bear his loneliness.

Thinking about his loneliness caused his mind to travel back to Leila and the last time they were together. His heart still hurt every time he thought about her and how they had broken up.

She'd wanted to change him, to make him who he wasn't. She wanted him to convert to her faith or she would not marry him. He had been so disappointed and hurt by that. He missed her terribly and would give anything to see her again, but he knew it was best that they stay apart. He could never be who she wanted him to be.

He bent down to look into Fanta's face and said softly, "You remember I told you that you would soon have a mother, don't you?"

Fanta nodded as she gazed intently at him.

"Would you like to see her now?"

Fanta shrugged and Malik sighed. He knew that would be the only reaction he would get from his daughter for now. Hopefully, when she met the girl he wanted to marry and they got well acquainted, she would be much more excited about his upcoming marriage and about having a new mother.

He stood up once more and took Fanta's hand. As they made their way to the bus stop, he talked to Fanta about his upcoming wedding and tried to prepare her to meet his fiancée. Since she would be staying with his soon-to-be bride and her grandmother, he hoped Fanta would like them. He would keep visiting her and his wife-to-be until he got married, and then he would move Fanta and his wife into his new house here.

They got to the bus stop, quickly found a bus going to Dogon, and got on.

Throughout the journey, Fanta said nothing, while Malik tried to coax her out of her shell. When they finally got to Dogon, his heart raced with anxiety as he and Fanta walked toward his fiancée's house. Hopefully Fanta would like her.

They finally reached the hut where his fiancée and her grandmother lived and Malik knocked on the wooden door. Seconds later, the door opened and Hauwa's cheery face peered out. A huge smile broke out on her face as she looked at him, and then she looked down at Fanta and whooped. "You brought your daughter!" she said, smiling down at Fanta.

Malik reached out and gave her a quick hug, and then entered the house with Fanta. Hauwa bent down to grin at Fanta, but Fanta hid behind his back. Malik smiled and said, "She's a little shy, but once she gets to know you, she will open up."

Hauwa shook her head. "No problem," she said, looking at him. "Do you want anything to eat? I just finished preparing lunch."

Malik said, "No, I won't eat anything now. I just ate not too long ago."

Hauwa looked down at Fanta again and said, "You will eat now, Fanta, won't you?"

Fanta didn't answer and Malik looked at her. She had settled on the stool beside him, playing with her doll. He asked, "Will you eat now, Fanta?"

Fanta shook her head.

Hauwa said, "You have to eat, Fanta."

"Don't trouble yourself, Hauwa," Malik said. "She ate with me before we came here. I guess she's not hungry yet. Since she's staying here, she will eat later."

Fanta took Malik's hand and held on tightly to it. He smiled at her and faced Hauwa again. "Where is your grandmother?"

"She went to the candy factory in the next town. She will probably be back in the evening." Hauwa looked at him. "Even if you won't eat anything, let me get Fanta some candy. She will like that. Won't you, Fanta?"

Fanta nodded and continued to play with her doll.

Hauwa smiled, stood up, and left the living room.

Malik stared after her and sighed. She was still so young and sometimes he forgot he was going to marry her. She had been just like a little sister to him since he came to Dogon and he still, in a way, thought of her as that.

He looked at Fanta playing with her doll and his mind traveled back to a year ago, when Hauwa's grandmother had first brought up the idea of marrying Hauwa. She had just turned twenty. He came to the hut to give her the small gift he had bought for her. After he had given her the gift, he lamented once more to Hauwa's grandmother about the fact that he had to leave Fanta again with his wicked father. "I can't wait until I have my own farm and get my own house. Then I can have Fanta live with me." And then he frowned. "What am I saying? I still won't be able to have Fanta live with me even if I have my own farm. Farm work is so stressful. I would be gone all day. I can't leave Fanta alone in the house." He sighed sadly.

"Why don't you get married again?" Hauwa's grandmother had asked.

His mind had immediately gone to Leila and a shaft of pain ran through him as he thought about her. He pushed her face away from his mind, along with all the pain that thinking about her caused him. Not even when his late wife, Fanta's mother, had died, had he felt such pain as he did after breaking up with Leila. He had loved her dearly.

He felt a hand on his shoulder and turned. Hauwa's grandmother was looking at him. She said, "I know you have suffered two great losses in your life. The first was when Fanta's mother died, and then when you and Leila broke up. However, I think it's time to move on, if for nothing else than just to have someone to take care of Fanta."

Malik sighed. "Well, I haven't found anyone I like enough to marry. I don't even have time for that right now."

"But you want a mother for your daughter, don't you?" Hauwa's grandmother had asked him.

"With all my heart."

"Then let me tell you something," the old woman said.

Malik raised his brows as Hauwa's grandmother asked Hauwa to go on an errand. Hauwa had reluctantly left, and then the old woman's eyes had settled on him again. "Malik, you should marry Hauwa."

Malik's mouth had fallen open and he stared in astonishment at Hauwa's grandmother. Finally, when he found his voice, he said, "I can't marry her!"

"Why not?" the old woman asked him.

He had blinked and said, "Well... because she's like a little sister to me. Besides, she's too young for me."

"She's twenty," the woman said.

"I know," Malik nodded, "And I am in my mid-thirties. I can't marry her. It's impossible."

"But don't you like her?"

"Of course I do," Malik said. "I like her as a sister. But that is it."

"And I like you as a son, Malik. Do you think Hauwa will be a good mother to your daughter?"

Malik had shot up from his stool. "I am sorry, Ma," he said. "I want a mother for my child but I cannot marry Hauwa. Maybe I will get someone to take care of Fanta while I am at work."

"You've known her for a long time and you know me. You can trust her with your daughter. But how are you sure you can fully trust Fanta with whoever you hire to take care of her?"

"I don't know," he said. He had to quit this conversation immediately. He began to make his way to the door and then stopped when Hauwa's grandmother called out to him. He turned around again.

"Please think about it," the old woman said.

He had left the hut quickly, baffled by the old woman's suggestion. He had been thinking about getting married for years but had never made the leap. When Leila had come back into his life, he had been overjoyed. Not only had he gotten the woman he loved back in his life, he'd found someone who could be Fanta's mother. Someone he could fully trust Fanta with. It was part of the reason why he had been so devastated after the breakup.

A year later he had begun to consider remarrying once more, and even as he went to Hauwa's house to give her the birthday gift, it had been on his mind. But never in a million years had he considered marrying Hauwa. It wasn't because he didn't like her. He did. Or was it because he didn't think she could be a great mother for his daughter? He was sure she would make a great mother for any little girl or boy. And it wasn't rare for girls her age to get married in their community. However, he'd never imagined marrying anyone that young. She was barely out of her teens.

He had gone back to his house on the farm thinking about what Hauwa's grandmother had said, and then he had forced it out of his mind.

However, days later, as he worried about Fanta again, the old woman's suggestion popped up in his mind. After that, he constantly thought about what she told him.

For some time, he avoided going to Hauwa's house. But one day, months later, he was in his house when someone knocked on the door. He went to answer it and his eyes widened in surprise when he saw Hauwa standing there. He let her into his house and sat on the couch. When she sat beside him, he shifted slightly and chided himself for his childish behavior. It wasn't as if she was privy to her grandmother's strange idea to get them married to each other.

What she said next, however, startled him. "You've been avoiding me, Malik, because you don't want to marry me."

For a few moments, he couldn't speak. And then he said, "I'm sorry. Your grandmother brought up the suggestion months ago, but I was not in agreement with it. You're just like a sister to me. I don't know why she thought it was a good idea for us to get married."

Hauwa said, "And why is it not a good idea? Is it because of Leila? I really like Leila as well, but she hasn't been back since she left."

He stared at her with his mouth open, and then he considered her question. Why indeed couldn't they get married? It wasn't as if he was looking for a love match. He liked her well enough. In fact, he liked her more than most other girls he had met. And she was a good girl. So she was only twenty, but she was quite responsible and acted older than her age. His heart began to beat fast as he looked at her. "Do you really want to marry me?" he asked her and waited nervously for her answer.

She chuckled. "I would not have come here if I didn't. And I love you, Malik. I've loved you since the first time I saw you. Yes, I will marry you."

He gazed at her for a long time and finally said, "I have to be honest with you. You know I don't feel the same way. I like you very much, but…"

"I know," Hauwa cut in. "You don't love me the way you loved Leila."

"It's not just that," he said. "I'm still in love with Leila. I still think about her every day. Can you live with that?"

Hauwa nodded.

He said to her, "How can you, though?"

She said, "Look around this village, Malik. There aren't any young men here who I can consider marrying. Unless I want to stay single for the rest of my life, which I don't, I will take whatever you give me. I love you, Malik, and I know you like me. For now, that is enough for me."

He couldn't argue with her logic. He sighed deeply and then nodded. "So we are engaged, then."

She broke into a huge smile and then he gasped when she squealed and hugged him tightly. She stood up and said with a grin, "I have to go and tell my grandmother the good news. She will be so happy."

He had bought her an engagement ring a few weeks later. They had been engaged now for about five months. In two weeks' time, she would be his wife.

He still thought about Leila every day and each time he did, he felt guilty for doing so. "You shouldn't be thinking about another woman when you are about to get married," he constantly chided himself.

He looked at Fanta, who was now braiding her doll's hair, and then looked up when Hauwa walked back into the living room.

"Sorry for taking so long," she said. "The stew I was cooking was starting to burn. I had to pour it into another pot and wash up the burnt one."

"No problem," he said.

He watched as she gave Fanta a packet of multi-colored candies. Fanta put aside her doll and began to gobble them up. He wanted to tell her to eat them slowly, but he changed his mind. He would allow her to enjoy her candy the way she wanted.

Hauwa sat beside Fanta on a stool and began to point out the different colors of the candies. Sometimes, she knowingly said a color wrong and when Fanta corrected her, she widened her eyes in feigned surprise and said, "Oh, I thought it was white."

Fanta laughed each time and exclaimed, "It's not white!"

Malik smiled, thankful that they were beginning to bond, even if it was over candies.

Soon, he and Hauwa began to talk about her grandmother's business at the candy factory and then about the wedding. Hauwa and her grandmother had mostly been in charge of the preparations. He and Hauwa had decided on a very simple wedding with only a few guests. The wedding would be held here in Dogon. He had only invited his mother and Khadija. Hauwa's grandmother and two of Hauwa's friends would be the only guests from Hauwa's side. Fanta would, of course, attend.

Finally, after an hour, Malik got up to go. He had to get back to his father's farm because he had some final business to take care of there. After that, he would go back to the village where he had built his new house. He looked down at Fanta, who was playing with her doll again. He had already told her she would be staying here but that he would come to see her every day. "I have to go, Fanta," he said to her.

Fanta looked up at him and smiled sadly. If it was any other child, they would probably cry and maybe throw a tantrum because they didn't want their papa to go. Fanta, however, took it all with her usual forbearance.

He bent down and hugged her tightly, and then straightened again.

Hauwa followed him as he walked to the door. Just before he opened it, she said, "Malik, I have something very important I need to tell you before we get married."

"What is it?" he asked her. He noted the apprehensive look on her face and became worried as well.

"Malik..." she looked down at the floor and didn't speak for a long moment.

"What is wrong, Hauwa?" Malik asked again.

Finally, she looked up at him and said, "Malik, I... I am a Christian."

His eyes widened in shock and he stared at her. At last he said, "No, you're not."

"Yes, I am," she said quietly.

He couldn't believe it. She was a Christian all this time. He had his suspicions on how she had come to be a Christian. It was probably Leila's doing. He voiced his suspicions and she nodded.

"Yes," she said. "Leila was the one who told me about Jesus. I've been a Christian since then, but I haven't been a very good one. I have been a secret Christian because I know that most people around here would not approve. I'm sorry for hiding it from you. If you are angry with me and don't want to marry me anymore, I understand."

He couldn't speak for a long moment. How was it that the two women he wanted to marry in a space of two years were Christians? He had known Leila was a Christian, but it had not bothered him. However, it had bothered her that he was not. How come it did not bother Hauwa? He looked intently at her and saw how worried she was. He quickly said, "It doesn't bother me. Leila was a Christian and I still wanted to marry her. Unfortunately, she wasn't interested in marrying me because I didn't share her faith."

Hauwa raised her brows as a surprised expression crossed her face. "I didn't know that was the reason you two broke up."

"Well, you know now," he said angrily. Hauwa stepped back slightly and he sighed. "I'm sorry, Hauwa. I'm not angry with you. Just with myself and a little with Leila."

Hauwa nodded and said to him, "You still miss her. I understand. I hope you come to love me one day the way you love her."

He smiled sadly and opened the door. She leaned in, clearly about to kiss him, and he instinctively stepped away from her. He was surprised that she'd tried to kiss him. They had never kissed. She bit her lip and he immediately regretted rejecting her kiss when he saw how hurt she was. Why, oh why had he stepped back when she tried to kiss him?

But he knew why. It was because of Leila. He still loved her passionately even though he had not seen her for two years. "I'm sorry," he said to Hauwa.

Hauwa nodded. "It's okay."

But he knew from the look on her face that it wasn't. He stepped out of the house, troubled. As he made his way to the farm, he kept scolding himself. Why hadn't he corrected his mistake by kissing Hauwa? And how could he marry someone he couldn't bring himself to kiss because he felt like he was cheating on his ex if he did? How could he marry Hauwa when another woman constantly consumed his thoughts?

He got to the farm still asking himself a myriad of questions. The questions had no answers and, finally, he did what he had become an expert at doing since he lost Leila: he buried every question and thought of her deep in his mind so he could concentrate on the matter at hand. Without a doubt, the questions would emerge later on, when he was alone in his house at night, to taunt and confuse him.

SEVEN

Faizan sat up on the sleeping rug. The tent was still dark and he could not see Zainah, but he could hear her soft breathing as she slept next to him. He stood up and went to light the kerosene lamp by the corner of the tent. He lifted it and walked back to the sleeping rug. Looking at the small clock that Miriam had bought for him and Zainah about a year ago, which now sat beside the sleeping rug, he saw the time was five-thirty a.m.

As he usually did whenever he woke up in the night to ease himself, he lightly put his hand on Zainah to make sure she was breathing and that she and the baby were okay. He knew his fears were irrational, but he had them anyway. As he usually did after he had confirmed that she was breathing, he stared at her, marveling at how beautiful she was and the fact that she was his. They had been married for a few years of complete bliss and he thanked God every day for giving her to him. Immediately after, he pulled Zainah close and went back to asleep.

Today, however, he was going to the men's camp that he and Zainah had stumbled upon some days ago. He was supposed to have gone the next day after they found the camp, but he'd had to help with setting up new tents, as half a dozen women had arrived to join the camp.

Today, he was eager to go to the men's camp. He loved the women in this camp and they had all been so nice to him, but he missed the company of his fellow men. He looked down at Zainah's face again as she slept peacefully. If only he could take her with him... but the older man at the camp had made it clear that it was strictly for men. Women were not allowed in that camp. He had to honor that.

He reached out and gently tapped her shoulder. When she opened her eyes, he smiled at her.

She stared quizzically at him and asked, "What is it, Faizan?"

He said, "You remember I promised that man at the men's camp that I would go back there. I want to go there now," he said, and then asked if she had any reservations about his going. Hopefully, she wouldn't.

She sat up and laid her palm on his cheek. She gently caressed him and said, "It's okay, Faizan. I don't mind you going to the camp without me. I know you miss having other male companions. You can go." She looked around and said, "But isn't it a bit too early to go that far?"

He looked at the clock beside her. "It's a quarter to six. That is not so early anymore." He smiled and then kissed her. "I'll be back as soon as I can," he said and stood up.

She slowly stood up as well and hugged him. "You can stay as long as you want today, Faizan," she said. "Leila will keep me company."

He smiled widely. "Thank you."

She shook her head slowly and grinned at him. "You know, though, that you can't make a habit of always going to that men's camp. I know how you men are. When you are all having fun together, you don't want to go home anymore."

He laughed. "I don't think I will make it a habit since I can't take you along with me. Plus, why would I want to stay with a bunch of men for long when I have such a beautiful wife waiting for me here?"

She stepped away from him, still grinning. "Well then, go quickly so you can hurry back to your beautiful wife."

He leaned down, kissed her belly, and then went to light the smaller kerosene lamp that was at the other end of the tent. He left with Zainah waving to him.

He made his way slowly down the path he and Zainah had taken that led to the men's camp. As he walked, he thought about what he planned to ask their leader. His excitement grew as he thought about spending the day with the men at the camp.

He had to ask them if his brothers-in-law could stay with them. If they could, they would be able to come here with Sienna, Audrey, and Trisha. With all his heart, he hoped the men at the camp would agree, because he had a feeling that his sisters would not want to travel without their husbands. He would be extremely disappointed if that happened. "Lord, please let them agree to my request," he prayed.

Soon he approached the men's camp and saw that it was already bustling with activity.

Multiple eyes turned to him as he made his way into the camp. One of those eyes belonged to the older man he had spoken with the day he and Zainah discovered this place. The man smiled widely, walked up to him, and gave him a huge hug as though they were old friends.

Faizan smiled, pleasantly surprised, and even more so when some of the other men surrounded him, hugged him, and pounded his back as though he had just won a competition on their behalf. Their greeting was simple and manly, and he found he had missed this sort of rough, masculine exchange. For some reason, he felt extremely touched by it all. A few of them said, "The peace of Christ be with you."

They led him into a small tent not unlike the one many at the women's camp stayed in, but smaller than the one he and Zainah occupied. He sat on a small mat, which was plain, different from the brightly colored mats and rugs in the women's camp. There were no embroidered pillows here either. His and Zainah's tent, like many others at the women's camp, were decorated with an abundance of pillows.

Someone brought him a jug and a cup and poured a white liquid from the jug into the cup. They handed it to him and he looked curiously into the face of the older man who was standing beside him. He asked, "What is it?"

"It's a special, non-alcoholic drink that one of us brought from his hometown. We all like it very much and told him to bring a large amount before we came here. It really works for this place because it can stay for a long time before going bad."

Faizan looked at the drink, wondering what exactly it was. He took a sip and then nodded at the older man, who seemed to be the leader of the camp. It was sweet but not too sweet and it had a slightly bitter aftertaste. He drank the whole cup and chuckled when the man who had poured him the drink poured another cup for him. This time, he took sips while the older man sat beside him. Three other men sat across from him.

He noted that just like the women's camp, the men here were from different parts of the region, with different skin tones and varying facial features. He thought about what Zainah had said concerning letting the women at the camp know about this men's camp because many of the women yearned to have husbands and children of their own.

But it was completely impossible. As much as he understood where Zainah was coming from and also wanted any woman who desired what he and Zainah had to have it, they had to respect the wishes of the men here. They had come to this place to separate themselves from the world, and specifically, as the older man had said, from women. It would not be fair or right for the women at the camp to come here. As a man, he understood the weaknesses of men, and if these men wanted to stay away from women, they needed to be allowed to do so in peace. Just as he had asked Zainah not to tell any of the women about the men's camp, he would tell the men here to say nothing about the women's camp.

The older man smiled and said to him, "My name is Ishaq." He pointed out the three men sitting across from them. "This is Jafar, and this is Abdul, and this is Reza."

Faizan looked at the three men, who he guessed were all the leaders of the camp. Jafar had a long beard, bushy eyebrows, and an olive complexion. From what Faizan noticed when he was standing up, Jafar was tall and lanky. Abdul was short with a thick mustache and dark skin, as dark as Zainah's. Reza was a strapping young man with a trim beard and the same olive complexion as Jafar. He seemed like the youngest of the three and was probably in his late twenties. Faizan smiled at the men and said, "My name is Faizan. I'm glad to meet all of you."

"So, where do you and your wife live, Faizan?" Ishaq asked.

Faizan's heart jumped slightly at the question. He had not considered that he would be asked about it. He had just made up his mind not to tell the men about the women's camp. Would it be wrong if he lied about where he lived? He decided to conceal the truth about where he and Zainah lived. No good would come of telling these men that there was a camp full of single young women somewhere near.

The men wanted to stay totally pure. He would not jeopardize that.

"My wife and I live just a short distance from here, in a tent. Nothing special," he added quickly in order to discourage any of the men from deciding to pay he and Zainah a visit.

"I might come and visit you on Sunday," Ishaq said.

Faizan's eyebrows lifted and his heart began to pound. What have I done? he thought.

"I hope your wife will not mind me visiting," Ishaq said. "I will come with my fellow brothers here."

Faizan's heart sank even further. He had to find a way to discourage them from coming. He said in a tone he hoped did not betray his concern, "I thought you had all moved here to stay away from women?"

Ishaq chuckled. "I take it you are talking about your wife. Well, she's just one woman and she's already married to you. There is no temptation there, even though she is a very good-looking woman, if you will permit me to say so."

In spite of himself, Faizan smiled and nodded in agreement. And then his heart filled with worry again. Neither the women at the camp nor the men here could know of the other's existence. He wasn't against love, but he would not be the cause of people breaking their vows to God. Their dedication must stay pure. It reminded him of Zainah's vow before they got married and how that had kept them away from each other for a long time. There had to be other women like Zainah who had taken that kind of vow. Since none of them had met any of the men here, their hearts were safe from falling in love and having to break their vows because of that love.

You're being selfish, a thought ran through his mind.

He pushed the thought away. It did not even make any sense.

"What is on your mind, my brother?" Ishaq said to him, his eyes searching Faizan's closely.

Faizan blinked and came out of his reverie. "I'm sorry. Nothing much," he answered.

"Well, you haven't given me an answer," Ishaq said. "Are we invited to your tent or do you want us to stay away? We will understand if you do."

Faizan couldn't speak for a long time. He thought about the favor he wanted to ask. If he told them for whatever reason that they couldn't visit him, how would he then ask them for a favor on behalf of his brothers-in-law?

He looked at the men. They were looking at him expectantly. He needed to give them an answer now. Without thinking about it much longer, he said, "Yes. You can come, but please give me some time and let me know when you will be coming so we can make preparations for you before you do."

Ishaq nodded. "Of course." He stood up and then motioned with his hand for the other men to stand up too. He smiled down at Faizan. "Come. Let me show you the whole camp."

Faizan stood up and followed Ishaq out of the tent. The other men followed behind.

They went around the camp from one tent to the other. Faizan greeted the other men in the camp as they went around doing their chores, or just sitting in their tent, chatting or reading the Bible.

They entered a bigger, partly open tent where three men were stirring a big smoking pot of food on an open fire. Two men came into the tent carrying buckets of water and dropped them near the men who were cooking. The scene was just like that in the women's camp whenever he visited the cooking tent. In many ways, life here was like that in the women's camp, only in that this camp was made up of just men.

They came out of the cooking tent and continued to their tour around the camp. Soon, they entered another big tent. Mats were placed on the ground all around this tent. Ishaq said, "This is where we all gather in the mornings and at night for our general prayers." He turned to look at Faizan. "Will you join us this evening for the prayers?"

Faizan didn't say anything for a few seconds while he thought about the man's request. If he joined them this evening, he would probably miss the evening prayers at the women's camp. Since he was the only man at the camp, his absence would be noticed quickly and Miriam would for sure want to know where he had gone. She worried about all the inhabitants of the camp, even him, which amused him a lot seeing that he was the one who was supposed to be the protector. He had taken on that role since he'd moved into the camp. Thankfully, there had been no attacks. Not that the women's camp had ever suffered attacks, except the one they'd had when he'd first arrived there, before he and Zainah got married. He had been the cause of that one, and as much as he was not expecting another similar attack, it was not totally unlikely, and part of him was always on alert in case it happened again.

He finally said to Ishaq, "I would love to join in your prayers, but I have to go home to my wife. She will be worried if I stay out too late."

"I understand," Ishaq said.

They continued to explore the camp and then finally came back again to the first tent. They all settled back down on their seats and started a lively conversation about football, of all things; or as his friends and sisters in America called it, soccer.

He had been a huge fan of soccer and had watched it a lot before his shameful life in the desert as a terrorist. Even during that life, he still loved the game and listened to it on the radio whenever he could. He was surprised that these men, who seemed austere and serious, spoke so fervently about the different European teams and the different games they had watched and supported. It took him back to his old life and some of the good things that he missed about it. When he lived in America, while the other men watched American football, he chose to watch his soccer matches and followed his teams very closely.

The conversation soon veered toward their old lives and what they had done and been. As the men talked about their different occupations, their ordinary and unique lives back then, Faizan listened, partly in apprehension. What if they asked him what he did in his past life? What would he tell them? He definitely couldn't tell them he had been a terrorist.

"And you, Faizan," Reza said, facing him. "Where did you live before now? What was your occupation before you moved to this desert? How did you grow up, and are your parents still alive?"

Faizan took a deep breath and said, "Well, I was born in Spain but lost my mother at a very young age. It's a long story but, umm... I lived for some time in Algeria... and then lived in America for a few years before I came here."

"That's very interesting," Abdul said. "You've lived in many places."

Ishaq smiled. "Well, you are a man of the world and you have lived in America. When I was much younger, I wanted to go to America but never had the opportunity."

"I am originally from Algeria," Jafar said. "Where exactly did you live when you stayed in Algeria?"

Faizan's pulse raced and a heaviness settled over him. He had lived deep in the desert as a dangerous terrorist during his years in Algeria. How was he going to get out of this one? He muttered, "It's been a while, so I can't really remember where I lived, but it was slightly deserted at that time."

He waved his hand and quickly changed the topic. "So, since you all came to this camp, how has it been living away from the world out there and everything it has to offer? Has it been hard?"

Ishaq answered, "I could ask you the same question."

Reza said, "I guess for you, being married has helped a lot."

Faizan looked at Reza. He looked serious and slightly forlorn. The expression on his face reminded Faizan of the look on some of the young women's faces at the camp whenever they visited him and Zainah in their tent. When he and Zainah had just gotten married, many of the young women who came to visit them in their tent just sat there, gazing at them with wistful expressions on their faces. At the time, he thought it was slightly strange. But then Zainah had explained to him that some of the young women had told her how much they wished they could have what she had.

Was it possible that this young man wanted a wife, even though he had left the world to escape what the men here called "distractions"? Once again, he thought about what Zainah had said about letting both camps mix, and then pushed the thought away again.

Once more, the men had begun to chat about their old lives, the lives they had left behind to come here. As they talked, he thought about how lucky, or rather blessed, he was to have Zainah as his wife. He hadn't really made much of his life before and certainly missed nothing about his life as a terrorist. The only thing he missed were his sisters and brothers-in-law. Thinking about his sisters and their husbands, he remembered what he wanted to ask these men.

Soon, two young men who seemed barely out of their teens brought a tray with steaming plates of food. One of them handed Faizan a plate and he looked at the food. It was rice, chicken, and steamed vegetables. He dug into the food as the other men did while wondering how they bought their food items. They probably brought all they needed with them before they came here, but their supplies would soon be depleted. He found the food really tasty and told the men so.

They ate as they continued to chat. When there was a lull in the conversation, he said, "Can I ask for a favor?"

"Go ahead," Ishaq said.

"My sisters and their husbands are planning to visit us very soon. Unfortunately, there is no space for my brothers-in-law, only for my sisters. Can my in-laws—there are three of them—can they come and stay here with you, my friends?"

He felt terrible for lying to them, but he had to respect their wishes and also the wishes of many of the women at the camp who did not want to mix with men. If he told them the full truth—that he lived in a women's camp, he was almost certain someone like Reza would, without permission, go and investigate and find the camp. Soon, neither of the camps would be a secret and there would be plenty of the "distractions" these men and some of the women wanted to avoid, and it would be his fault. He couldn't let that happen.

Ishaq rubbed his beard and looked at the other men across from them. "Do any of you oppose the idea of Faizan's brothers-in-law coming here to stay with us?"

The men shook their heads and said that they did not.

Ishaq turned to Faizan and said, "I don't have any problems with them staying here and neither do these men. I doubt any of the men at the camp will have any problems, either. Your brothers-in-law are men like us." He looked up thoughtfully and then looked at Faizan again. "Are they Christians?

Because if they are not, we hope to make them so."

Faizan smiled, relieved. "They are all Christians. They love the Lord and will be good guests."

Ishaq nodded. "Then they are welcome to stay here."

"Thank you so much," Faizan said, smiling widely. "I am relieved." He silently gave thanks to the Lord in his heart. He couldn't wait for Ken to call again so he could give him the good news. Audrey, Sienna, and Trisha would be very relieved by this, and their spouses would be happy as well.

Faizan continued to chat with these warm believers who had embraced him even though they did not know him well. He really liked them and he knew that this place would soon become a place he came to regularly.

When another man came into the tent holding a tray with plates of food again, Faizan's brows lifted in surprise. How was it already time to eat again? They had been sitting here talking for so long. He guessed that time did really fly when you were having fun.

After they had eaten, they continued to talk. When there was another lull in the conversation, Faizan said, "I think it's time for me to go." He stood up and the men stood up as well.

Ishaq reached out and hugged him; so did the other men. They all stepped out of the tent together and the men walked him to the edge of the camp.

Ishaq said, "So, my friend, when will you be back?"

"I'll come tomorrow or the next. It depends on what is comfortable with my wife."

"The trials of a married man," Ishaq said, laughing.

"It's not much of a trial." Faizan grinned.

Ishaq nodded and said, "We will be looking forward to your visit again. Won't we, brothers?" He looked at the other men.

"We will," Jafar said.

"I hope you will be able to join us in our general prayers the next time you come," Abdul told him.

Reza smiled at him. "I wish I could come and visit you now and just see how you live."

Faizan ran his fingers through his hair and prayed that the man's curiosity would not lead him to the women's camp one day.

Faizan waved to the men and left. He walked quickly back to the women's camp, this time with his heart full. He had enjoyed the men's company tremendously, and he couldn't wait to go back again.

When he finally got to the camp, he went straight to his own tent, hoping Zainah was there so he could tell her about his day. He was disappointed when he didn't see her. He guessed she was with Leila.

He left his tent and began to make his way to Leila's, and then smiled when he saw Zainah walking toward him.

Zainah reached him, hugged him, and then pulled away again. "Halima told me just now that she saw you entering our tent. A lot of people noticed your absence today."

Faizan kissed her on the cheek and said, "What did you tell them?"

"I told them you were somewhere around, but a few of the women actually made it their duty to go searching for you. You know how much joy some of them take from observing us every day."

Faizan chuckled and said in a teasing voice, "I hadn't noticed."

She shook her head. "That's a lie. You haven't noticed how the women here sometimes follow us around and ask all those questions about our married life?"

"Okay," Faizan smiled. "Of course I have noticed. Thankfully, most of the questions are directed at you."

Zainah took his hand and whispered, "Come and tell me all about your time at the men's camp. Did you enjoy yourself?"

Faizan beamed. "More than I thought I would. I enjoyed talking to them and I told them I would come back again."

They entered their tent together and sat on one of the rugs, surrounded by soft, embroidered pillows. Faizan began to tell her all the things he had talked about with the men and then looked up when someone yelled from outside the tent, "Can I come in?"

Since the tent had no doors, in order to respect their privacy as a married couple, anyone who wanted to come in let them know first from the outside. It was the usual way and Faizan was grateful for it, even though once in a while he had been a little put out when a visitor came and interrupted his time with Zainah. Thankfully, that did not happen a lot. Most people made them aware beforehand that they were coming for a visit.

He yelled back to whoever was outside the tent, "You can come in!"

Sherifat, a girl in her early twenties who had taken to Zainah and Faizan and followed them around the camp, came in. Sherifat had been very helpful to him and Zainah, constantly asking if Zainah was okay and always wanting to help since Zainah was pregnant. She beamed at Zainah and then said to Faizan, "Miriam wants to see you. I think you have a phone call."

Faizan immediately stood up, excited. He said to Zainah, "That must be Ken calling. He will be happy when I tell him the good news."

"What good news?" Zainah asked, and then her brows rose and she nodded.

Faizan left Sherifat and Zainah in the tent. As he made his way to Miriam's tent, it suddenly occurred to him that Miriam might be near when he told Ken on the phone about the men's camp. Maybe it was time to tell Miriam about the camp. He knew Miriam well and trusted her. She would also keep the existence of the men's camp secret while helping him with whatever he needed to make his brothers-in-law's stay comfortable. In addition, she would help his sisters settle down well in the women's camp for the duration of their visit.

He got to Miriam's tent and then smiled in greeting as she handed him the satellite phone. He held it to his ear. "Hello," he said, and then looked back at Miriam.

She was staring at him with a look of mild curiosity.

He sighed and stepped out of her tent. He would tell her about the men's camp after the call.

"Hi, Faizan," Ken said.

"Ken, I have good news. There is a men's camp some distance away from our own camp and the feel of the place is just like ours. I visited them and asked if you, Frank, and Bryan could stay there, and they said you could. It's not too far from our camp so you and the guys can visit your wives and vice-versa."

He immediately recalled that the men at the camp did not want female visitors and said quickly, "Well, none of your wives will be able to visit you, but I guess you can visit them here. You just can't stay. I'll have to find some excuse to tell the women here about where you guys will be staying."

"Okay. It's not a perfect situation, but it is good news," Ken said. "Our plans to all travel to see you had already begun to disintegrate. Audrey and Sienna had said they could not come if I and Bryan were not going to go. They will be really happy to hear that we can come after all."

"I can't wait for all of you to come here. I have missed you all so much. You'll have a great time here."

"I know we will." Ken chuckled.

"Where is Audrey?" Faizan asked.

"She and Sienna went to see Trisha. Trisha called them this morning about something very important she wanted to tell them. I don't know what it is, but I guess Audrey will tell me when she gets back."

"Okay," Faizan said. Once again, his heart soared with excitement and anticipation. "There are just a few days left for you all to come here."

"Yes," Ken said.

"Well, I better start making preparations for your arrival. I have to set up new tents for the girls."

"So, our plane will land in that town. Blima, isn't it?"

"Yes," Faizan answered. "I've made arrangements with the driver who takes Miriam to town to come here on the day before you arrive. We will leave very early the next day to pick you up and bring you here."

"I will see you in a couple of days, then," Ken said.

"Yes, you will," Faizan said gleefully. "Greet my precious sisters when they come back and tell them I can't wait for them to come."

"I will, Faizan."

After the call ended, Faizan took a deep breath and then looked back at Miriam's tent. It was time to tell Miriam about the men's camp. As much as he trusted her levelheadedness and her ability to keep a secret, there was always a chance that she might want to investigate the men's camp for herself and even take a few of the women there with her. If that happened, Ishaq and the other men would feel that he'd betrayed them by bringing women to their camp.

He sighed. "Lord, please don't let that happen." He walked toward Miriam's tent. Before he entered, he took another deep breath and prayed once more that Miriam would keep his secret.

EIGHT

Trisha exhaled and looked at Sienna and Audrey, who were sitting beside her on the couch. She sighed heavily. Since Stan had come and threatened her with that lawsuit, her mind had been going around and around the conversation. She'd asked the Lord over and over again why Stan had come back now.

Sienna reached out and touched Trisha's shoulder. She said, "What is it, Trisha? You look awful and you're scaring me. What's wrong?"

Audrey searched Trisha's eyes and said, "Please, Trisha, tell us. What's the matter?" Her forehead furrowed. "Please tell me nothing has happened to Frank or the kids." Audrey looked around the living room and said, "Where are they, anyway?"

Trisha shook her head. "Frank and the kids are okay. He took the girls to see his mom and dad."

"Then what's the matter?" Audrey asked.

"Stan came here yesterday."

"What?" Audrey exclaimed and leaned forward to gaze at Trisha. "Stan, your slimy ex-husband, came here? What did he want?"

Trisha put her hand on her forehead as details of her angry conversation with Stan came rushing back to her. She said, "He came to tell me he was suing for custody of Ruby. Full custody."

Sienna's mouth dropped open and Audrey gave a short laugh.

"He has gone mad, that Stan!" Audrey said. "He's not been around for years and he thinks he can just waltz in and get full custody of Ruby?"

Sienna said, "I don't really think he has a case, Trish. I know it's hard, but I don't think the court will grant him shared custody, not to talk of full custody."

"I am pretty sure the case will be thrown out," Audrey said. "He's never really been in that child's life. Not when she was born, and not for all these years. You and Frank are the only parents Ruby has and Frank has been her father for years."

Trisha listened to her sisters tell her that Stan had no case. It was the same thing Frank had been telling her throughout yesterday and even today, but it still hadn't stopped her from worrying continuously. Trisha finally said, "Unfortunately, because of all this, I won't be able to go and see Faizan anymore."

Audrey sighed and Sienna nodded, looking sad.

"That's understandable," Audrey said. "But that means none of us will be going. Faizan will be so disappointed. Who knows when we will be allowed to go and see him next?"

Sienna shook her head. "If only they would let him back into the country, it would solve everything."

"That will probably never happen," Audrey said. She looked at Trisha and put her hand on her sister's shoulder. "Don't worry, Trish. We will be here for you. Stan is not going to take Ruby away and when that custody case is over, if it even begins at all, I think you should file a restraining order against him. He shouldn't be allowed to come near you or your kids anymore."

In spite of herself, Trisha smiled, albeit sadly. "What will I give as a reason for filing the restraining order? It's not like he is dangerous or has threatened me, Frank, or any of the kids physically."

"He is a rogue, that Stan," Audrey said. "Even if he hasn't threatened any of you physically, he has been threatening your well-being ever since he came back into the picture a few years ago, and then now."

Trisha smiled sadly. "Our plan to mark Mom and Dad's anniversary by taking that trip to North Africa has disintegrated before our eyes."

"Well, we can still throw a party here, even if it's a small one," Sienna said.

"But we wanted to do something more meaningful than just throwing a party," Audrey said.

Trisha nodded. They had briefly talked about using a part of their inheritance to do something tangible for the women at the camp where Zainah and Faizan lived. They hadn't yet discussed what exactly they would do, but they had already started to make a budget for whatever it was. Now that would not happen.

"We could just donate the money even if we can't go," Sienna said.

"I guess that could work." Audrey sat back on her seat. "I would have loved to go, but unfortunately this is the time when Ken and I have to double down on trying to have a baby. It's become so tiring and I'm about to give up."

"Don't, Audrey," Trisha said. She took Audrey's hand. "It will soon happen for you. Don't worry about it. The doctor told you there's nothing wrong with you or Ken so it will happen soon."

Sienna sighed. "So no one is going to see Faizan. He will be pretty hurt by that."

"I know," Audrey said. "Ken told me the last time he called, Faizan was really excited about our upcoming visit. And so was Zainah. If only just one of us could go." Audrey stared quizzically at Sienna. "You haven't told us why you decided not to go, Sienna."

Sienna shrugged. "I just decided that if Bryan can't go, then neither will I."

Trisha shook her head and said, "That might be true, but I know you, Sienna. There's something else bothering you. That day... when you told us you and Bryan were going to move back to the United States soon, there was something about the way you looked. I knew that day that something was wrong. I planned on asking you what it was later on, but I guess I forgot. Please tell us what it is."

Audrey shifted closer to Sienna and put her arm around her shoulder. "What is wrong, Sienna? I'm so sorry I haven't noticed like Trisha has. I've been so preoccupied with trying to have a baby that I haven't bothered to really see what is going on around me."

Sienna bit her lip and looked away.

Audrey kept rubbing Sienna's back while Trisha waited patiently for her to turn around and tell them what was wrong. After a while, when Sienna still did not speak, Trisha said, "Please, Sienna, tell us what is bothering you. We can't help you in any way if you don't, and we are terribly worried about you."

Sienna finally turned to look at Trisha and Audrey again and said in a small voice, "The panic attacks and crippling fear are back." She shut her eyes and a look of dread appeared on her face.

Trisha's heart sank and fear gripped her. She remembered the last time Sienna had those panic attacks and crippling fear. She and Audrey had not known how bad it was until Sienna had attempted to take her life. Thankfully, she had not succeeded. Trisha and Audrey had gone to stay with her in her New York apartment for some time, and even Bryan had stayed with them as well. That was before he and Sienna got married. It had been a dreadful time and Trisha had breathed a huge sigh of relief when, months later, Sienna seemed totally okay and married Bryan. As far as she knew, the fear and anxiety had not returned. But maybe she was wrong. Maybe Sienna had been living in fear for a long time without telling anyone about it, just like she had years ago.

At last, Sienna turned around again. Worry was etched on her face.

Audrey took Sienna's hands and looked into her eyes. "When did it all start again?" she asked, her voice tinged with worry.

"It began some months ago."

"Why didn't you tell us?" Trisha said, unable to hold back her tears.

"It started gradually and so I did not really pay attention to it until just about a month ago, when it became serious."

Trisha's hand flew to her mouth. "Please tell me you didn't try to..." She couldn't bring herself to complete her sentence, but clearly Sienna knew exactly what she meant because she shook her head.

"No, I didn't try to take my life again. Thankfully Bryan is helping me through it, and I have the word of God to battle it. But still, there are days when the fearful thoughts swamp me and I feel like I'm being suffocated. If Bryan is not around when I have a panic attack, I almost feel as though I'm about to lose my mind. I am grateful that I have Ethan to think about. Whenever I begin to fall apart, I think about him, that I have to take care of him, and then I gather myself together as best as I can. I have done what I did in the past to try to get rid of it, but it's just not going away this time. I am so tired."

"But if Bryan is helping you through it like he did years ago, why is it not going away?" Audrey asked.

"I don't know," Sienna said. "Unlike all those years ago, when the fear and attacks caused me to run away from God and try to kill myself, this time I have no such thoughts. However, deliverance seems so far away and I don't know why. Maybe it's because I've gotten so used to the word from the scriptures that delivered me the last time. I just don't know."

"Are you under more stress than usual?" Trisha asked, and then shook her head. "What am I saying? Of course you are. You're a wife and mother now. Plus, you've been running that orphanage. I'm so glad you and Bryan are coming back so I can keep an eye on you."

"We will help you through it, Sienna. I promise you that."

Sienna smiled, and Trisha reached out and gave her a hug. "I love you, little sister," she said.

"I love you too, Trisha," Sienna said. "Thank you so much." She held out her hands and hugged Trisha and Audrey, and they stayed that way for about a full minute.

Audrey was the first to draw back. She said, "I have to go, you guys. Let's make some kind of plan to speak to Faizan together. Even if we all can't go, we should at least talk to him and maybe give him some kind of explanation as to why we can't make the trip."

"You're right," Trisha said.

Audrey got up and looked down at Sienna. "Are you staying here with Trisha today, Sienna, or are you coming with me?"

"No, I'll stay here with Trisha." Sienna wiped the tears from her eyes. "Before Bryan took Ethan to the park, he said we would be staying here today. They will probably come back soon." She smiled through her tears. "Besides, you and Ken need your privacy. You know... to make a baby."

Audrey groaned and then laughed. "Stop it, Sienna! You know our house is huge. Ken and I have all the privacy we need."

Sienna chuckled and Trisha shook her head in amusement.

They waved to Audrey as she left, and then Trisha hugged Sienna again. "I'm always here for you," Trisha said to her. "Remember that. Remember that you can always talk to me."

"Thank you, Trish," Sienna said. "But soon Bryan and I will have to go back to Peru. During the day I'm mostly at the orphanage while Bryan is at the church or off on one of his mission trips. When I get home whenever Bryan is away on a mission trip, I get lonely. That is when the panic and anxiety start. I don't know what I would have done if I didn't have Ethan."

Fear knocked on Trisha's heart, but she refused to pay any attention to it. She focused fully on Sienna. "I'll be praying for you, Sienna. The Lord is your strength and He will bring you out of all this."

Sienna gave Trisha a weary smile. "I hope so." She sighed and stood up. "I think I will go and take a short nap. Once all the kids return, this place will be in complete chaos again."

Trisha watched her go with a heavy heart and then shut her eyes. She began to pray and ask the Lord to deliver her sister from all her fears and the root cause of the attacks. He had done it before and He could do it again. She was rounding off her prayers when the doorbell rang.

Must be Bryan and Ethan, or maybe Lauren, she thought. Lauren had promised to come by this afternoon to talk about how her blind date went.

Trisha stood up and went to the door. She opened it and scowled. "Stan!" She glared at him and made no attempt to hide her disdain.

He did not wear the sneer or smug smile he had when he'd come by yesterday. Instead, he had a subdued expression on his face. "Can I come in?" he asked her.

"No! No, you can't!" she said to him.

"Please."

"I'm sorry, Stan, but I am not letting you into my house."

"It was once my house as well."

"Well, it's not anymore."

"Your husband is in, isn't he? That's why you won't let me in."

"No, that's not why. It's because you're threatening to take my daughter away from me, and that is just wrong."

"Ruby is my daughter as well."

"She hasn't been for years."

He sighed loudly and Trisha was surprised when he nodded. "Well, if you will not let me in, I guess I will have to tell you why I came out here."

"I guess you will," she said.

"I've come to make a deal with you."

She gazed suspiciously at him. "I'm not interested in making any deal with you," she said.

"You will be when you hear what I have to say." Before she could say anything, he continued, "I will not pursue the custody case anymore on one condition."

Her eyes widened and then suspicion once again replaced her surprise. She said slowly, "And what is that condition?"

He looked down for a few seconds and then looked up at her once more. The smug smile had returned.

She folded her arms across her chest and glared at him. "Well, are you going to tell me what it is?"

"I won't file for custody anymore if you will make it worth my while."

She frowned. "And what do you mean by that?"

"I mean I want money from your inheritance, Trisha. You inherited a lot of money from your father and I want some of it."

Trisha's mouth fell open and then she began to laugh.

"What is so funny?" he growled.

"Stan, you want some of my inheritance. Wow! That is what you always wanted, wasn't it? That was why you came back the last time. When I broke off our engagement, you went away, sulking. It wasn't me you wanted. It was the money."

"So?" Stan growled. "Are you going to accept the deal or not?"

She looked at him with burning hatred in her heart and then asked the Lord to forgive her for how much she hated him. She took a deep breath to try to let go of her angry feelings and said, "Fine! How much do you want?"

Stan smiled again and said, "I want a large sum. Fifty million dollars."

"That is impossible!" Trisha said. "Why would I give you 90 percent of my money?"

Stan shrugged. "Well, it's your decision. It's either that or we go to court to fight for custody of Ruby, but just know that I am also hiring the best lawyers. I will not make it easy for you."

"You have no case, Stan."

"You wait and see," he said. "I want that money and I will do whatever it takes to get it." He began to back away and she stopped him.

"Wait!" she said. She glowered at him. "Aren't you ashamed of yourself? You want money in exchange for your daughter. You are truly a terrible person."

Stan shrugged. "I have been told that before. Are you going to give me the money or not?"

"I don't even have that kind of money to give you."

"You're a liar, Trisha!"

Trisha sighed loudly and silently asked the Lord for help. "Okay, Stan, I will give you the money, but you have to be patient. It will take some time for me to get it for you."

"How much time are you talking about?"

"About a year," she said, hoping to buy some time while she decided on how to proceed. She would contact her lawyers and see if she could call Stan's bluff. She would get advice and know if she should go to court to battle Stan for Ruby or if it was better to just give him the money.

"No can do," he said.

"That's the best I can do, Stan. The money is tied up in a lot of investments and it will take time to liquidate it. I will get the money for you but you need to be patient."

"I can only wait three months," Stan said.

"Three months is too short," she said to him.

"Well, have it your way. I'll see you in court, then." He turned around and began to walk away, and she called him back once more.

"Alright, three months it is."

He smiled widely. "Good! And don't try to double cross me, Trisha, or I will make your life a living hell."

She said nothing and watched as he walked to his car and drove away. After that, she shut the door quietly and threw herself onto the sofa. This was all wrong. She wanted to curl up on the sofa and weep, but she gathered herself together, reached for her phone, and called her lawyers. She would find out what her options were and then, if she had to fight, she would fight Stan with everything in her. One thing she knew was that no one was taking Ruby away from her. No one.

*****

Audrey walked into her house and found Ken sitting on the living room couch, flipping through the channels on TV. He turned, smiled at her, and patted the seat beside him. "Audrey," he said. "I've got good news to share."

She sat beside him and smiled curiously. "Did you speak to Faizan?"

"Yes, I did," Ken said.

"What did he say?" Audrey asked.

"He said that Frank, Bryan, and I can come to the camp. He found a men's camp near the women's camp where he and Zainah stay. They agreed to let us stay there for the duration of our trip."

Audrey whooped. She reached out and hugged Ken, and he squeezed her tight. Her heart flooded with joy. Finally, she would be able to go and see Faizan and Ken would come along, too. And then she remembered what Trisha had just told her and her heart sank. She turned away from Ken and shut her eyes as sadness replaced her joy.

"What is it, Audrey?" Ken asked.

Audrey sighed loudly and opened her eyes. "I still can't go, Ken," she said.

"Why not?"

"It's Trisha. She told me and Sienna just now that Stan visited her and Frank and told them he was going to file for custody of Ruby. Trisha is distraught and right now Sienna and I have to be there for her."

Ken thinned his lips and nodded. "I understand." He smiled sadly. "This is so weird. First, no one except Trisha could go, and now that we can, Trisha can't, and because of that, we can't either." He shook his head. "Maybe Bryan can go."

"No, I don't think so," Audrey said. "Sienna is going through some stuff right now and she needs Bryan beside her. And I am pretty sure he won't want to go without her."

"Great!" Ken shook his head, dismay written on his face. "Now I have to call Faizan and tell him that none of us is going again."

"He is going to be so disappointed," Audrey said ruefully. "And we were all looking forward to the trip. If that idiotic Stan had not returned, things would not be like this."

"What is Trisha going to do now?" Ken asked, looking at Audrey.

"She said she is going to fight him. I don't think he can ever win the case. He hasn't even been there for Ruby."

"Frank is definitely the only real father she's known," Ken said.

Audrey nodded.

"Well, I guess I have to call Faizan now. Let's just hope Miriam's phone goes through, because if it doesn't Faizan will still think we are coming."

Audrey sighed. "And we were supposed to leave in just five days. We have to get him on the phone, Ken. It will be really bad if we are unable to and he keeps expecting us and we don't show up on the day we are supposed to." She sighed again. "Tell me why Faizan can't get a satellite phone like Miriam's as well."

"The camp has to be kept as private as possible. Multiple phones wouldn't be a good idea."

Audrey nodded. She knew that, but it made reaching Faizan really difficult. That lady, Miriam, didn't have her phone charged regularly and so a lot of times, the phone battery was dead. Ken picked up his phone and began to dial Miriam's number while Audrey prayed that they would get through to Faizan. If they didn't and couldn't reach him quickly, he would go to town to pick them up on the day they were due to arrive and not see them. And then his hopes would be dashed.

Ken put the phone to his ear and Audrey eagerly gazed at him, praying that they would reach Faizan, but at the same time, nervous for them to. She wasn't looking forward to hearing how utterly let down he would feel when they told him they wouldn't be able to come.

After a while, Ken shook his head and removed the phone from his ear. "Miriam's phone isn't ringing. The battery is probably dead again."

Audrey covered her face with her hand. "Oh… no! And who knows when she will go back to town to charge her phone? Poor Faizan. I wish we could solve all these problems so we could go and see him. I wonder what he will think when we don't show up on the day we are supposed to. I hope he doesn't think something happened to us."

"I will keep trying to reach him," Ken said.

Audrey said, "It would be so unfair to leave him in the dark."

"It's not really our fault."

"I know, Ken. Still…" Audrey felt despondent. First, it was her inability to get pregnant, and then Stan's return to try to take Ruby away from Trisha, and Sienna's awful panic attacks. Now it was the fact that they couldn't go and see Faizan nor could they even inform him that they couldn't go. Who knew when they would next get the opportunity to go and see him? It was all too much. Audrey felt like weeping, but crying would do no good.

"Maybe we should just return to Miami," Ken said. "This vacation is a bust. Plus, we will see Esther again. I miss our precious daughter."

"I miss Esther too, Ken. But I would love to stay and be here for my sisters. They need me now. Besides, Esther is having a great time with her grandparents and cousins. Remember how happy she looked and sounded when we facetimed her yesterday."

"I know," Ken said. "Well, if you want to stay here, I will stay with you."

She beamed and then looked up at the clock on the wall. It was three p.m. She said to him, "Talking about Esther, I have an overwhelming desire to call her."

"So do I," Ken said. "We should facetime like yesterday."

Audrey stood up. "Let me go get my laptop. I want to see her beautiful face on a big screen."

"Okay," Ken said. He put his hand on his chest as she started to walk away and pretended to have a heart attack. "Hurry back to me, my darling," he said in a dramatic voice, still clutching his chest. "I cannot live without you."

She laughed at his silliness and shook her head before turning around and walking out of the living room.

NINE

Leila's eyes flew open as someone called her name and tapped her on the shoulder. The tent was dark but she immediately recognized the voice of the girl who had called her name. It was Sherifat, the young woman who was both her friend and Zainah's. Immediately after Sherifat had arrived at the camp, she had stuck to Leila and Zainah's side.

At first, Leila had been irritated when the young woman started to follow her and Zainah everywhere. She just wanted alone time with Zainah, especially as Zainah spent most of her free time with Faizan, but Sherifat got in the way of that. She insisted on tagging along wherever they went. After a while, Leila began to grow fond of her. The girl was spunky and beautiful, with skin almost as dark as Zainah's. And she was a very nice person and very helpful, too. When Sherifat wasn't busy running errands for Miriam or a few of the older women, she was with Leila or Zainah, or with both of them.

Leila sat up and whispered so she would not wake up the other women in the room. "What is it, Sherifat? What time is it?"

Sherifat switched on a flashlight she was holding and Leila instinctively shut her eyes. She opened them again and said, "Where did you get that?"

"Miriam bought it the last time she went to town."

Leila shook her head. Sherifat was Miriam's only tentmate and the camp leader trusted Sherifat with her things. But somehow, Leila knew Miriam had not given permission for Sherifat to take the flashlight. "You took Miriam's flashlight without her permission," Leila said incredulously. "And what are you doing here at this time, anyway?"

Sherifat said, "I need you to follow me some-where."

Leila stared at Sherifat. "I'm not following you anywhere. What time is it?"

"It's almost five o'clock."

Leila's eyes widened in surprise. "You want me to go somewhere with you at five o'clock in the morning? What is wrong with you?"

Sherifat stooped down and whispered, "Some days ago, I overheard Zainah and Faizan talking about a camp… a men's camp near us. At first, I didn't know what to think, whether to believe it or not. But they both said they had been there and so I had to investigate. The day after, early in the morning, I took this flashlight and headed out. And guess what I saw? Another camp in the distance. I was too scared to go near, but Zainah and Faizan are right. I think there is a men's camp some dis-tance away from here."

Leila stared at her with chagrin as she listened to Sherifat's words. So Sherifat had found the men's camp that Zainah had talked about. That wasn't good. If she told someone else and they found it, soon the whole camp might know about it, and then what would happen to their little haven? It sure would not be a haven anymore. It would become just like the outside world, with all its distractions and hang-ups. She couldn't let that happen.

Sherifat stared at her and said in a high-pitched

voice, "You know about the men's camp, Leila!"

"Shh! Lower your voice, Sherifat! Do you want to wake up my tentmates?"

Sherifat said in a hushed tone, "So Zainah told you about the men's camp. Have you been there?" Her voice was now animated and full of curiosity.

"No," Leila answered. "And I am never going there. Neither are you."

"I'm going there now," Sherifat said. "Will you come with me?"

"You're not going," Leila said to her. "You don't even know what type of men they are."

"From what I heard Faizan and Zainah say about them, I think they're Christians and they are harmless. Faizan spent a day with them."

"Aren't you ashamed, listening in on other people's conversations?"

Sherifat straightened. "I'm going, Leila. If you don't want to go with me, then that's fine. But I am going."

Sherifat began to leave the tent and Leila sighed. She didn't want to go to the men's camp, but someone had to keep an eye on Sherifat or she would do something stupid like alerting the other women. She stood up from her sleeping rug and went after Sherifat. "Wait!" she called out as soon as she was outside the tent.

Sherifat turned around, shining her flashlight in Leila's direction. Leila hurried over to her and both of them walked away from the camp.

They walked on together in silence. Leila sighed as she went. This was so typical of Sherifat. The girl was like a fairy, restless and skipping from one place to another. The first time Sherifat had discovered the men's camp, she hadn't gone in because she was too afraid. Now, without a doubt, she would enter boldly and who knew what else she would do? Leila had to restrain her from doing anything stupid. "Stop walking so fast, Sherifat!" Leila said.

"Where are you going?"

Leila's heart stopped and she froze. That was Miriam's voice. How did she find out? Leila turned around at the same time Sherifat did.

Miriam had a kerosene lamp with her and she was walking toward them with a scowl on her face. She reached them and glared at Leila. She turned her eyes to Sherifat and shook her head before turning back to Leila. She said, "Where are you going, Leila? No, don't tell me. I already know where you're going."

Leila's mouth flew open. Miriam was so intuitive. Still, how did she know about the existence of the men's camp? Because from the look on her face, Leila was sure she knew about it.

Miriam said, "You are going to that men's camp, aren't you? You and Sherifat. I expected more from you, Leila."

Leila finally found her voice and asked in a small voice, "How did you know about the men's camp? And how did you know that was where we were going?"

"I saw when Sherifat took my flashlight. I was awake, but she didn't know. At first, I thought she was just going out to ease herself or something, but when she didn't return, I knew something was up. And Faizan told me about the men's camp. I somehow guessed that Zainah had also told you about it since you are best friends. And knowing how Sherifat follows you around, Leila, I knew this one here was going to get you to be her accomplice. When I saw you both sneaking away from the camp, I had to follow you."

Sherifat looked down at the ground and said in a trembling voice, "I'm sorry, Miriam. I was the one who asked Leila to come with me. She didn't want to go, but I'm sure she came along in order to keep an eye on me."

Leila said, "Stop it, Sherifat! You don't have to

cover for me." She said to Miriam, "I didn't know anyone else in the camp knew except for me and, of course, Faizan and Zainah, who told me about it. I really didn't want anyone else to find out, but Sherifat overheard Zainah and Faizan talking about it in their tent."

Miriam stared at them for a minute and then said, "Well, let's go. Why are you both standing here, looking at me?"

Leila nodded and began to head back to the women's camp.

Miriam called out, "Where on earth are you going?"

Leila turned around again and Sherifat turned, too.

"I said let's go to that men's camp. Since we are out here and this far from our camp, we might as well go on."

Leila lifted her brows in disbelief. Miriam, the responsible and logical one, wanted them to go to the men's camp? Leila turned and looked at Sherifat. She had an incredulous look on her face too.

Miriam waved her hand and began to walk forward. Leila and Sherifat ran to catch up with her. "Do you know the exact directions to the camp?" Miriam asked, looking at Leila and Sherifat.

"I know the way," Sherifat said. "I investigated some days ago and found it."

"Of course you did," Miriam said in an amused voice.

They continued to walk on in silence. Sherifat walked one step in front of Leila while Miriam walked slightly behind her. They walked for about twenty minutes and then Leila gasped. She could see in the distance an open fire and tents just like theirs back at the women's camp. She pointed. "Is that it, Sherifat? Is that the men's camp?"

"Yes," Sherifat said. She pointed her flashlight in the direction of the camp and Leila's eyes scanned the vicinity. She saw a man standing some distance away from where they did. As they came nearer, she saw there was a huge pot on the open fire.

"Let's stop here," Leila said. "I don't think we should let them see us."

The man who was near the fire walked away and Leila was grateful he had not looked their way. Around this place, there was nowhere to hide, and once it was daybreak and this men's camp awoke fully, it would be impossible not to see them.

"But we just got here," Sherifat said.

"You are right, Leila." Miriam looked at her. "It is best that the men don't see us. We certainly don't want them knowing there is a women's camp anywhere near here. Even if they are not dangerous, we don't want them invading our camp and getting our women all excited and worked up."

But rather than turn around and go back to the camp, they stood watching in fascination as two other men dressed in white tunics and pants strode out of one of the tents. Another man who looked older than them also walked out of the tent.

Just as Leila repeated again that they should leave before they were found out, the men turned around and looked at them.

"They have seen us," Sherifat said, but not in the alarmed voice that Leila had expected. She sounded happy to have been discovered by these men.

Leila's eyes widened in shock as Sherifat began to walk toward them. "Come back, Sherifat!" Leila called out to her.

Sherifat kept walking and Miriam said sharply, "Sherifat, come back now!"

Sherifat turned around and then turned back again toward the men and moved toward them.

Leila went after her with Miriam close behind. The men did not speak or move. They just stood transfixed, the expression on their faces ranging from shock to eagerness.

Sherifat reached them and Leila got to them at almost the same time. When she looked into each of their eyes, the men turned away. The older one turned around again and said, "You shouldn't be..." He stopped mid-sentence; his eyes planted on something.

Leila turned to see what he was looking at and saw it was Miriam. His eyes were fixed on her face, and Miriam's on his. Her eyes where wide and glassy, and she had an expression on her face that Leila had never seen before. If Leila didn't think the situation was so detrimental to their camp's well-being, she would have thought it was funny. The man and Miriam were staring so intently at each other.

Leila blinked. Come to think of it, Sherifat has said nothing since we came here and she always has something to say, especially when she's nervous.

Leila turned to Sherifat and saw that just like Miriam, her eyes were fixed on one of the men—a handsome young man who was staring at her with equal parts shyness and hunger.

Leila groaned. This can't be happening, she thought. She had been in love before and she knew the beginnings of it. This was it... or infatuation at its worst. And of all people to be struck by infatuation, it was the last person she expected. Miriam was still staring at the man who looked like the leader of this camp as though she had never seen a man before. It was just ridiculous.

Well, someone has to put an end to this madness, Leila thought. She snapped her fingers and said loudly, "Miriam, we need to go now." She grabbed Sherifat's hand and said, "Come on, let's go!" She looked at the men, who seemed to be coming out of their trance-like state, and said to them, "We're sorry for intruding. We will just be on our way now and not bother you anymore."

Leila began to pull Sherifat away, but the girl

wrenched her hand from Leila's. She turned around again and fixed her gaze once more on the young, handsome man.

Leila put her hand on her forehead and shook her head. Miriam had not moved an inch since she told them to come away to the camp.

"Do you want to come into our camp?" the young man asked.

Leila was about to say, "No," when Sherifat smiled and said, "Yes, we do."

The older man shook his head and then slowly turned his face away from Miriam. "We shouldn't invite women into the camp," he said to the young man.

Miriam blinked rapidly and said, "That's okay. We can't come into your camp. We have to go now." She turned to Leila and Sherifat. "Come on, ladies, let's go."

Leila exhaled, greatly relieved. Hopefully this small adventure they'd had today would be kept only between them. Hopefully Sherifat would not go and spill her guts to the other women in the camp. Miriam turned around and walked away quickly without speaking to Leila or Sherifat again.

Leila grabbed Sherifat's hand once more and this time held on tightly as she pulled her away from the young man. He was still gazing at Sherifat and the girl's face was turned toward him as Leila dragged her away.

Miriam was walking way too fast and Leila had to almost run in order to catch up with her. Sherifat lagged behind as they made their way to the camp.

They got to the camp quickly. Miriam made her way straight to her tent while Leila stood at the edge of the camp and waited for Sherifat to get to her.

"You can't tell anyone what we saw today," Leila said when Sherifat finally got to her.

Sherifat had a dreamy and faraway look in her eyes. "I know," she said. "I won't tell anyone."

She began to walk away, but Leila held her hand. "I'm very serious, Sherifat. You cannot tell anyone about that men's camp and you cannot go back there, either."

Sherifat looked her in the eye and gave a wistful sigh. "Why can't I go back there, Leila?"

Leila stared incredulously at her and said, "I can see it in your eyes, Sherifat. You're planning on going back soon to meet that guy, aren't you?"

"And what if I am?" Sherifat said in a sharp tone.

Leila knit her brows, surprised. Sherifat had never spoken to her in that tone of voice. She put her hands on Sherifat's shoulders and studied her friend's face for a long moment. Finally, she said, "You have to trust me. Don't go back there. I know what I'm talking about."

"I don't understand why I can't."

"Trust me, Sherifat. Just don't go back. I have been in love before. You will just end up getting your heart broken."

Sherifat shook her head and said, "But what about Zainah and Faizan? Faizan did not break Zainah's heart and they are married and about to have a child. I want that. I thought I would never have that when I came to this camp. But now I know it can happen for me."

Leila sighed wearily. "I had that same dream years ago," she said. "But it was just that—a stupid dream."

Sherifat said, "I don't know what the future holds, but I am going back to that camp. I like that man…"

Leila cut her off. "You don't even know him! You don't know what kind of person he is! And besides, this is not about you alone. It's about the entire camp. If you go back there, he might want to return the favor and come here. Soon, other men will follow him, and then the women in this camp will discover that men's camp. What do you think will happen then? Most women here are here in order to dedicate themselves totally to the Lord. What do you think will happen when men overrun our camp and the women here start to go to the men's camp? The very reason why we exist here and have succeeded in staying away and being protected from the outside world would be lost. Others will probably find out about this place, and then what?"

Sherifat shut her eyes as sadness took over her features. Leila felt sorry for her, but there was nothing she could do. She had to make the young woman understand the implications of her actions if she went back to that men's camp.

A thought crossed Leila's mind. Is this really about protecting the women in this camp or is it about protecting yourself from getting hurt again?

Leila blinked and brushed aside the confusing thought. This was not about her. This was about the camp and its safety. She looked at Sherifat, who looked so downcast that Leila's heart filled with pity for her. Still, it was important for Sherifat to understand that it would be wrong to go back to that men's camp. "Sherifat, promise me you will not go back there."

Sherifat did not answer for a long moment, and then she looked up at Leila and nodded. "I promise I won't go back."

Leila let out a huge sigh of relief. "Thank you. You'll find out one day that you made the right decision." She placed her fingers on Sherifat's cheek and smiled at the young woman. And then she walked back to her tent, satisfied that Sherifat would keep her word.

But as she sat down on her sleeping rug, a voice echoed in her mind: You are not doing this to protect the women's camp, Leila. You're doing it because you got your heart broken by Malik and now you are bitter and don't want anybody else to find love.

"That's a lie," Leila said.

Halima, who was just waking up and was sitting on her sleeping rug, stared at Leila with a curious expression on her face.

Leila turned away and picked up her Bible from beside her. Before she opened it, she asked the Lord to speak to her from His word and show her if she had bitterness and unforgiveness in her heart. She wanted to know if her motive for not wanting the women in the camp to know about the existence of the men's camp was right or selfish. When she finished praying, she started to open her Bible and then blinked when the bell for morning prayers rang.

She frowned. It was already time for morning prayers. That meant they had spent more time at that men's camp than she had thought. She closed her Bible and stood up. Halima and Binta also stood up.

Leila left the tent and made her way to the prayer tent. She saw Zainah and Faizan in the midst of the small crowd in front of her. They were holding hands and smiling into each other's eyes. She felt the familiar pang of envy in her heart. Her mind went to Malik again, and pain tore through her. She groaned. Will it ever get easier? she thought.

She looked around as the women in the camp went toward the prayer tent, conversing with smiles on their faces, and sighed. Conviction settled in her heart, and she knew she was doing the right thing by keeping the existence of the men's camp a secret. Hopefully, the few other people in this camp who knew about it would do the same. Then the women here would continue to be protected from the fickleness of men and the terrible effects that a love-gone-wrong could bring.

TEN

Trisha opened the door and smiled at Audrey. "Good," she said. "You are here. I was just about to call you so I could speak to you and Sienna at the same time."

"What is it?" Audrey asked.

"Let me go and get Sienna," Trisha said.

"I'm coming."

Audrey sat on the sofa and Trisha left the living room to go and find Sienna. She had already put Molly and Ruby to bed. Frank was still at the restaurant, but he would return soon, as it was already almost six in the evening.

She stopped in front of the guest room where Sienna and Bryan slept. Bryan and Sienna had been out with Ethan for most of the day. They had gone to Green Valley to spend the day with Bryan's parents and had returned with Ethan sleeping in Sienna's arms. They'd gone straight to the bedroom to put Ethan to bed while Trisha called Audrey to tell her she wanted to speak to her and Sienna.

Trisha knocked on the door. When Sienna called out, "Come in," she opened it. Smiling at Bryan, Trisha said to Sienna, "Can I speak to you now? Audrey is here in the living room."

Sienna nodded. She kissed Ethan's chubby cheeks as he slept on the bed, smiled at Bryan, and told him she would be back soon.

Sienna walked down the hallway with Trisha until they got to the living room. Sienna hugged Audrey and then settled down on the couch beside Trisha, while Audrey sat on the sofa across from them.

"Stan came back after we talked yesterday."

Audrey said, "So he's really serious about this custody thing."

Trisha laughed without humor. "Actually, that really wasn't why he came. He came to make a so-called deal with me."

"What deal?" Sienna asked, frowning.

"He came to tell me he would not file for custody if I gave him money." Trisha shook her head. "A lot of money."

Audrey's eyes grew round and she said, "How much did he ask for?"

Trisha laughed bitterly. "Fifty million dollars."

"What?" Audrey and Sienna said in unison.

"That Stan is a joker," Audrey said. "He wants you to give him fifty million dollars so he can stay away from his daughter."

"He's so greedy," Sienna said. "And totally heartless. He wants to substitute his own daughter for money."

"What are you going to do?" Audrey asked, leaning forward on her seat.

"I'm not sure," Trisha answered. "I told him to give me three months to get the money together for him."

"No, Trisha," Audrey said. "You cannot be thinking about giving him all that money. That is so not right."

"I'm trying to buy some time," Trisha said. "But I really want him to go away and not bother me and my family anymore. If that means giving him the money he wants, then maybe that will have to be what I'll do."

"But he really has no case," Sienna said. "I don't see any court granting him full custody of Ruby."

"Even joint custody would drive me crazy," Trisha said, sighing.

"I'm not sure they would even give him that," Audrey said. "He hasn't been around for years. He abandoned his daughter and went to God-knows-where. I think you should not give him the money and you should call his bluff and allow him to file the custody suit. You should go to court and bring up his request for you to give him money."

"My lawyer told me as much," Trisha said, "but I am still scared. What if something happens and for some reason, he is granted full custody of Ruby?"

"That isn't going to happen, Trisha," Sienna said and put her arm around Trisha's shoulder. "Ruby is your daughter and you and Frank have been the only ones who have been there for her since she was born."

"But Stan is Ruby's biological father," Trisha said. She shut her eyes as fear gripped her heart. "I can't let him take my Ruby away."

"You are being irrational," Audrey said. "He's not going to take Ruby away. He can't."

"Are you sure I shouldn't just give him the money and get this over with?"

"No, Trisha," Audrey said. "You shouldn't give him anything. And that is a lot of money. Besides, who is to say he won't come back for more once you give him what he requested this time? Stan is a terrible person. I wouldn't be surprised if the following year, he comes back to ask you for more money. He will not rest until he has drained you of every cent. I am sure of that."

"Audrey is right," Sienna said. "Don't give him any money. If he wants to file for custody, let him. He's never going to win."

Trisha felt better and less afraid as she listened to her sisters' words of comfort and encouragement.

Sienna rubbed her back soothingly and smiled brightly at her, and Trisha smiled back. "I still have three months before I have to deal with Stan again. I won't tell him anything for now. Let him think I am gathering the money for him until his three-month ultimatum is over, and then I'll let him know I am ready to fight him in court."

"Atta girl," Audrey said.

"Okay, I feel much better now," Trisha said. "I think I will probably go and see Faizan, then."

Audrey stood up and came to sit beside Trisha on the couch. She took Trisha's hand and smiled at Sienna. "So, about that. I have good news," she said. "Trisha, I didn't want to say it earlier because I thought there was no need if Sienna and I were staying with you to support you in the custody case. Since you don't have to be in court for another three months, let me tell you the good news." she smiled at Trisha and looked at Sienna. "Faizan found somewhere… a men's camp a short distance away from the women's camp. The men there agreed to let our husbands stay at their camp while we stay at the women's camp."

Trisha smiled as happiness flooded her heart for the first time since Stan appeared in her life again.

Sienna clapped, the look on her face gleeful. "Yes! Thank God! Bryan and I can go together now. I felt so down when I thought I couldn't go and see Faizan. I've missed him so much." She said smiled at Audrey and Trisha. "We will have such a great time, especially with the guys coming as well."

"We will have a fabulous time," Trisha said.

Bryan walked into the living room and Sienna immediately stood up and went to hug him. Bryan had a surprised expression on his face. "What are you guys celebrating?" he asked, kissing Sienna's cheek, and then looking at Trisha and Audrey.

"You can come with Trisha, Audrey and I, Bryan. Ken and Frank will come, too."

"Come where?" Bryan asked.

"To see Faizan," Sienna said excitedly. "We can all go now."

Bryan lifted his brows and said, "I thought they said no men were allowed at the camp."

"Ken called Faizan, and he said that he found a men's camp some distance away from the women's camp. They've agreed to let you, Ken, and Frank stay there. You can come and visit us whenever you like."

"Wow! That's great news," Bryan said, smiling widely. "I was so disappointed when we were told we couldn't go. I can't wait to see the place.".

Bryan sat down on the loveseat and Sienna sat beside him. He drew her close and wrapped his arms around her.

Trisha smiled at Sienna and then remembered her confession about her struggles with anxiety and fear. She asked, "How are you really doing now, Sienna? Do you still have the panic and anxiety attacks?"

Sienna turned to look at Bryan and then turned back to Trisha. "Sometimes, but I believe the Lord will deliver me completely soon," she said. "Bryan and I study the scriptures about God's grace and faithfulness regularly and they help to calm me down."

Trisha nodded and Audrey said, "I'll keep praying for you."

Frank walked into the house just then, and Trisha smiled up at him. "We have good news, babe," she said.

He sat down on the sofa near the door and Trisha told him about the men's camp and what Ken had said about the men there agreeing for them to stay at the camp for the duration of their trip.

Frank was thrilled about the news and said he was looking forward to it.

"We should celebrate the good news," he said.

"Let's wait for Ken to come," Audrey said. "He said he would be here at about eight or nine o'clock."

"Alright, then," Frank said.

They chatted about the trip and the plans they had to put into place before they left. Twenty minutes later, Ken walked through the door and Frank said, "Time to celebrate, everyone!"

Frank stood up and went to the kitchen, and the rest of them continued to talk about how they were going to prepare for their trip. Twenty minutes later, Frank came back with drinks and snacks.

They continued their conversation well into the night while they munched on their snacks and drank their root beers. Audrey soon yawned and stood up. "I feel sleepy. I think it's time to go." She looked down at Ken. "We should go, honey."

He nodded and stood up. "Okay, everyone. Goodbye and see you all tomorrow."

The rest of them bid Audrey and Ken goodbye. After they left, Bryan turned to Sienna and said, "We should go to bed, too."

Sienna stretched. "I think we should."

"Goodnight, you two," Trisha said to them as they strode out of the living room together to go to their bedroom.

After they left, Trisha stood up and went to sit on Frank's lap. He put his arms around her and kissed her. She looked down at him and then let her worry show. "My sisters told me the same thing you and the lawyer said about Stan not having a case. They said I shouldn't give him money at all."

Frank nodded. "I told you. That's the right thing to do."

"I'm still scared, though, Frank. What if the court decides to give Stan custody because he is Ruby's biological father? I won't be able to bear it if he's given joint custody. I know the kind of person he is. I don't think I want him alone with my daughter. He doesn't even care about her. Who is to say he won't just abandon her while he has custody of her? All he wants and cares about is money." She laughed without humor. "Money and lots of women."

Frank threaded his fingers through hers and kissed the back of her hand. "Stop worrying about it, Trish," he said softly. "Everything will be alright. You'll see."

Trisha sighed and said, "I hope you're right."

Frank nodded. "We've been praying about it, Trisha. Everything will work out for the best. Ruby is staying here with us where she belongs."

Trisha bent her head and kissed Frank. She drew back slightly to look into his eyes. "What would I do without you, Frank?" she said, love for him flooding her heart.

He beamed. "I should be asking you that, Trisha," he said. "Every day, when I wake up beside you, I have to pinch myself to make sure I am not dreaming. I cannot believe you are mine now. All I've ever wanted since I was a teenager was for us to be together, and now we are. It's more than I could ever have hoped for. This life I have with you."

She kissed him again, putting aside all her worries, and let herself bask in their love for each other.

ELEVEN

Malik squinted at the sun as he straightened. He had been working on his farm with two of the farmers he'd hired some days ago. Hopefully the seeds they had planted would produce a bountiful harvest that would provide for his daughter and his soon-to-be wife. He dropped his cutlass on the ground and hollered to the farmers, "I'm going! When you both finish, you can go as well. You will be paid at the end of the week."

They both nodded and Malik walked away toward his new house. He entered the house and went straight to the tiny bathroom to shower. He had to go to Dogon to see Hauwa today so they could put finishing touches on their wedding plans.

As he showered, his heart filled with worry as he thought about Hauwa. He had visited her almost every day in Dogon because the wedding was very near. But for the past week, she'd been acting really distant. The day he went to take Fanta back to Nira to stay with his parents until after the wedding, she had hardly said a word to him. He had asked her what was wrong, but she only shrugged and said it was nothing. However, he had known something was wrong. She loved him, he knew, and usually whenever he visited, she fawned over him. But that day had been different, and so had the next time he visited, and the next. Today, he would find out what exactly was wrong, no matter what.

He finished showering and went to his bedroom. He put on an off-white T-shirt and a new pair of jeans he'd bought when he went to Bamako some days ago. He was worried that she might be falling out of love with him and would soon change her mind about marrying him. If that happened, his well-thought-out plan to get a mother for his daughter so she didn't have to stay in his father's house again would fail. Plus, he had introduced Hauwa to Fanta as her soon-to-be mother. She would be disappointed once she knew she wouldn't have a mother again.

A thought crossed his mind. But you don't even love Hauwa.

He sighed. That wasn't true. He did love her.

But you're not in love with her.

He brushed away the thoughts from his mind. He didn't have to be in love with her to marry her. He liked her and she would make a great mother for Fanta. That was enough.

He groaned when his mind immediately traveled to Leila. Her face was firmly planted in his mind now, and it would take everything in him to push it away. But he had to. He was about to marry someone else. He couldn't keep thinking about Leila.

He quickly ran a comb through his hair, slipped on a pair of sneakers, and left his house. He walked quickly to the bus stop and paid for his bus fare. Ten minutes later, the bus was speeding toward Dogon.

All through the drive there, he struggled to focus on Hauwa, but his mind kept going back to Leila; to the day they broke up. He had replayed the events of that day in his mind what felt like more than a million times over the last two years. It was odd that after two years, he still hadn't gotten over her. What was worse was the fact that he remembered the day they broke up as though it were only a few days ago. The pain it brought to his heart felt like the pain he'd experienced on the day they parted ways.

As the bus approached Dogon, he realized he had not bought Hauwa a gift as he sometimes did when he went to visit her. He decided he would ask for her forgiveness and promise to get her a present the next time he visited. It was still early evening, which meant she would still be at the bus station, selling her candies. He would sit with her until she was ready to go back to her grandmother's.

The bus drove into the station and immediately when Malik got out of the bus his eyes settled on her. She was in her usual spot where she sold her candies. He frowned when he saw that she did not smile at him as she usually did.

He walked up to her and she stood stiffly. She gave him a smile that seemed forced and said, "Welcome, Malik." Sitting down again, she focused on the candies on the table in front of her.

He put his hand on her shoulder and asked, "What is wrong? Really."

She turned to look at him. "Nothing," she said, frowning.

"No, something is definitely wrong. Something has been wrong for some time now. I need you to tell me what it is. Don't you want to marry me anymore?" he asked, his heart beating fast.

She didn't say anything for a few moments and then she sighed loudly. When tears trailed down her cheeks, Malik blinked.

"What is it, Hauwa? Please tell me."

She swiped at the tears falling down her face and said, "I'm sorry, Malik." She looked at the ground. "You know I love you."

He put his finger beneath her chin and lifted her face. Searching her eyes, he said, "You can tell me what's wrong."

"I'm so sorry, Malik," she said in a shaky voice. "I can't marry you."

His eyes widened. "What? Why?"

"Your heart still belongs to Leila," she said. "I thought I could just go ahead, ignore it and marry you because I love you, but I can't. I don't want to be married to a man who loves another woman."

Malik groaned, but he did not say anything.

Hauwa said. "Plus, I remember what you told me some days ago. Something you told me Leila said before you both broke up."

His heart pounded at the mention of Leila's name. "What did I tell you Leila said?"

"You said she told you she could not marry you because you did not share her faith."

He frowned deeply and shook his head. "What does that have to do with your decision not to marry me now?" he asked, but he could already guess what she was going to say.

Hauwa smiled sadly. "Remember I told you I was a Christian? Though I have not been a very good Christian. Not like Leila. Hearing you tell me what Leila had said, I knew she was right and I knew I had to do the same thing. I shouldn't marry anyone who does not share my faith in Jesus, no matter how much I love that person."

Malik shut his eyes as pain overwhelmed his heart. This was the second time this was happening. First it was Leila, now Hauwa. Why did it have to be him? Anger bubbled up from within him at the injustice of it all. He had given up on love after he broke up with Leila, and all he wanted was a mother for his daughter. Why couldn't he have that? He had Christianity – Leila and Hauwa's Jesus to blame for it. He had never asked either of them to change their faiths for him, but they had chosen to let him go, even though they said they loved him, because of their faith. He stared angrily at Hauwa. This time, he would not fight. There was no use. He stood up and nodded. "All right, then," he said to her. "I guess the wedding is off."

Hauwa stood up with fresh tears running down her face. "I'm so sorry, Malik. I wish things were different. If only you were..."

"Don't say it!" he spat out. "Don't you dare!"

Hauwa frowned. "I'm sorry."

Malik sighed and said in a small voice, "I'm sorry, too. I should not have yelled at you." His anger dissipated, replaced by despair. What would he tell Fanta now? Two years ago, when he was sure he was going to marry Leila, he'd told his daughter about her and told her to expect a new mother. That had not worked out and he'd had to explain to her that she was not going to have a new mother at that time. Now, she had bonded some with Hauwa. How would he tell her that he would not be marrying Hauwa and that she would not be her mother anymore? Even though Fanta was a quiet child, she had been looking forward to finally getting a mother of her own so she could be like other children.

Hauwa put a hand on Malik's shoulder and said again, "Please forgive me, Malik."

He looked at her and nodded. It wasn't her fault that he did not love her. Why should she marry him and spend the rest of her life with someone who loved someone else? "It's okay," he said. "I have to get back to my farm." He quickly started to walk away, but she called his name and he stopped.

"Malik, I think you should think about going to find Leila."

His mouth fell open. "Why would I do that?" he asked.

"You know why," Hauwa replied.

He looked away for a second and then looked back at her. "I have no idea where she is. And even if I did, I know she won't have me. She made it clear before we broke up. Just as I told you, she said she could not marry me or be with me unless I became a Christian. But that isn't going to happen. I cannot change who I am."

Hauwa said, "I know how you feel, Malik, but have you ever considered why you love Leila? Everything that makes her who she is is really because of her faith in Christ."

He shrugged. "Maybe it is, but she said she loved me as well and my faith is part of who I am. I didn't ask her to convert to Islam, so why would she ask me to convert to Christianity if she really loved me?"

"I know it's not right for me to ask you to convert to Christianity just because you want to win Leila's heart, but will you try to find out the truth for yourself, Malik? I know it was the joy and peace that I saw in Leila that attracted me to her and ultimately led to my salvation. Wasn't there something in you that wondered about Leila? That something about her was different? Special?"

"Of course," Malik said. "That was why I loved her so much."

"And you know what that thing is?"

Malik sighed and then said, "I really have to go, Hauwa." He smiled at her even though his heart was aching. "I'm sorry. I wish I could stop loving Leila and love you instead."

She shrugged. "You can't do anything about it, Malik. You love who you love. Please think about what I said. As much as I'm sad that we won't be together, I still want you to be happy, Malik. And I know you won't find true happiness until you find Leila. And most of all, until you find Jesus."

Malik wanted to tell her to stop preaching to him, but the sincerity in her voice gave him pause. He said goodbye to her and started to turn around. And then he stopped and turned back to her. "Just because we are not getting married anymore doesn't mean we cannot be in each other's lives. I hope we can still be friends."

Hauwa nodded. "I would love that."

Malik smiled genuinely at her and then walked away. On the bus, he kept thinking about what Hauwa told him and how similar their breakup was with his and Leila's breakup and yet how different. With Leila, he had been shattered and he knew after the breakup that he would never be the same again. With Hauwa, he felt sad because his daughter would not have a new mother, but he also felt relieved.

When he got to the tiny town where he now lived, he went straight to his house. Rather than change into his work clothes and head for his farm, he sat on the bed and recalled everything he had talked about with Hauwa. He marveled at how increasingly relieved he felt. He especially played in his mind what Hauwa had said about searching for Leila.

He thought about that for a long time. After two years, he was still in love with Leila. Maybe it was the logical thing to do. Something in the depths of his mind cautioned him against following that train of thought. What if she had moved on? Surely, by now, she would have found someone else.

He shook his head. She had loved him dearly. Their love had been special and that kind of love did not come twice in a lifetime. Even if she had found someone else, she would not love that person the way she loved him.

The voice grew insistent. But what if she has married that person?

He sighed. It was a valid point. However, he had to try. If he didn't because he was afraid she had moved on, he would one day come to regret it. If he found her and indeed she had moved on, then he would live with it, no matter how painful it would be.

Hope and anticipation began to rise in his heart. But still, there was one major obstacle, apart from the fact that he did not even know where to start looking for her. And that was her faith. Surely she would still insist that he convert even if she was still in love with him and wanted them to be together. Could he convert for her sake? Could he change who he was, who he had been since he was a child… for her?

He wrestled with that thought as he sat staring at the wall in front of him. After a long time of thinking about it, he finally came to a firm conclusion. He had tried as best as he could to forget about her for these past few years, but he had not been able to. The pain that their breakup had caused him was great, and if there was a chance to win her back, he would take it, no matter what it cost him. He knew without a doubt that he was ready to do whatever she wanted him to and if that meant converting to her faith, he would do it. He didn't want to live without her anymore.

He said out loud, "So, there is just one thing I have to do now. I have to find out where Leila is." All he knew was that she had told him she lived in some camp in North Africa for years with his sister, Zainah. Where exactly that camp was, or whether she was still there, he had no idea. She could be anywhere. However, he was determined to find her.

He didn't know where Zainah was, either. The only person he knew to ask about her now was his sister, Khadija. It was unlikely Khadija knew where Leila was. Still, he would start by asking his sister if she had any idea where she was. If she didn't, he would have to find other options to trace Leila's whereabouts.

He stood up and opened his wardrobe. He had kept a stash of cash—some of the money he had saved for his wedding and for getting furniture for his house. The rest was in the bank in Bamako.

He brought out a wad of cash and put it in his pocket. He went out of his house and walked to his farm. One of the farmers had left, but the other was still there. He brought out some of the money, paid the man, and gave him money for the other farmer.

The man looked at the money and then looked up at him with a surprised expression on his face. "This is much more than what we agreed on," he said.

Malik nodded. "I know. I want you to do something for me."

"What is it?" the farmer asked.

Malik said, "I want you to watch over my farm for me and also my house. I'll be traveling soon and will probably be away for a long time. Keep working on the farm. I will send you more money if I don't return in time."

"Okay," the man said and smiled. "I can do that."

Malik patted the man's shoulder. "Good," he said. He left the man and went back to his house. Bringing out his suitcase from his wardrobe, he threw his clothes into it. It was a large suitcase and he packed most of his clothes in it. He wasn't sure how long he would be away. He had to go to Nira first and see his daughter at his parents' house. After that, he would talk to Khadija and try to find out everything she knew about Leila's whereabouts. Hopefully, she would know something.

He finished packing and then wheeled his suitcase out of his bedroom to the living room. He stepped out of the house and before he locked the door, he turned to look at the house once more. He had built this house in preparation for a new life with a new wife. But it had not worked out the way he had planned. However, he was hoping for a much better outcome this time, and a much happier one.

If everything went well, he and Leila would get married immediately and they would probably come and live here. If things went badly, he would come back a very lonely and sad man. But at least he would know he had tried his best to look for the love of his life. And if he lived in regret for the rest of his life because he had broken up with her the first time, then he would have to deal with it.

He shut the door, locked it, and began to walk to the bus stop to go in search of the only woman he'd ever loved, and who he knew he would never stop loving.

TWELVE

Leila stood up from her sleeping rug and rubbed her eyes. After her eyes had adjusted to the darkness, she went to the corner of the tent where the kerosene lamps where usually kept, along with a box of matchsticks, and lit one of the smaller lamps.

The tent flooded with light and she could see her tentmates sleeping all around the tent. She straightened as she picked up the lamp.

Careful not to wake any of the women, she slowly made her way outside. She walked a short distance away from the tent to ease herself and then staggered back, yawning.

Suddenly, her eyes widened in surprise and shock as she heard male voices whispering some distance away. The voices drew near and she bit her lip as fear flooded her heart. What were they looking for in the camp? Were the women here in danger?

With nowhere to hide, she stood frozen while the voices came nearer and nearer, and then she saw who it was and blinked. She immediately recognized the men that she, Sherifat, and Miriam had seen at the men's camp some days ago.

She marched up to them, her lamp lifted and her stomach boiled in anger. "What are you doing here?" she asked angrily.

They stood gazing at her, the calm expression on their faces causing her anger to grow. They did not look surprised to see her; neither did they look ashamed that they had come to a women's camp at night looking for God-knew-what.

The bearded handsome one came closer to her and said, "I am sorry. We did not introduce ourselves on the day you came to the camp. I am Reza and this is Abdul."

"I don't care what your names are," Leila spat out, scowling at both of them. "All I want to know is why you are here at this time of night."

The other one, Abdul, came closer and spoke. "I am actually here to see you."

Leila stared at him as though he had gone mad. "You are here to see me? Why?"

The one called Reza said, "I am here to find the other girl that came with you to the camp." His eyes lit up. "The one with dark, shiny skin, and the most beautiful face I have ever seen. Can you tell me where she is?"

Leila stared at him. His eyes sparkled as he described Sherifat. She shook her head. There was no way she would tell him where Sherifat was. All she wanted was for them to leave before any of the women found them here and the existence of their camp became known.

"You have to leave before anyone sees you," she said harshly and looked back to make sure no one was around.

Reza said in a desperate voice, "Please, I just want to speak to her." He put his palms together in a pleading gesture. "Please help me."

Leila shook her head again.

"I am begging you. Please."

"And I am begging you... please go now," she said. She looked around again and prayed earnestly that none of the women came out to find the men here.

Neither of the men moved an inch and she glowered at them. "Why are you both still here? Please leave now! Right now!"

Her eyes widened in shock as Reza lowered himself before her and knelt on the sand. "Please," he said, looking up at her.

She put her hand on her forehead in frustration. "What are you doing?" She stared incredulously at him. "Why are you kneeling down?"

"I am begging you to help me," Reza said to her. "I just need to speak to the girl of my dreams. Please… just for a minute. It won't take long. I promise."

Leila stared down at him as he looked up at her. She sighed wearily. He looked so desperate and so earnest. What would it really hurt to get Sherifat for him? She shut her eyes briefly. This wasn't right. She started to shake her head slowly, but Reza began to plead again.

Leila groaned and then said, "Okay… okay. Just stand up! I will get Sherifat for you. But please stay here." She looked at the other man and then faced Reza again. "Please do not go farther into the camp. Do you hear me? Stay here. I will go and get her for you."

Reza smiled widely and said, "Thank you so much. Thank you." He stood up.

Leila went away, scolding herself for what she was about to do. Why on earth was she going to get Sherifat for that man? Still, she continued toward Miriam and Sherifat's tent and smiled in self-derision. She knew why. In spite of the pain of her breakup with Malik and her vow to keep the women here away from the men's camp, she still believed in love in the depths of her heart. As Zainah had accused her of some years ago, she was a hopeless romantic. Her breakup with Malik had buried all that, but now, seeing the beginnings of true love between two young people, that side of her had risen up again.

The whole camp was deathly quiet; everyone was still fast asleep. She knew what she was doing was wrong as she tiptoed into Miriam's tent after leaving her lamp outside the tent. She knew the corner where Sherifat slept. Even though the tent was pitch dark, she had been in here many times, especially since Sherifat had arrived and become Miriam's personal assistant and sole tentmate.

Leila's heart drummed as she bent down and tapped Sherifat's arm, and she prayed earnestly in her heart that Miriam would not wake up.

Sherifat grunted but continued to sleep.

Leila groaned inwardly and tapped Sherifat's arm again. She whispered, "Sherifat! Wake up!"

"Leila!" Sherifat said. "What are you…?"

"Shhh! Come with me," Leila whispered.

"Why?" Sherifat muttered.

"Just come! I have something to show you."

Leila tiptoed out of the tent, hoping Sherifat would follow behind. When she was outside the tent, Sherifat stumbled out as well, and Leila sighed in relief. She picked up her lamp and walked back to the spot she'd left the men.

"Where are we going?" Sherifat asked drowsily, following Leila.

"You'll see," Leila answered.

They rounded a tent and Sherifat stopped when she noticed the men. She turned to Leila and said, in a voice heavy with disbelief, "That man… at the men's camp… He's here, Leila. How come he's here?"

"He came because of you," Leila sighed. "And apparently the other one came because of me."

Sherifat ran forward to meet Reza and Leila thinned her lips. The one called Abdul was staring at her, but she turned away and avoided his gaze. She focused on Sherifat and Reza. A smile tugged on her lips as she watched them. They looked like long lost lovers who had been separated for a long time and were finally reunited again, rather than strangers who had only met once before.

Reza reached out and slowly took Sherifat's hands. They looked into each other's eyes and for some time, neither of them said anything. Finally, Reza spoke. "Since you came to our camp that day, I have not been able to stop thinking about you."

Sherifat said, "I haven't stopped thinking about you, either."

Leila's heart ached as she watched them, though it was a sweet ache. Love was blooming right before her eyes and, as much as she fought all of this, she couldn't help feeling a sense of joy. And yet she also felt despondent. She yearned for the love she had once had and lost. Sherifat and Reza walked hand in hand some distance away from the camp, whispering to each other.

Leila kept watching them and then started when someone touched her arm lightly. Turning around, she saw it was the other man, Abdul. She had completely forgotten about him. "What is it?" she asked, slightly irritated.

He told her he had also been thinking about her since the day she came to the camp. She wanted to tell him that, unfortunately, she had not given him a thought, which would be true, but he sounded so earnest that she said nothing.

After he had told her he was interested in pursuing a relationship with her, she said, "I thought you men were not supposed to have anything to do with women."

"It's not a law for us. We are not bound to anything," he said. "It's just that many of us left the world to avoid all distractions, which included women. Many of us have a past of living in sin and we left all that behind to focus on God. That doesn't mean we cannot pursue a relationship that will lead to marriage if we want. It is just not encouraged."

"That was not what I heard from your leader

and from one of my friends who has been in your camp," she said. "From what I heard, you all are supposed to be totally sworn off relationships with women." She really wasn't interested in him or this conversation, but she didn't want to be rude.

He insisted that as much as what she said was true, there was no law in the camp that actually forbade them from getting married if they found someone. As long as their intended was a sister in Christ.

"But as you said, relationships and marriages are not encouraged, are they?"

He didn't respond.

She was over this conversation. She shook her head and said, "I am sorry. I am just not interested in a romantic relationship." And it was true. She wasn't interested in being with anyone except for Malik. But she and Malik were no more. For all she knew, he was probably married now. He had been really eager to get a mother for his daughter; someone who would take care of the little girl while he was at work and be a mother to her. There was no way he would still be single now. And even if he were, they could not find their way back to each other, especially since he had refused to consider giving his heart to Jesus.

She felt Abdul's eyes on her and remembered once again that he was standing beside her. She looked at him and he said, "Won't you at least consider what I am asking?"

She smiled weakly. "I'm sorry. I don't want a relationship, and I certainly don't want to get married."

He didn't say anything for a long moment and then he nodded. "Okay. I understand."

Leila looked at Sherifat and Reza again. They were way too close to each other now, almost about to kiss. From the way they were looking at each other, she wouldn't be surprised if in a few moments, they actually did. She had to put an end to it all.

Still, she did not move an inch as she watched them. They seemed so enthralled by each other that she did not want to break up their moment together. When Reza cupped Sherifat's face with his hands and stared at her lips, she knew it was time to separate them. Quickly marching up to them, she put herself between them and pulled Sherifat away. "Enough!" she said.

Sherifat followed Leila reluctantly while still looking back.

"I will come back to see you," Reza called out.

Leila groaned. What have I done? This will not end well. Who knew if he would come back with more men next time? Now that this Reza and Abdul knew there was a camp full of women, they would tell the other men at their camp. It would be way too difficult for the young men, even those who were dedicated to Christ, to resist a camp full of young women who looked like Sherifat. Soon, the young men would swoop down on this camp like Reza had done, looking for brides... and God knew what else.

Lord, please don't let that happen. She turned and shook her head at Reza. "Please do not return."

He did not say anything.

She looked at Abdul and he gave her an anxious smile. She turned around again and groaned when Sherifat pulled her hand away and began to walk back to Reza.

"Sherifat, come back!" Leila called. She quickly went and grabbed Sherifat's hand again. She shooed the men away and Reza said, "I will come back, Sherifat!"

He and Abdul jogged away and Leila watched them until they disappeared from sight.

Sherifat gave a long sigh. "I cannot wait to see him again," she said wistfully.

"You shouldn't see him again, Sherifat," Leila said.

"Why not?"

"I told you what would happen if more of the women in this camp found out about the men's camp, and vice versa."

"But would it be so bad if that happened, Leila?" Sherifat asked. "Would it be so bad if we mixed; if some of the women here decided to marry some of the men?"

Leila did not answer. She had already explained her concerns to Sherifat. The girl was blinded by her budding love. Nothing Leila said would make any difference.

Sherifat left Leila and went back to Miriam's tent. When she entered, Leila turned around and walked back to her own tent.

Lying on her sleeping rug, Leila turned and tossed. She had just opened Pandora's Box by getting Sherifat for Reza and allowing them to fall even deeper for each other. She thought about what Sherifat had said. What was she really afraid of? Was she scared that if more of the women here began to fall in love with the men, she would feel left out because she knew she could not love anyone except for Malik?

"No!" she whispered fiercely in the darkness. That wasn't why. She was concerned because this place would be totally different if all that happened. It would not be the haven it now was. Women who were persecuted from all over came here to find solace from the world. That peace would be lost if it was overrun with men.

Are you sure of that? a small voice in her head asked.

She sighed. She was not sure of anything anymore. Maybe tomorrow, she would ask Zainah about it.

She struggled to fall asleep for a long time, and then thankfully, after what seemed like an eternity, sleep came.

The next day, after the morning prayers and breakfast, she went to Zainah's tent. She was relieved to find that Zainah was alone in the tent, which was an unusual occurrence. Zainah and Faizan were mostly together, except when Faizan had chores to do for the whole camp.

Zainah smiled widely as Leila entered and sat beside her on the sleeping rug. Pillows surrounded Zainah and she had her hand on her huge tummy. "This baby has been so active these past few days," Zainah said to Leila. "She keeps kicking me."

Leila smiled in spite of herself. "How do you know the baby is a 'she'?"

"I don't know. I said that because I am hoping it's a girl. But if it's a boy, that will be great as well."

"Where is Faizan?" Leila asked.

"He went to town with Miriam right after breakfast. He has to make preparations for the arrival of his sisters and brothers-in-law in a few days' time."

Leila lifted her brows. "I thought only his sisters were coming. Where will his brothers-in-law stay?"

"At the men's camp," Zainah said. "Faizan asked them if his brothers-in-law could stay there and they agreed."

Leila groaned. The men's camp again! She looked at Zainah and said, "Speaking of the men's camp, do you know what happened?"

"What?" Zainah turned to look quizzically at her.

"Two men came here."

"What? When?" Zainah's eyes grew as round as saucers. "No, they did not!" she exclaimed.

"Yes... yes, they did. In the middle of the night."

"What did they want?" Zainah asked, her eyes still round.

"One of them, a young man named Reza, was looking for Sherifat."

"Reza... Reza... I think I know him," Zainah said. "The day Faizan and I went to the men's camp, I saw him. I know he was one of the men we saw because Faizan told me his name after he went to the camp on his own." Zainah frowned. "He came here looking for Sherifat? How come?"

"You remember I told you about the day Miriam, Sherifat, and I went to the men's camp?"

"Yes, I remember."

"Well, Sherifat and Reza apparently made a connection that day. He came looking for her and I think they are falling in love, even though they hardly know each other. I can see it in their eyes."

"You seem dismayed by that," Zainah said. "What's the harm?"

"You know what the harm is. Think of the implications."

Zainah sighed loudly. "Not again, Leila. I don't want to argue with you about all that. I don't think we will ever see eye-to-eye on this matter."

Leila pressed her lips together and said, "Zainah, it's why I came to talk to you. I still miss Malik terribly. After two years, I still haven't gotten over him. I think about him every day. I am beginning to think that the pain caused by my breakup is coloring the way I see this whole thing about the men's camp. I am not sure if I am trying to protect the hearts of the women here, or if I'm being selfish."

Zainah gave her a sympathetic smile. "I understand how you feel, Leila. Remember the time after Faizan left this camp, before I finally decided to go find him? I felt the same way you do now. I thought love was too difficult, too heartbreaking. I didn't want anyone to go through the same thing. Remember all I told you at the time?"

Leila smiled sadly. "Yes, I remember."

"I think in spite of what happened with you and Malik, you should still open your heart to love. Who knows, you might meet someone . . ." she grinned. "…in that men's camp."

Leila pursed her lips and said, "Speaking of that, the other man that came with Reza told me he came to see me. He said he had not stopped thinking about me since the day we came to the camp. The thing is… I'm not interested in him, not when I am still in love with Malik."

Zainah nodded. "I understand. Do you want to know what I think?"

"Yes," Leila said. "That's why I came here to see you."

"I think you should either decide to go back and find Malik again since you still love him or give this new man a chance; see where it goes with him."

Leila closed her eyes and for a long moment, said nothing. Finally, she opened her eyes and said sadly, "There's a huge chance that Malik is married now. Even if he isn't, he might still not want to accept the Lord, and I cannot be with him unless he does. Besides, I certainly don't want him to convert just because of me. It would not be real."

"I know," Zainah said. "I was hoping you would come to that conclusion yourself. So you know what the other option is."

Leila sighed softly. "I should consider moving on with this other man."

Zainah nodded. "Yes, I think you should."

Leila bit her bottom lip and said, "I guess you are right. If I still want to have children of my own, I need to open my heart once more to finding love. And if not love, at least a husband who I can have a child with." She smiled again in spite of herself. "I'm not getting any younger." She looked at Zainah's belly and sighed. "Who knows? If it works out for me with that man, I might be as heavily pregnant as you are soon."

"Yes," Zainah grinned. "Our children will be like siblings. That would be wonderful."

Leila nodded, but the thought of marrying Abdul

was as appealing to her as eating stones. She wanted what Zainah had; not a part of it, but everything. Not just a child, but a husband that she loved. And the only man who had her heart, the only man she had ever loved, was Malik. She wanted to marry Malik and have children with him. Unfortunately, she could not.

Zainah put her arm around Leila's shoulders. "Just give it time, Leila. You might come to discover one day that you have found love again."

"I hope so," Leila said.

"It will happen for you, Leila," Zainah told her. "I am sure of it."

Leila smiled but she was not so sure it would. Still, she listened as Zainah told her with great excitement about her expectations once she had her baby and imagined herself sharing her excitement about having her own child one day. But she could not fathom having a baby with anyone other than Malik.

As she listened to Zainah, she prayed desperately in her heart that the Lord would take away her love for Malik. Then she could start a new relationship and have her dreams of starting a family of her own come true.

She knew what she would do in order to make that dream happen. When Reza returned to the camp, she would tell him to inform Abdul that she was ready to give him a chance, if he was still interested in her.

THIRTEEN

Malik opened the door of the taxi he had hired to Nira and got out. He paid the driver and brought out his suitcase from the trunk of the taxi. When the driver drove away, Malik carried his suitcase to the front of his father's house and knocked on the gate.

He waited, hoping his father would not be the one who opened the gate. Karim Keita was the last person he wanted to see. It was impossible for him not to see his father now he was in Nira, but he preferred to see everyone else first—Fanta, Khadija, his mother and other siblings, before his father.

He had come straight here rather than go to his house because he could not wait to see Fanta, and it was also imperative that he speak to Khadija right away.

The gate opened and his heart lifted with happiness when Khadija peered out at him. She gave a small scream and hugged him quickly. She pulled back again. "Malik, you're here!" she exclaimed. "You didn't tell anyone you were coming today."

He nodded. "I did not know I was going to come until just this afternoon."

"Come in." She took his suitcase before he could respond and wheeled it behind her as she walked through the gate.

Malik entered the compound behind her and shut the gate. He asked, "Where is Fanta? I hope she's at home." His mother sometimes took Fanta to the market with her and they didn't return for hours.

"Yes, she is," Khadija answered. "She's with your mother. They are both in the kitchen. You know how Fanta is. She asks if she can help cook the meals all the time."

"She likes to do things that older people do," Malik said.

They entered the house and Malik groaned when he saw his father sitting on the sofa in the living room.

His father looked up from the book he was reading and removed his glasses. "Malik, so you're here. I thought you had cut all ties from your family when you decided to stop working on my farm."

Malik scowled at him. "What are you talking about? I come here often to visit my daughter."

"Well, you hardly speak to me when you come."

Malik did not respond. Instead, he turned to Khadija. "I have something very important to discuss with you. Please don't go out. Let me just go and see Fanta and Mama, and then we will talk." He walked toward the kitchen, while Khadija left his suitcase in a corner of the living room.

He stopped when his father called out his name in a stern voice. Turning around, he stared at his father. "Yes, what is it?"

Karim Keita shook his head and said, "I am not your enemy, Malik."

"Really?" Malik said. "I'm not even going to get into it with you. I just want to see my daughter and mother in peace."

Keita glared at him for a long time and then said, "You have apparently decided to stay angry with me, but you cannot keep on being angry forever. At some point, you'll have to forgive me."

Malik thought about everything his father had done to him, to Zainah, and even to Khadija. Most of all, to Leila. Hell would freeze over before he ever forgave his father. He did not bother to respond. He turned around and made his way to the kitchen.

Fanta beamed when she saw him. She ran to him and put her little hands around his waist. "Papa," she said. "You're here!"

He hugged her and lifted her off her feet. Kissing her forehead, he grinned at her and then put her down. His mother came to him and he smiled and hugged her as well.

He took his daughter's hand as his mother put her hand on his shoulder. "You didn't tell us you were coming today," she said to him.

"I didn't know I was going to come. I just decided a few hours ago."

His mother nodded. "I am glad you're here." She looked down at Fanta and smiled. "Your daughter has missed you," she said. "I cannot wait for your wedding day to come. I am so excited. I have already sent the fabric I want to use to make my outfit to the tailor. It will be ready by..."

"No, Mama!" Malik interrupted her and then whispered in her ear so Fanta would not hear, "The wedding has been called off."

She raised her eyebrows and looked at him with sadness in her eyes. "What happened, Malik?" she asked.

He shook his head. "I don't want to talk about it with Fanta here." He would tell his daughter that the wedding had been called off soon enough. Just not right now.

His mother gave a weary sigh and said, "So you came to Nira to rest and get away from it all." She rubbed his back to soothe him. "I'm so sorry, Malik."

He gave her a small smile and said, "I actually did not come to Nira to stay."

"You're going back to your farm?"

"I am not going back yet, Mama."

Confusion crept into her features. She asked, "Then where are you going?"

"I'll tell you later on," he said to her. "I need to speak to Khadija first." He bent down and looked at Fanta. "I will be back, Fanta. Let me speak to Aunty Khadija."

Fanta nodded.

He left the kitchen quickly. He found Khadija still in the living room and said to her, "Can we talk in my house privately?" He glanced at his father, who was glaring at him, and then turned back to face his sister.

"Okay," she said.

He carried his suitcase from the corner of the living room and went out the door. Khadija followed him, and they walked out of the gate. They walked to his house without speaking. He unlocked his front door and they both entered the house. Taking his suitcase to the bedroom, he came out immediately and sat next to Khadija on the couch.

She said to him, "What do you want to speak to me about?"

"I called off my wedding, Khadija."

"You what?"

"Actually, my fiancée, or ex-fiancée, broke up with me."

"I'm so sorry, Malik," Khadija said.

He shook his head quickly. "No… no! I am actually relieved about it."

She raised her eyebrows and stared at him with a surprised look on her face. "You are relieved that your fiancée broke up with you just days before your wedding?"

"Yes," Malik said. "The truth is that I did not love her and she knew it. Apart from that, I found out she was a Christian, and just like Leila, she said she could not marry me since I did not share her faith."

"Again!" Khadija said, an incredulous expression now on her face. "Leila broke up with you because you would not convert to Christianity, now another woman has broken up with you for the same reason. You sure know how to pick them, Malik." Khadija grinned.

"Stop it!" he said. "It's not funny, Khadija. It's actually heartbreaking."

"I know," Khadija said. "I'm truly sorry. What you said about being relieved that Hauwa broke up with you—what do you mean by that?"

"Just like I told you, I didn't love her and she knew it. I have decided to find Leila. She's the only woman I have ever truly loved. I don't think I want to go on living without her. I have to find her, Khadija. That is why I asked to speak to you. Do you have any idea where she is?"

Khadija blinked rapidly and said, "The only thing I know is that when Zainah called me and Mama some weeks ago..."

"Zainah called? You didn't tell me she called!"

"I actually did not remember to tell you. The last time you came here, you were preoccupied with your wedding plans and with Fanta finding a new mother. Anyway, she called to tell us she was pregnant and would soon be having a baby. I think she said she was seven or so months pregnant, I cannot remember. She should be preparing to give birth to her baby any time now, I guess."

His mouth dropped open and then he closed it. "Wow! Zainah is going to be a mother. Is she happy in her marriage?"

"She sounded extremely happy," Khadija said.

"That's good. I'm really happy for her. But... what does that have to do with Leila? Does Zainah know where Leila is?"

Khadija's eyes searched his and she said, "Leila is actually in the camp where Zainah is."

"She is?" Malik sat up straighter. "Please tell me

you know where that camp is, Khadija."

"Unfortunately, I don't," Khadija said. "I asked her where it was but she refused to tell me. She said the location of the camp is a secret."

Malik groaned. "How will I ever find Leila if no one knows where she is? Can I at least call Zainah and ask her myself? She might tell me where that camp is if she hears how desperate I am."

Khadija bit her lip.

He sighed. "Oh, Khadija, don't tell me you didn't save her number in your phone after she called you."

"It wasn't me she called. It was our mother. You know Papa hasn't allowed me to get a phone of my own yet. Anyway, I did get try to call her on Mama's phone several times, but I haven't been able to reach her."

Malik put his hand on his forehead and shut his eyes. "How will I ever find her, Khadija?"

"I'm glad you want to get back with Leila, Malik," Khadija said. "But have you converted to Christianity, or are you planning to? Because if you aren't, I don't think there's any point. Besides, it might be almost impossible for you to find her. Maybe you should not have broken up with your fiancée."

"I did not break up with her. She broke up with me, and I am glad for that. No matter what it takes, I am going to find Leila and we will get married."

Khadija stared at him as though he had lost his mind. She finally said, "Let me go and get my mother's phone. Zainah's number is saved on it." She got up and dashed out of the house.

Malik felt his emotions roiling with a mixture of worry and anticipation. He had to believe that, somehow, Zainah would answer her phone when he called, and that he would be able to speak to Leila.

His front door opened and Khadija walked in again, panting. She sat down beside him once more.

"I ran all the way to the house and back," she said.

He nodded and watched as she began to scroll through different numbers on her mother's phone. Finally, she settled on one and pressed it to initiate the call. She put the phone on speaker and Malik held his breath. The line did not even ring and Malik's heart sank.

Khadija looked up at him and said, "I am sorry. We can try again tomorrow."

Malik moaned. "I have to find her, Khadija. Every day that goes by means that I might be too late. If she isn't married now or in love with someone else, it'll only be a matter of time before she is. I have to think of something... another way to find her."

He shut his eyes once more as his mind ran through different possibilities and ways in which he might track Leila down. However, he came up with nothing.

And then he thought about Leila's ex-husband, Dauda. Not long after he and Leila broke up and he went back to Dogon, Leila's ex-husband had come to Nira and so had Leila. The marriage had been dissolved. Khadija had told him about it and his heart had ached at the fact that they were not going to get married anymore. Their plan had been to wed immediately after Leila's marriage was dissolved. He had been despondent for months after that.

"What about Dauda?" he asked Khadija. "Do you think he'll know where she is?"

"That's unlikely," Khadija answered.

"What about one of his wives? Do you think any of them will know?"

"I don't think so." Khadija shook her head. "But what does it really matter? Right now, Dauda and his wives are in Saudi Arabia. No one knows when next they will visit Nira."

"Do you, by any chance, have Dauda's number?" Malik asked.

She gave a short laugh. "You know I don't, but Papa surely will."

Malik groaned and rolled his eyes. "I don't want to ask that man for anything."

"You don't have a choice," Khadija said.

"I know." Malik stood up and Khadija did as well. "I guess I'll have to speak to him and ask if he has Dauda's number." He wasn't looking forward to doing that. The last thing he wanted to do was ask his father for anything and then be beholden to him. But he had to find Leila, so he had no choice.

He walked out of his house with Khadija and went back to his parents' house. Entering into the living room, he saw his father was still there. He sat across from the man and waited until his father looked up from his book. "Can I ask you for a favor?" he said reluctantly.

His father's eyes lit up. "What is it?" he asked, way too eagerly for Malik's liking.

He couldn't help the anger in his voice as he said, "Dauda, your friend who you married Leila off to, can I have his number?"

"Why do you want his number?"

Malik did not reply for a long moment and then he said, "I need to ask him something about Leila."

His father said nothing for some seconds, and then he sighed loudly. "You want to ask him about his ex-wife. I hope you know it's not a good idea." Putting his hand into his shirt pocket, Karim brought out his phone. "I will give you his number. At least he is better than his brother, Jibril. Now, if you had asked me to give you Jibril's number, I would have said no."

Malik brought his phone out from his pants pocket and typed out Dauda's number as his father dictated it. When his father finished, Malik dialed the number he had been given.

He waited with his heart in his throat as the phone rang. Finally, Dauda's voice came on the other end. "Hello, who is this?"

Malik struggled to keep his voice even and polite as he said, "Hello, sir, this is Malik, Karim Keita's son."

"Okay..." Dauda's voice sounded wary. "What do you want, young man?"

"Umm... I'm trying to find Leila, your ex-wife. I was wondering, do you have any idea where she is?"

Dauda gave a harsh laugh and said, "I have broken ties with Leila. I don't know why you're asking me where she is."

"I was just wondering if you knew where to find her. She seems to have disappeared since..."

"Listen, young man," he cut Malik off, "I have no idea where she is. It's none of my business now."

Malik sighed and then said, "Okay. Thank you for your time." He ended the call and then put his hands on his head, frustrated and dismayed.

He stood up as his father asked, "So what did Dauda say?"

Malik answered coldly, "He doesn't know where Leila is." He walked quickly out of the living room before his father could ask him any more questions and went back to his house. He sat on his sofa and then roared in anger as his frustration took over. "Where on earth am I going to find Leila now?"

A clear but unfamiliar voice in his mind whispered, "Pray!"

He blinked. Pray? That's the last thing on my mind. He opened his mouth and surprised himself with the words that came out. "Please..." he hesitated for a few seconds, and then went on, "please, Jesus, help me find her."

It was a strange prayer for sure, and he felt slightly guilty for saying it. But it seemed fitting since Jesus was the one Leila had dedicated her life to; the one she followed. He would know where she was and how to find her. He added, surprising himself even more, "If you help me find her, I promise that I will give my life to you."

He opened his eyes and then leaned back against the sofa and sighed deeply. After a while, he stretched out and shut his eyes. He felt drained and weary. Tomorrow, he would resume his search for Leila, because he had to find her. Right now, apart from his daughter's well-being, finding her was all that mattered to him.

FOURTEEN

Sienna got out of bed, her heart pounding. She took a deep breath to try to still her racing heart and went into the bathroom. Switching the lights on, she stared at herself in the mirror. Her heart was still drumming. She took deep breaths but it did not stop.

"Lord, what is wrong with me?" she whispered. The panic attacks and fears had subsided for a couple of days, but they had now returned with a vengeance for reasons she did not understand. She felt guilty all the time, as though she were living in sin, and yet she could not think of any major sin she had committed. True, she made mistakes all the time, but she repented constantly, which was also really tiring.

Just now, she'd had a nightmare where she was locked in a dark room with a dark personality she couldn't see. She had cried out for the Lord to help her, but He had not. She had felt completely alone. God had not heard her cries in spite of her constant prayers.

She felt more out of tune with the Lord than she had ever felt, except for the years before she married Bryan, when the scrupulosity had been at its worst.

She went back into the bedroom, leaving the light from the bathroom on. Climbing into bed, she looked at Bryan's sleeping form. She could not see his face clearly, but she ran her fingers through his hair and kissed his cheek. She stretched out beside him and sighed. Just lying next to him made her feel a little better, but her heart was still pounding.

Bryan turned around, stretched out his hands, and drew her close. She smiled in spite of herself, knowing it was a reflex action. Even asleep, he still thought about her and wanted her close to him.

She rested her head on his chest and felt herself drifting off to sleep once again. She resisted, knowing she would have another nightmare if she fell asleep now. She sat up on the bed again, gently extricating herself from Bryan's arms. She had to find the root cause of this present battle with scrupulosity. She'd thought she was done with it, but obviously something had brought it up again and, in spite of her continuous prayers and confessions, it remained.

She whispered to the Lord, "Please help me find the root of this and a solution… a permanent one."

She climbed out of bed again and snatched up her Bible from the bedside table. She went into the bathroom, shut the door, and sat on the edge of the bathtub. Opening her Bible randomly, her eyes settled on a scripture and she read it out loud. "'But to him that worketh not, but believeth on him that justifies the ungodly, his faith is counted for righteousness.'"

She suddenly blinked as a thought crossed her mind. She read the scripture one more time and immediately knew in the depth of her heart why the scrupulosity had come back. It had come back gradually, and she hadn't taken it seriously until it began to really bother her. But now she could trace the first time it had actually started. It was about the time she took the reins of the orphanage and also began all the ministerial roles as a minister's wife.

She understood now what had happened. Because of her history with scrupulosity and then her deliverance, she had held on to her relationship with Christ and her righteousness in him by faith, knowing she was justified by faith alone. But when she began ministry, she started to depend way too much on what she did for the Lord to make herself right before him, rather than on his unconditional love. The more she did for him, the better she felt about herself and her place in God. At least, at first. But gradually, her good works seemed never to be enough and she had to do more and more in order to feel like she was a true Christian and that God was pleased with her. This was how the anxiety attacks had started again.

She looked up from her Bible and said, "Lord, I'm so sorry. After everything I went through and how you delivered me the last time, I should have known better."

She prayed and asked the Lord to help her come back to the basics, the simple gospel—that she was loved by the Lord, no matter what.

After she'd finished praying, she smiled as a supernatural peace descended on her. She knew that from now on, she had to keep believing that God loved and accepted her unconditionally.

When Dr. Lincoln told her and Bryan that they were going to be transferred somewhere else, she had begun to panic. She loved running the orphanage, but she had let it become her identity; the reason for her being.

She'd told herself, even unknowingly, that without running the orphanage, she wasn't really working for God. That had added to her panic and anxiety attacks. Now she had to let go and let God lead her into His will for her now. She would miss the orphanage, but she was looking forward to whatever the Lord had planned for her future.

She looked up as the door opened and Bryan walked into the bathroom.

He had a surprised look on his face as he stared at her. He came and sat beside her and said, "When I awoke and didn't see you in bed, I wondered where you had gone in the middle of the night and then saw the light streaming from under the door. I waited about ten minutes. When you did not come out, I began to worry." He put his hand around her shoulder. "Are you okay, sweetie? Did you have another nightmare?"

She turned and smiled brightly at him. "I did."

His brows lifted. "And you're happy about that?" he asked her, looking both surprised and slightly confused. "You're smiling as if you had the best dream in the world."

She said to him, "I had a nightmare and I was scared as usual. I came into the bathroom asking the Lord what exactly was wrong with me. I wanted to know the root cause of this problem and why it had returned. I opened my Bible and my eyes fell on this scripture." She read the scripture that she had read out loud earlier to him. "After I finished reading it, I immediately realized what the root problem was. It was as if the Lord immediately dropped it into my heart and I could clearly see how the scrupulosity started again."

She told him what she had realized after reading the scripture; about how she had depended on how much she did for the Lord to feel that she was righteous and loved by him. "I love being a minister's wife," she told Bryan and smiled at him, "but I cannot depend on that and all that I do in ministry to feel like I am accepted by the Lord."

Bryan nodded. "I understand, Sienna. I have to struggle with that as well. I'm glad for everything the Lord showed you. I'll try to remind you about it as much as I can from now on."

He combed his fingers through her hair and said softly, "I love you, Sienna. We will overcome this together."

"I already feel a lot better," she said. "At least I know exactly what to do now when I start feeling like I have to do more and more in order to please God."

Bryan stood up and held his hand out to her.

She took his hand and walked into the bedroom with him.

Without even talking to each other about it, they both headed directly to Ethan's cot. Sienna switched on the light and they both stooped down to gaze at their precious son. Sienna's heart filled with an overwhelming love for him, and she reached down and gently caressed his cheek. She turned to Bryan and said, "I hope he grows up to be just like you, Bryan. I hope he becomes the sweet, kind, and godly man that you are."

Bryan beamed at her and said, "And I hope one day we have a little girl who grows up to be just like her mama— beautiful, kindhearted, and the most amazing woman I know."

She straightened and hugged Bryan tightly. She sighed in contentment as she rested her head on his chest. "I am so glad I have you in my life, Bryan," she said. "I know I can conquer anything with you by my side."

He kissed the top of her head and his arms tightened around her.

They stayed wrapped in each other's arms for a long time and then Bryan said, "Let's go back to bed, sweetie."

She pulled back slightly from him and they both climbed into bed again. She snuggled up to him and, this time, quickly drifted off to a dreamless sleep.

*****

Audrey opened the car door, got out, walked to her front door and then opened it. Walking into the living room, she saw Ken sitting on the couch and smiled brightly at him. She had decided to go to the station today to see some of the officers she had worked with for years before she traveled with Ken in a few days' time.

Ken smiled at her and said, "Come and sit beside me, Audrey."

She went to sit beside him and tossed her purse on the coffee table.

"How was your day, Police Chief Baylor?" he asked her.

She laughed and shook her head. "Ex-police chief Baylor."

He shrugged. "Once a police chief, always a police chief."

She chuckled and then frowned. "Something one of the officers told me immediately after I got to the station is still on my mind."

"What?" he asked.

"Derrick asked to speak with me."

"Who?" Ken frowned.

"Derrick. The man who kidnapped Sienna on the day she married Bryan."

He smiled wryly. "The one who went insane?"

"Yes, him. The officer who was in charge of his case with me at the time told me Derrick was getting better at the psychiatric hospital and had asked to speak with me."

"And what did you say?" Ken asked.

"Nothing. I don't want to speak to Derrick."

"But you don't know why he wants to speak to you, Audrey," Ken said.

"Why else?" Audrey said. "Probably to spin one of his tales and tell me he made a mistake and wants to get out of the psych hospital. Actually, he's lucky to be there or he would be in prison now, rotting away."

"Maybe you should go and hear what he has to say," Ken said.

Audrey shook her head. "No, I don't have the time for that. I haven't even packed for our trip."

"Okay, then," Ken stood up. "We should go and pack now. I haven't packed a thing, either."

"Yes, I think we should," Audrey said. She stood up and they both went into their bedroom together.

Audrey went into her closet, brought out her traveling bag, and packed her clothes into it. She folded each outfit neatly and carefully and tucked them into the suitcase. She looked over at Ken as he threw his clothes into his suitcase and shook her head. "What are you doing, Ken?" she asked him, staring incredulously at him.

"I'm packing, Audrey. What does it look like I am doing?"

"You are packing your things like that?" Audrey frowned. "Why are you not folding your clothes into your suitcase?"

"I'll probably not wear most of them anyway... but just in case..."

"That does not explain why you're not folding your clothes," Audrey said, chuckling.

Ken shrugged. "What's the point?"

"What will I do with you, Ken Baylor?" she asked, laughing.

They continued to pack while enjoying each other's company and talking about random stuff. After a while, Audrey said to Ken, "I wish Esther could travel with us. It's a shame that this opportunity to go and see Faizan came while school was still in session."

"I know," Ken said. "But at least she's having a good time with her grandparents and her cousins. We should call her after we finish packing."

"We should," Audrey said. She suddenly felt nauseated. Before she could throw up all the food she had eaten that day, she stood up quickly and ran into the bathroom. Bending over the toilet bowl, she threw up into it.

Ken came and stooped beside her. "What is wrong, baby?" he asked in a voice that rang with alarm. He rubbed her back and said, "Do you have a bellyache?"

"Just a little discomfort," she told him. She stood up and smiled at him. "I'm okay. Maybe it was something I ate."

He looked at her with a strange expression and she frowned. "What?"

"Maybe you are pregnant, Audrey,"

Her eyes widened and her mouth fell open. She had been feeling a little tired for some time now, but she thought it was just stress. But if Ken was right... "Oh my God, Ken! Maybe I am! That would be so wonderful if I was pregnant." Her heart began to race with excitement, but she told herself to calm down. They weren't yet sure she was.

"You have to take a pregnancy test," Ken said, the excitement in his voice clear. "I could go get some pregnancy tests for you from the pharmacy."

She nodded. "That would be a good idea. Oh Ken, if I am, I might die of happiness!"

He reached out and hugged her tightly, and then pulled back. "Let's not get ahead of ourselves, though. Let me go to the pharmacy." He walked out of the bathroom and she followed him into the bedroom. He grabbed his wallet and car keys from the bedside table and left the room quickly.

She followed him to the living room and after he had left, she looked out the window as he entered the car and drove off. She stepped back from the window and took deep breaths. "Calm down, Audrey. What if you are not really pregnant?"

She went to sit on the sofa, but her excitement would not subside. If she was, it would be an answer to her and Ken's prayers.

She could not sit still anymore and stood up

again. She paced the living room impatiently. She looked up at the clock and whispered, "Where are you, Ken?" She scoffed. "Calm down, Audrey! He just left a few minutes ago."

She began to imagine what it would feel like to find out she was pregnant. The first people she would call would be Sienna and Trisha. She could imagine how excited they would be. They would be so happy for her, knowing how long she had been wanting to have a baby, how hard she and Ken had been trying, and how worried they had both been.

She paced the living room again, clenching and unclenching her fists, her stomach roiling both with worry and excitement. Her stomach suddenly lurched when she heard Ken's car outside and she thought she would puke again.

She opened the door before Ken got out of the car, and then waited at the door, tapping her foot impatiently as he walked briskly toward her and entered the house.

He handed a bag to her and said, "Here it is. How long will it take for us to know if you are pregnant or not?"

In spite of herself, she chuckled at the impatient tone in his voice. She headed toward the bathroom and smiled when he followed her. He waited at the door while she went in.

Inside the bathroom, she took another deep breath to try to let go of her nervousness and then brought out the pregnancy test kit. After she had peed and followed the directions, she came out of the bathroom.

Ken immediately walked up to her, looking nervous. "Well?" he said. "Are we pregnant?"

"We have to wait for a few minutes before we know."

They both sat on the bed in silence. Audrey's heart kept drumming. Finally, after a few minutes, though it felt like ten, she stood up. She went into the bathroom again and slowly picked up one of the strips. Ken had bought three of them.

She hesitated for a long moment and then finally mustered up courage and looked. Her heart sank to her feet. There was only one line on the stick, showing she wasn't pregnant.

"No... no!" she cried and picked up the second stick. It showed the same thing. She picked the last one up and then shook her head as it still showed that she wasn't going to be a mother. She sat on the floor and wept softly.

Ken came into the bathroom and sat beside her. He took the sticks, looked at them, and dropped them back on the sink. "I am sorry, Audrey," he said. He wrapped his arms around her and she continued to cry. Why had she let her hopes rise so much just because she had puked once? She wanted to be pregnant with all her heart, and she had made herself believe she was because she'd thrown up. Now her hope had been crushed. Her heart ached.

"Why, Ken? Why am I not pregnant?" she cried.

Ken said nothing, and she knew he was hurting, too. He rubbed her back soothingly and kissed her hair.

She cried some more and then she gathered herself together and stood up. Ken did as well, and they both went into the bedroom again.

She walked back to her suitcase on the floor, threw open her closet again and mechanically continued to pack.

"Are you sure you don't want to rest for now? We can continue tomorrow," Ken said.

"No," she said to him. "I want to finish packing. At least I have control over this if not over my body." Sadness flooded her heart again. She bent down and folded her clothes into the suitcase. This false hope had been a bad blow, but she would not let it keep her down nor dim her excitement at their upcoming trip. No matter what, she would try her best to enjoy this trip. Most of all, she would continue to be grateful for what she had now.

Thinking of what she had now made her think of Esther. She looked up at Ken, who was sitting on the bed and had given up packing his own clothes. "We should call Esther," she said. "Hearing her voice will definitely make us feel better."

He nodded eagerly.

She straightened and went to sit beside him as he brought out his phone. As she spoke to Esther on the phone, she smiled genuinely and thanked the Lord for her daughter. She might not have the baby she wanted, but she had this precious girl, and for now, that would have to be enough.

FIFTEEN

Audrey laughed as Trisha told her about Ruby and Molly's latest antics.

Sienna shook her head and said, "I'm sure Ethan's presence here has made them even more boisterous than usual. He's such an energetic child, that one."

Audrey looked at her sisters and said, "So we're leaving tomorrow evening. Has everyone finished packing?"

"I have," Sienna said. "Bryan hasn't even packed anything."

"What?" Trisha's eyes widened and she chuckled. "Bryan has not packed his things at all?"

Sienna grinned. "That's the way he is. He leaves his packing until the last minute. He'll probably start until an hour or two before we have to leave."

Audrey laughed. "Okay, then. As long as he doesn't make us late for our flight."

"We are flying on a private plane. Doesn't the pilot have to wait for us or something?"

"I don't know, but I can't imagine that he will be happy if we are late for our flight," Audrey answered. "Anyway, Bryan has taken Ethan to his parents' house in Green Valley?"

"Yes," Sienna said.

"Frank will take Ruby and Molly to his parents' this evening. We need a full day to prepare without them here." Trisha chuckled. "I love them, bless their little hearts, but they will not allow us to pack anything if they are here."

"Speaking of Ruby," Audrey leaned forward and looked intently at Trisha, "have you heard anything from Stan since the last time he came to your house?"

"No, I haven't. Thank God. He has probably left town again to God-knows-where. I just wish he would stay wherever he is so that I never have to see him again."

"If only he would do that," Audrey said. "But unfortunately, knowing him, he will soon be back to make your life a living hell."

Trisha laughed. "That was exactly what he told me the last time he was here."

"It's a good thing you're deciding not to give him the money and call his bluff."

"It was a hard decision to make, Audrey," Trisha sighed. "But you all convinced me. I hope it's the right one."

Audrey opened her mouth to tell her it was, but the doorbell rang.

"I wonder who that is," Trisha said. She stood up and then went to the door.

"I'm so glad you had that divine intervention from the Lord," Audrey said to Sienna. "I've been really worried about you. After you told us the anxiety and panic attacks had come back, it took my mind back to that time when you nearly died."

"I know," Sienna said. "It was terrible, but every day now, I am resting in God's unconditional love for me."

"Thank God—" Audrey frowned as she heard Trisha telling someone off. And then she heard Stan's voice. "Oh no! What is that jerk doing here now?" She stood up at the same time Sienna did and went to the door. Stan and Trisha were arguing about something. Audrey glared at Stan and said, "What do you want, Stan? I thought you agreed to give Trisha some time to get the money for you."

Trisha turned to Audrey and Sienna with an angry expression on her face. "Stan has decided he cannot wait three months. He wants me to give him the money in two weeks instead."

"You have got to be kidding me!" Audrey said. "Stan! Didn't Trisha tell you that she needed some time in order to liquidate some assets and then give you the money?"

Stan shook his head. "Audrey, you have always been a character." He turned back to Trisha and said, "I know what your plan is, Trisha. You just want to buy time. You don't plan to give me the money, do you? Well, your plan isn't going to work. I'm giving you two weeks to get the money for me or I'll see you in court."

Trisha folded her arms across her chest and shook her head. "You know what, Stan? I am sick and tired of this. If you want a fight, then I will give you a fight."

Audrey scowled. "We are calling your bluff, Stan. We know you don't really want Ruby. All you want is money. Well, let's see how your case will stand in court. No judge is going to grant you custody of the daughter you abandoned."

"Well, I hope you start to prepare to only see Ruby once a year, because when I win the custody case, that will be the only time you will get see her."

Trisha laughed without humor and Audrey chuckled. "That is not going to happen and you know it!" Trisha said.

"Are you really sure about that? Even if the court doesn't grant me full custody, then they will grant me joint custody, especially since I am Ruby's biological father. I have a clean record, a good job, and a very convincing reason, which I will not tell you, for being absent from her life. I bet you'll enjoy sharing me with your daughter. Just like you have always said to me, I'm not a very responsible person. Who knows how Ruby will fare when she is with me?"

Trisha's mouth fell open and Audrey barked at him, "You are a monster, Stan Coleman!"

Stan shrugged. "Just get my money ready in two weeks, Trisha." He turned around, walked to his car, and drove off.

Trisha put her hand on her forehead and shut her eyes as fear gripped her. "What am I supposed to do now? Are you sure I shouldn't just give him the money he is asking for?"

"No, you shouldn't!" Audrey said. "He's blackmailing you now. I promise you he won't stop even after you give him the money. It's your share of the inheritance Dad gave to you and to your family. Stan has no right to it."

"But you heard what he said. What if the court grants . . ."

"Trisha, I agree with Audrey," Sienna said, interrupting Trisha. "Don't give in to Stan and his blackmail."

"I wish I could get him arrested now," Audrey said. "But unfortunately, we don't really have anything on him." She sighed and put her arm around Trisha's shoulders. "Let's go back inside," she said.

They went back into the house and Trisha sat between Audrey and Sienna. "I don't think I can go on that trip anymore," Trisha said.

Audrey did not know what to say. She wanted to tell Trisha not to let Stan's words affect her and to come on the trip with them, but Stan's threats were serious and at this time, Trisha was right. She had to stay in Rosefield and try to find a solution to it all.

"Maybe I should stay behind and be with you, Trisha," Sienna said.

Audrey nodded. "I think I want to stay as well, Trisha."

"No, no!" Trisha complained. "Both of you should go with Ken and Bryan. Frank will be with me. I will be okay."

"No, Trisha," Audrey said. "Remember that last trip we took to Spain? You couldn't go because you gave birth even though we all planned to go. We can't let that happen again. We will stay and solve this problem together. Besides, it will not be the same without you on the trip."

Trisha smiled at Audrey and then at Sienna. "Thank you so much. But are you guys sure? Because I will understand if you go without me."

"We are sure," Sienna said.

"Our plans to go and see Faizan have been such a rollercoaster ride," Audrey said. "One day we are excited about going, and the next we are deciding that we can't go, and then changing our minds once more."

"All because of Stan," Trisha added.

"Not just Stan," Audrey said. "It was also because we thought our husbands could not go and we didn't want to go without them." She recalled the incident that had happened some days ago when she thought she was pregnant. She said to Trisha and Sienna in a small voice, "I took a pregnancy test a few days ago."

Sienna's mouth dropped open and Trisha's eyes widened. "Are you pregnant?" Trisha asked.

"Unfortunately not," Audrey answered. "I felt nauseated and was throwing up and I really thought that I was pregnant; so did Ken. When I did the test, however, and found out that I wasn't, I was so crushed. I never want to experience that feeling again." She leaned back on the sofa and closed her eyes. "Guys, I think it might be time for me to give up on having a baby."

"No, Audrey," Trisha said. "You will have your baby. You just need to stop stressing about it."

"Trisha is right, Audrey," Sienna said. "Just trust the Lord and give it time."

Audrey smiled, but in her heart, frustration was building up. The doctor had said nothing was wrong with her or Ken, and yet they couldn't get pregnant. She put aside her concerns and frustration and changed the topic.

They began to talk about the small party they would throw to mark their parents' anniversary. After about an hour, Audrey stood up and said, "Well I need to get home now. I have to tell Ken that we cannot travel anymore."

"Oh, Faizan will be so disappointed," Trisha said.

Audrey nodded. She hugged her sisters and left Trisha's house. She got home and made her way to the bedroom to find Ken. Just as she stepped into the bedroom, her cellphone rang. She opened her purse and brought out her phone, and then answered, "Yes, who is this?"

The officer she had spoken to about Derrick said, "It's Hammond, Chief." Audrey smiled. They still called her Chief at that station.

Ken entered the room. He had apparently been in the bathroom. He smiled at her and she smiled back. She raised a finger to let him know she was on the phone.

"Yes, Hammond. What is it?"

Officer Hammond told her once more that Derrick was still asking for her. "He keeps insisting that he needs to speak to you about something important. Something about Stan."

Audrey raised her brows. "Did you say Stan?"

"Yes, I think that's the name he's been calling. The staff at the psychiatric hospital told me he's mostly recovered now, and he sounded sane enough when I spoke to him."

Audrey frowned, wondering why Derrick wanted to speak to her and how it concerned Stan. Finally, she said to the officer, "Okay, thanks. I will go and speak to him tomorrow."

After the call ended, she turned to face Ken.

"What was that about?" he asked.

She told him what the officer had said about Derrick. "I will go and see him tomorrow and hear him out."

"Tomorrow? But we are supposed to travel in the evening tomorrow, Audrey."

"About that. Ken, we won't be able to make the trip anymore." She told him everything that had happened when she was with Trisha; how Stan had come and demanded that the money he was asking for should be given to him in two weeks instead of the agreed three months.

"Trisha is distraught," Audrey said. "Sienna and I promised that we would stay here with her since she cannot travel with everything that's going on."

"Oh my Lord!" Ken exclaimed. "We're changing our minds again? And I still haven't gotten through to Faizan. I'll have to try once more and see if I will get him on the phone and tell him that we can't come anymore." He put his hands on Audrey's shoulders. "I was really looking forward to the trip."

"I was, too," Audrey said. "I was looking forward to seeing Faizan and that women's camp. It's unfortunate that Stan has ruined our plans."

Ken sighed and brought out his phone from his pocket. He dialed a number and put his phone to his ear. After a while, he removed his phone from his ear and said, "The number is still unavailable."

"Well then, Faizan will be angry with us, but there's nothing we can do," Audrey sighed.

"I'll keep trying to call him," Ken muttered.

Audrey nodded and went to get something to eat.

The next morning, she went to the psychiatric hospital. She sat on the manicured grounds, waiting for Derrick to be brought to her. A few minutes later, Derrick walked toward her, led by a young woman in white scrubs. As he came closer, she studied his face. She had expected his eyes to look wild like they had years ago when she had interrogated him after he was arrested for trying to kidnap Sienna. Instead, he looked almost like his old self. He had the same smirk on his face that he usually did, and he walked confidently. Soon, he would leave this place, but, unfortunately for him, he would be going to jail.

"It's so good to see you," he said to Audrey as he sat on the chair in front of her.

Audrey said nothing. She continued to study his face while he looked at her with an amused smile. Finally, she said, "You wanted to speak to me, Derrick?"

"I decided that since I'm going to jail once I leave here, I'm not going down alone."

Audrey leaned forward and nodded. "Okay. I am listening."

He began to narrate a long story of betrayal. The more she listened, the angrier she got. He told her about how her father had confided in him about the inheritance and how he had plotted for a long time to marry one of them in order to get his hands on it.

He had succeeded in winning Sienna's heart, but when she walked away from him, he got angry. Without her, he could not get the money. And that was why he had kidnapped her. When he was caught and realized that he would never be able to have the money and that all his plans had been in vain, something broke in him and he lost his mind. But now, he could think clearly again. He told her that Stan had been involved in his plans. "He would have left Trisha a long time ago if not for the inheritance," Derrick said. "Stan was to stay with her until we could get the money, but his philandering ways ruined our plan, at least temporarily. The only option I had then was to kidnap Sienna and try to force her to marry me."

After Derrick finished narrating his story, Audrey leaned back in her seat and said, "So Stan was your accomplice." She smiled as an idea presented itself to her; an idea on how to get rid of Stan once and for all so he would stop bothering Trisha. Stan was not the only one who knew how to make threats.

"Since I have told you all this," Derrick said, "Can you help me so my sentence will be reduced?"

Audrey shrugged and stood up. "I can't help you," she said. "I am not a police officer anymore."

"What?" he stared at her in disbelief.

"You're worse than I even thought you were. I hope I never see your face again."

He began to plead, "Surely there is a way you can help reduce my sentence?"

She walked away without looking back. He had taken advantage of her baby sister and their father's trust.

She hurried to Trisha's house. If they could get Stan back to the house in time, she could tell him what Derrick had just revealed to her and solve this issue once and for all. Then they could all still travel this evening to see Faizan.

She got to Trisha's house and rang the doorbell. When the door opened, she immediately walked into the house.

Trisha looked at her. "You are here, Audrey. Was Ken able to get through to Faizan yesterday?"

"No," Audrey answered. "But I have very interesting news for you. Where is Sienna? She will want to hear about this, especially since it concerns Derrick."

"Derrick, Sienna's ex?"

"Yes," Audrey answered.

"Let me go and get her," Trisha said and immediately left the living room. She came back a minute later with Sienna, and they all sat together on the couch.

Audrey told them about the call she'd received and about going to see Derrick in the psychiatric hospital. She told them everything Derrick had said to her. When she finished, the expression on their faces ranged from anger to dismay.

Sienna said, "I can't believe this. So Derrick plotted from the beginning to marry me just so he could get his hands on Dad's inheritance."

Trisha shook her head, disbelief etched on her face. "And Stan did the same to me. He is truly a monster. I cannot believe I was married to such a person."

"That's why I came here quickly," Audrey said. "We need to get Stan here as soon as possible and let him know his secret is out. That is how we will get rid of him once and for all."

Trisha shot up from the couch and picked up her phone from the coffee table. She dialed a number and put it on speaker.

Stan's voice came on the phone and Trisha said to him, "Stan, please come over right away. I have something to tell you about the money."

"You have my money now?" Stan asked in an eager voice.

"I have information about the money. Just come now."

"I'm on my way," he said.

When the call ended, Trisha hissed and said, "What a greedy soul! I cannot wait to get rid of him permanently!"

They started discussing specifically what they would tell Stan until they heard the doorbell ring.

Trisha stood up from the couch and went to the door. Audrey and Sienna followed behind.

Trisha opened the door and nodded at Stan. She looked back at Audrey and Sienna and then faced Stan again. She said, "You have something to tell Stan, Audrey."

"I sure do," Audrey said.

Stan stared at her with a curious expression on his face as she began to tell him about her visit to the psych hospital to speak with Derrick. She told him everything Derrick had said to her and watched with satisfaction as the smug smile on his face melted away. As she spoke, his face grew redder and redder. Finally, after she finished, Stan closed his eyes and did not utter a word.

"Don't you have anything to say now? You wicked blackmailer!"

Stan still did not speak and Audrey said, "Now you listen to me, Stan. If you don't want me to call the police and have you arrested, you will leave Trisha and Ruby and everyone in this house alone. In fact, you will get out of town and never return."

Stan opened his eyes and nodded eagerly. "I will get out of town," he said. Audrey could see that he looked relieved. He had obviously expected them to call the police.

"You better leave now," Audrey said to him. "By the time I leave Trisha's house, you must have left Rosefield. If I spot you anywhere in this town, you will be spending a very long time in prison. Do you understand?"

He nodded, backed away, and then turned around.

Audrey called his name and he turned back to her. "I don't want to hear that you ever tried to call or contact Trisha ever again, do you hear me?"

"Yes," he said.

"Go!" Audrey ordered.

He hurried to his car, got in, and zoomed away.

Trisha fell into Audrey's arms and hugged her tightly. "Thank you, Audrey," she said. "What would I have done without you?"

Audrey smiled and said, "That's what big sisters do."

Sienna wrapped her arms around Trisha and Audrey and said, "Thank God that is over."

Audrey was the first to pull back from her sisters. She wiped away the tears from Trisha's cheeks. Turning to look at Sienna and then back at Trisha, she said, "Well, I guess we should all get ready to leave for the airport. Sienna, tell Bryan to start packing!"

Sienna chuckled and Trisha beamed.

"As for me," Audrey said, "I'll have to go home and tell Ken that our trip is back on. Poor Ken. I hope he has not gotten through to Faizan because we will have to call him again to tell him we're still coming."

Trisha laughed. "I hope this is the last time we change our minds."

"I hope nothing else comes up," Sienna said.

Audrey nodded. "Okay, girls, I'll see you in the evening. Who is driving us to the airport?"

"Certainly not you," Trisha said, laughing again. "You drive as though you're chasing a gang of criminals."

Audrey laughed. "That is not true."

Sienna said, "It is true, Audrey. But I guess that is what happens when you've been in the police force for years."

"Okay, then," Audrey said, "See you guys later." She turned around and left the house, her heart filled with joyful anticipation.

SIXTEEN

"Leila, please wake up!"

Leila's eyes flew open and then she shut them again as someone shined a bright flashlight in her direction. She rubbed her eyes and slowly opened them. Looking up at the person who had shined the flashlight, she whispered harshly, "What in the world, Sherifat? Why are you waking me up in the middle of the night again?"

Immediately after she asked the question, she knew exactly why Sherifat had woken her up. Reza was probably here again. But why did Sherifat need her to go with her on her secret rendezvous with Reza?

"Reza and Abdul are here. Abdul wants to speak with you."

Leila groaned. "That Abdul doesn't give up, does he?"

Yesterday, Sherifat had begged Leila to accompany her to the men's camp to see Reza, but Leila had refused. Even though she had told Zainah that she would give Abdul a chance, she was still reluctant to do so. However, time was running out for her. Since there was no chance that she and Malik would ever be together, and since she wanted children, she had to move on and take what she was given now.

Leila sighed. "Hold on, let me get my scarf," she said. She stood up and went to get a scarf, which was folded with some of her clothes near her sleeping rug. She wrapped the scarf around her shoulders, quickly braided her hair, and went out of the tent with Sherifat.

Reza and Abdul were waiting some distance away from the tent. Sherifat ran to Reza while Leila walked slowly toward Abdul, who had an uncertain smile on his face.

Sherifat and Reza were already whispering to each other when Leila reached Abdul. She forced a smile and said, "How are you?" That was all she could think to say to him.

"I'm very good, now that I have seen you," he said to her.

She stamped down the urge to roll her eyes. She had told him she wasn't interested the last time he was here, yet he had come to see her again. She said to him, "So, Abdul, I have decided to give you a chance."

His eyes immediately lit up and he beamed. "You have?"

"Yes," she answered him.

"Thank you. You have made me very happy," he said.

She nodded but said nothing. She turned to look at Sherifat and Reza once more and then her breath caught in her throat when she saw the way they were looking at each other. She looked away, envying them. She'd once had this—a love that shined so bright it could light up the whole camp. But now, she had to settle for someone whom she felt absolutely nothing for. It was so unfair.

Abdul glanced at Sherifat and Reza and said to her, "Should we move to the other side so we can talk privately?"

She nodded. They might as well.

He moved to the back of her tent just a short distance away, and she followed him. He said, "I want to marry you, Leila."

She narrowed her eyes and let out a tired sigh. "Okay," she said to him. "But we need to take things slow. Can you do that?"

"Yes," he said quickly. "If that is what you want."

"Yes, I will be more comfortable with that."

She suddenly started when she heard someone call her name. But it wasn't just someone. That was Miriam's voice. "Oh no!" she exclaimed. "That's Miriam. You have to go now, Abdul."

Abdul's eyes widened and for a few moments, he did not move. Leila gently pushed him away and then he began to jog away from the tent. "Thank you, Leila," he called out to her. "I will come back tomorrow."

Leila saw Reza walking briskly away from Sherifat as well. Apparently, he had also heard Miriam's voice. Sherifat looked like she wanted to go with him and Leila quickly went and grabbed her hand. "Come on, before Miriam finds us here!"

Before they could walk back into the camp, they stumbled into Miriam.

"Both of you... what have you done?"

Leila bit her lip. From the expression on Miriam's face, she had most likely seen Abdul and Reza.

Miriam said, "Why would you invite those men to the camp? Especially you, Leila! I expected more of you."

Leila sighed. If she was going to marry Abdul, this was the time to tell Miriam about it. Before Leila could speak, Sherifat said, "I'm in love with Reza. We want to get married."

Miriam stared at her with a confused expression on her face. "Married? What are you talking about, Sherifat?"

Sherifat said in a small voice, "Reza and I want to get married, Miriam. We love each other."

Miriam stared at her for a full minute and then turned to Leila. "Don't tell me you are in love, too, and plan to marry that other man."

"I won't say I'm in love, Miriam, but yes, I want to marry him. I was going to tell you soon."

"Now that you two have opened the floodgates, you know what will happen. This camp will be overrun by men looking for brides." Miriam sighed loudly, but she did not look as angry as Leila had thought she would once she told her about her plans to marry Abdul. In fact, she looked somewhat relieved.

"Why do you look so surprised, Leila?" Miriam said, smiling warily. "You thought I was going to rage at you, didn't you? I thought about that, but what's the use? Maybe it's just as well that those men moved near our camp. Many women in this camp constantly talk about how they always dreamt of having husbands and children of their own but had to give up those dreams when they came here." She gave Leila a smile. "With you two getting married to those men, I guess more marriages will follow soon."

Sherifat screamed and then hugged Miriam. "Really, Miriam… you approve?"

Miriam smiled. "I have no choice, Sherifat. I guess I do approve. It all seems like the Lord's doing so who am I to stand in the way?"

Sherifat drew back and then beamed at Miriam. "Thank you so much. I can't wait to marry Reza."

"Don't be so eager," Miriam said to her, gently patting her cheek. "Faizan already told me about the men's camp. He said that those men left the outside world to come here partly because they wanted to do away with every distraction… and apparently, women are the worst distractions to them. You heard what they said the day we went to their camp. Women are not welcome there. Going there will definitely be an intrusion to some of them who are not interested in marriage and relationships."

"I guessed as much," Leila said. "But isn't it the same with our camp? After all, men aren't allowed to stay here. Faizan is an exception, of course, because we saved his life and he has been here for a long time."

"I guess the Lord is about to shake things up," Miriam said. "Our camp won't be just for women anymore, and neither will theirs only be for men."

Leila frowned but Sherifat squealed and clapped her hands in glee. "It's so exciting," Sherifat said. "My friend, Aisha, has been telling me how sad she is that she will never have children of her own. I couldn't tell her about the men's camp because Leila told me not to tell anyone. But now I can. Maybe she will meet someone in the men's camp that is handsome and nice like my Reza and get married."

Miriam laughed. "Don't get ahead of yourself, Sherifat. Let's just see how things play out."

Leila listened to them with a sense of detachment. She and Sherifat, apart from Zainah, were going to be the first women in the camp to actually change things and get married. And yet, she did not share Sherifat's excitement or eagerness. Instead of thinking about the man she was soon going to marry, Malik's face remained in her mind. Even now, she could clearly see his handsome face, as though she had only seen him the day before instead of two years ago.

"Both of you should go back to sleep now," Miriam said. "We will leave for the men's camp early tomorrow. For now, we won't tell any of the women where we are going. We have to talk to the men first of all and see how they really feel before telling the women in the camp about them."

Sherifat literally skipped back to her tent with Miriam while Leila went thoughtfully to her own tent. As she lay on her sleeping rug, she tossed and turned, wondering if she had made the right decision by agreeing to marry Abdul.

Knowing that she and Malik would never be together and that Abdul was her chance to have a family did not dampen her uncertainty. However, she had to take the right and wise path. She might not love Abdul now, but she would grow to love him. Besides, love was not a necessary ingredient to a happy marriage or relationship. If it was, Malik would not have broken up with her. They would still be together today.

She finally drifted off to sleep and then groaned when she heard someone calling her name again. She opened her eyes and saw it was already morning. Quickly, she sat up and found Miriam standing next to her. Miriam had said they would leave for the men's camp this morning. She was probably here to get her so they could leave.

"I'm sorry, Miriam," Leila said, rubbing her eyes. "I overslept. You want us to leave..."

"No, Leila," Miriam said, looking at her with an urgent expression on her face. "It's Zainah. She has just gone into labor and is calling for you."

Leila's heart jumped into her throat and she sprang up from her sleeping rug. She ran out of her tent to Zainah's. When she entered, Zainah was lying on her sleeping rug, drenched in sweat. Sherifat and Aisha were holding her hand, and Bisma, a petite woman who had arrived at the camp about six months ago and had midwifery skills, was kneeling in front of her, telling her to breathe. There were towels and buckets of water near Zainah and she looked wary.

"Leila!" Zainah called out when she saw Leila. "You're here, finally!"

Leila hurried over to her. "I am," she said brushing back Zainah's hair from her face. "You'll be alright, Zainah."

Zainah smiled and then her face screwed up in pain as another contraction hit her. Zainah gritted her teeth, obviously in great pain, and Leila bit her lip. She looked around the tent. Where was Faizan, anyway? Had the midwife sent him out?

Zainah took a deep breath as the midwife instructed and then smiled once more when the pain seemed to ease up. She looked at Leila. "I cannot give birth to this baby right now, Leila. I have to wait for Faizan to come back."

"Where did Faizan go?" Leila asked, her heart racing with worry and excitement at the fact that her friend was about to have a baby.

"He went to pick up his sisters and brothers-in-law from town. He left very early this morning. I wish he was..." she moaned again in pain.

Leila gently smoothed down Zainah's hair and then backed away slightly when the midwife told her and the other women to give Zainah some breathing space.

"Now, you're going to push hard, Zainah," the midwife said.

Zainah shook her head. "I can't give birth to this baby until my husband comes."

"Yes you can, and you will," the midwife said sternly.

Leila said, "It's all right, Zainah. I'm here and I'm sure Faizan will be back any minute. Faizan will want you and the baby to be healthy, so you need to push for him and for your baby."

Zainah closed her eyes and then let out a loud scream as she bore down.

"Push," the midwife encouraged, and once more Zainah groaned and she pushed.

Leila felt overwhelmed with both pity and excitement for Zainah. She wished she should bear the pain for her friend, but it was not possible. She just hoped that this labor would not be a prolonged one and that Zainah would give birth to her baby soon.

The midwife ordered Zainah to push again, and

she did this time and let out a scream that pierced the air. She was in so much pain that Leila wanted to look away, but couldn't. And then Leila's mouth fell open as the baby's head popped out.

Zainah laughed as she looked at the head and then ground her teeth in pain again and pushed once more. The baby slipped into Bisma's hands and Leila let out a sob as the tent filled with the baby's cries.

"It's a girl, Zainah!" the midwife said exultantly and then cleaned the baby up.

Zainah laughed and held out her arms, tears streaming down her face. "She's so beautiful," she said, looking down at the baby in her arms. "Come and see her Leila." She turned to Leila and then looked down at her baby again.

Leila came near while the midwife cleaned Zainah up. She felt tears flood her eyes as she looked down at the beautiful baby in Zainah's arms. When Zainah handed the baby to her, she swallowed a sob and smiled, overwhelmed with emotions. "She is perfect, Zainah," Leila said. "And she looks like you, I think."

"You think so? I was hoping she would look like Faizan."

"She looks like both of you, actually," Leila said. She handed the baby back to Zainah, feeling suddenly too overwhelmed to speak or even remain in the tent. "I'll be back," she forced out her words, and then quickly left the tent.

Outside, Leila let the tears flow down her face. Zainah had a beautiful baby girl now and the moment was so special, even more so because she'd had the baby with a man that she really loved. That was what Leila wanted, but unfortunately would never have.

Leila dashed angrily at her tears. "Get yourself together!" she whispered harshly. She would come to love Abdul in time. "You have to go back in there." She had to be there for Zainah, especially since Faizan was not around. She needed to put all her hang-ups aside and go back in. And she was truly happy for her friend.

She took a deep breath, and when she heard the baby crying, it dawned on her fully that Zainah had a baby girl now. Her best friend's dream had come true. She smiled genuinely now, her heart flooding with joy, and then quickly re-entered the tent.

*****

Faizan looked out the window as the jeep sped to the airfield in Blima where the private plane carrying his sisters and brothers-in-law would land. His heart raced with excitement as he thought about seeing his sisters again and getting to hug them. It felt so surreal. After two years of not seeing them and hardly speaking to them, they would finally be reunited.

He turned to the driver of the jeep, the one who usually came to take Miriam to town every month, and asked impatiently, "How much longer is it to Blima?"

"About half an hour," the driver answered.

Faizan nodded and then turned to look out the window again. The wind blew through his hair as the car sped on. It was a beautiful day, fitting for the day his sisters and their husbands would arrive.

The trip to the airfield took him back to the day he and Zainah had come back to the camp and the events leading up to it.

He had gone to Nira to rescue Zainah. Somehow, she had been mistakenly shot and had almost died. Fortunately, she had not. He had been able to take her away from Nira. They had left the town as soon as she was well enough to travel. Once they stopped in Blima, Zainah had given directions to their taxi driver and they had been taken to the women's camp.

He remembered how joyful Miriam and all the women at the camp had been when Zainah arrived safely. Most of all, he remembered the day he married her. He had left everything behind in America to be with her in the desert and had never regretted it. But still, he had missed his sisters. He had missed Audrey's quick wit and frankness, Trisha's wise advice and sometimes smothering love, and Sienna's kindness and tenderness with him. His heart leaped with joy as he thought about hugging his sisters and seeing their pretty faces again. Zainah was also excited. She had bonded with them when they were in the United States and couldn't wait to see them once more.

Thinking about Zainah, he was eager to get back to the camp once he picked up his sisters and their husbands. Zainah was due to give birth at any moment. He could not afford to miss the birth of his baby. He couldn't imagine leaving Zainah to go through the childbirth without him.

The driver increased his speed and Faizan was happy about that. The sooner they got to the airfield, the sooner he could be reunited with his sisters.

They finally got to the airfield. It was little more than an expanse of land with a narrow strip where only small planes could land. The driver parked near the airstrip and Faizan glanced at his wristwatch. It was ten a.m. already. The plane carrying Audrey, Sienna, Trisha, and their better halves was scheduled to land at about this time. Any moment now, their plane would arrive.

He got out of the jeep and stood, tapping his foot with impatient anticipation. He waited for five minutes and then ten, and then more minutes ticked by, but still the plane did not arrive. He glanced at his watch again. It was now half past ten. He frowned deeply. Where were they? If only he could call them.

When at about eleven o'clock, they still hadn't arrived, he began to worry that something had happened.

Calm down, Faizan, he told himself. There has to be a reason for their delay, but they will be here soon.

At about a quarter past eleven, his pulse raced as fear gripped his heart. You are being paranoid, he thought.

"Are you sure they are coming today?" the driver, who had been waiting in the car, asked, sticking his head out the window.

"They will be here," Faizan said with irritation. "Lord, please bring them here safely."

He looked up at the sky as he heard the sound of an approaching plane. His heart jumped for joy and he smiled broadly. That had to be them.

He kept looking up as the plane descended slowly. It landed and began to taxi down the airstrip. Faizan could not stand still anymore. He ran toward the plane and waited for it to stop. Once it did, he shook his hand and took a deep breath as he waited for his sisters and brothers-in-law to disembark.

The first person out of the plane was Ken, and Faizan walked toward him with a huge smile. And then Audrey came out behind Ken and Faizan's heart soared. He felt overwhelmed with emotions as he ran toward his sister. When she saw him, she raced toward him. They met halfway and she fell into his arms. He squeezed her tight and then saw Sienna and Trisha coming down the steps of the plane. He stepped away from Audrey, ran to them, and gathered both of them in a huge hug. He kissed their cheeks. Audrey came and put her arms around them and the four of them stood that way, embracing for a long time.

Faizan finally stepped back from his sisters and looked at each of their faces. He grinned. "I can't believe you are all here," he said with a voice choked with emotion.

Tears slipped down Sienna's face while Trisha reached out and hugged him again. He held her tight and then drew back and wiped Sienna's tears away with his thumb.

"We've missed you so much, Faizan," Audrey said.

"I cannot tell you how much I have missed you girls," he said to them.

He finally stepped away from them and went to hug Bryan, Ken, and Frank. After that, his sisters grabbed his hands and giggled excitedly as they all walked back to the jeep.

He looked back at his brothers-in-law, who were carrying the luggage, and said to his sisters, "Wait, I have to help with some of the suitcases."

"No," Audrey and Trisha said in unison. "Our husbands will manage," Audrey said. "We haven't seen you in ages and we plan to spend every moment with you and Zainah."

Faizan laughed and shook his head.

"Well, not every moment, though," Audrey added. She looked back at Ken and smiled at him, and then faced Faizan again. She said in her usual blunt way, "Ken and I are trying very hard to have a baby and we will keep trying in the camp."

Sienna's eyes widened. "Audrey, must you say everything?"

Faizan chuckled. This was the Audrey he remembered. She said whatever was on her mind and he loved it.

"Talking about babies, Zainah is due to give birth soon, isn't she, Faizan?" Trisha asked.

"She is," Faizan answered as he opened the front door of the jeep to get in. Trisha took his hand once more and said, "No, Faizan, you'll be sitting at the back with us. The guys will sit in the middle and front seats." She turned to Frank, Ken, and Bryan and said, "Won't you, guys?"

The men shrugged and dropped the luggage at the back of the jeep.

Faizan smiled fondly at Trisha and then helped the driver get the luggage into the trunk of the jeep.

Everyone had settled into the car when he got into the backseat with his sisters. As the jeep raced back to the camp, his sisters peppered him with questions. After that, he asked them questions of his own; questions about the church he'd attended in Rosefield, the school where he'd taught Arabic, and life in Rosefield in general. He did miss that place, even though he didn't want to live anywhere else but the camp now.

"We have a new mayor," Trisha said to him.

"You do? Wow! So Mayor Stanley is no longer the mayor?"

"No," Audrey answered.

When there was a lull in the conversation, Ken asked Faizan about the men's camp where they would be staying. Faizan told them how he and Zainah had found the camp and about the men they had spoken to that day. He also told them about his subsequent visits to the place. "It's a lot like the women's camp," he said to his brothers-in-law. "They have regular prayers and general chores there, too. You will like the place. The only thing, however, is that your wives cannot go and see you there, and you cannot really come and stay in the women's camp. However, I set up some tents where you can visit each other when you need privacy." He coughed and looked at Audrey. "I'm talking to you, Audrey."

Audrey laughed and said, "Yes, we will need lots of that, won't we, Ken?"

Ken shook his head and chuckled.

"As long as I can get to see Bryan every day, I will be alright," Sienna said and then beamed when Bryan turned and grinned at her. Frank also turned around and Trisha smiled affectionately at him.

Faizan looked at his sisters and their husbands and couldn't help smiling with joy. They all looked so happy and in love with each other.

The drive back to the camp seemed faster than the drive to the airfield. The driver parked the jeep at the edge of the camp and Faizan told his brothers-in-law to wait inside the jeep since the women would not be very comfortable having so many men come into their camp.

Women and children milled around the camp and Faizan exhaled. He grinned at his sisters as they stepped out of the jeep. They hugged and kissed their husbands and then carried their luggage out of the trunk.

Faizan frowned in confusion as a few women called out his name and ran toward him, yelling. At first, he could not make out what they were saying, and then Sherifat got to him, panting, and said, "Zainah has given birth, Faizan. She had a beautiful baby girl."

Faizan's jaw dropped and he froze for a few seconds. And then he ran toward the tent he shared with Zainah, his heart pounding.

He got to the tent and before he entered, he looked back and saw his sisters had followed him. He was grateful for their presence and asked them to come inside with him. He took a deep breath and entered.

Zainah was half-asleep on their sleeping rug. He felt a sob rise in his throat. A small bundle was wrapped in a blanket in her arms. He went to her, overcome with emotion, and sank to his knees as he gazed at his baby, their baby. He kissed Zainah on the lips and then his gaze returned to the baby in her arms.

Zainah opened her eyes and smiled at him. "You're here, Faizan," she said. "Thank God. We have a beautiful baby girl."

He nodded as tears filled his eyes. "Yes, we do." He went to wash his hands in a washbowl in the corner of the tent and then went back to Zainah. He gently picked up the tiny bundle and lifted her into his arms. He looked into her face and gasped as an overwhelming love flooded him. His heart ached at how much he loved this tiny bundle, how much he wanted to protect her from every evil in the world. He kissed her forehead and then her soft cheeks, and said softly, "I cannot believe you're mine. I love you so much, little girl."

He bent down and kissed Zainah again and then brushed back her hair from her face. He said, "Zainah, my sisters are here to see you."

Zainah slowly sat up and turned to look at Audrey, Trisha, and Sienna. They immediately surrounded her and gently hugged her. And then they surrounded Faizan and cooed at the baby in his arms. Their eyes were moist, especially Audrey's.

"She is gorgeous," Trisha said.

Audrey smoothed her fingers over the baby's hair. She looked at Faizan and then at Zainah with tears in her eyes. "What will you call her? Have you picked out a name for her?"

Faizan looked at Zainah and smiled. "We both agreed that if we had a girl, we would name her after my late mother and her precious mom. So, her name is Isabella Zainah Gardner."

"That's a lovely name, Faizan," Audrey said softly.

Sienna and Trisha nodded and Faizan smiled. Audrey was gazing at the baby with such a look of longing that Faizan's heart went out to her and he could not help but tell her she would soon have her own baby.

Audrey gave him a small smile. "Thanks, Faizan," she said.

After a while, his eyes widened, and he said, "I have forgotten about your husbands. I need to go get them to the men's camp." He bent down and kissed Zainah. He felt reluctant to leave her. "Will you be okay while I am gone?"

She nodded. "Yes. Besides, I have your dear sisters to keep me company."

He smiled and then straightened. He gazed at Isabella, now in Trisha's arms, and bent his head to kiss his baby on the forehead.

It felt so surreal that he was now a father. He made his way out of the tent and looked back once more at Zainah, who he loved with everything in him, and then at his precious sisters, and, finally, at the little baby who had stolen his heart. He smiled as a deep sense of contentment washed over him. This was what he had always wanted growing up—a large, loving family. Now the Lord had blessed him with one. He left the tent whistling happily.

SEVENTEEN

Malik walked slowly to the bus station with his shoulders sagging. Khadija walked beside him. He had done everything he could to find Leila, asked everyone around if they knew where she was, but no one did. He didn't know what to do or where to look for her anymore. The only thing left was for him to go back to his farm. Not only had he not found the woman he loved, but he was going to an empty house with no hope of a wife or mother for Fanta.

They got to the bus station and Khadija followed him into the building to buy his ticket. After they bought it, he wheeled his suitcase behind him out of the bus station terminal. He went out to wait for more passengers to come to the bus station.

Khadija put her hand on his arm and said, "Malik, I'm worried about you. For Fanta's sake, please try to put away your despair. It will all work out for you in the end. You'll see."

Malik sighed and mustered up a smile for his younger sister. He was glad for her company but her words did little to lift his spirits. "Thank you, Khadija. Please take care of Fanta for me."

Khadija smiled. "I will. When will you come back to Nira again, Malik?" she asked him.

"I'm not sure, but I will try to come back soon." He grimaced as he remembered how sad Fanta had been when he told her Hauwa would not be her mother anymore because they were not getting married. "That means I will never have a mother," Fanta had said, her eyes sad.

Malik had not known what to say to her. He'd simply hugged her, while his heart broke for her and for himself.

A small bus near him soon began to fill with passengers as the driver called out the name of the small town where he now lived. Malik turned to Khadija and gave her a big hug. "I guess it is time to go," he said, sounding despondent.

Khadija pulled back and looked into his eyes. "Please take care of yourself, Malik. And keep praying and hoping."

Malik shrugged. Prayers did not work. He had even prayed to Leila's Jesus, asking... no, begging for help in finding Leila, and promising to surrender his life if Jesus helped him find her. But his prayers had not been answered. Now he was going back without Leila.

Malik waved to Khadija as he stepped away from her and began to make his way to the bus. After the driver had put his suitcase into the trunk, he got into the back seat and closed his eyes as he settled in.

As the bus moved away from the station, he sighed sadly. If only he could sleep now so he could forget about his failure in finding Leila and block out the pain in his heart. Why was he still so consumed with thoughts of Leila after all these years, anyway? Why couldn't he stop thinking about her?

He opened his eyes to look out the window but the people who sat on both sides of him were blocking his view. He shut his eyes again and willed himself to fall asleep. He knew that sleeping now would only delay the pain he would continue to feel once he got back to his farm and to the house where he would live alone.

A cool breeze drifted in through the window, lulling him to sleep. As he thankfully began to drift off, words from the conversation the two men on his left were having sparked his curiosity. He opened his eyes and listened carefully to what they were saying. The more he listened, the more curious he became.

"How does that trader manage to go to the desert and come back with so many beautiful rugs?" one of the men asked.

"I have no idea, really. He just told me he goes to some remote camp in the desert where only women live. Those women are the ones who weave those beautiful rugs. He goes there once a month, purchases the rugs, and then sells them at his shop for exorbitant prices. I am very sure the women sell those rugs cheaply to him, but see how expensive the one I bought from him that other day was."

Malik frowned. Leila told him many times about the camp in the desert where she and Zainah had lived for years. She'd also told him how they wove rugs there and sold the rugs to some people who came to collect them from time to time. Could these men be talking about the same camp?

He turned to the men and apologized for interrupting them. "I was just curious about your conversation," he said. "I am looking for beautiful rugs to buy and I was wondering if you would tell me where this trader who sells all those rugs is, or better yet, where the camp in the desert is?"

One of the men said, "We don't know where the camp is, but we do know where the trader is. We are actually going there now. You can come with us if you like."

Malik's heart began to race. Was it possible that God had actually answered his prayers? Was the camp these men were talking about really the camp where Leila lived? If it was, that would be a miracle and an answer to his prayers.

He began to pray as the bus drove on and the men continued their conversation. He prayed earnestly, but to Leila's Jesus, since it seemed it was him leading the way to her. Malik prayed and asked that the trader these two men were going to take him to truly did go to the camp where Leila lived to get the rugs. He remembered clearly the prayer he had said some days ago—that he would give his life to Jesus if his prayers were answered. He would do anything to find Leila, and if Jesus actually answered his prayers, it was definitely worth giving his life over to him.

The bus passed Dogon. Just before they entered the small town where he now lived and where his farm was, the men told the driver to stop. The driver did and the men got off the bus. Malik followed them out and after their suitcases had been brought out from the trunk of the bus, the bus drove away again.

Malik looked around him. He had passed by this town many times on his way to and from Dogon, but he had never paid any attention to it. It was a pretty small town with nothing remarkable about it; it was just like the town he now resided in.

The men said nothing as they carried their bags and crossed the road. Malik crossed the road after them and continued to follow as they made their way along a clear dirt path. On both sides of the path there was nothing but trees and shrubs. Soon, however, tiny huts and small houses began to appear. Malik wondered where the men were taking him as they walked on. Hopefully, I'm not being kidnapped, he thought cynically. In his mind, however, he did not really care. The risk was worth it to find Leila.

They passed several huts and houses, and then came to another road; one with cars passing by. It surprised Malik. The road seemed to be a major one. He'd had no idea that there was a major road on the other side of this town.

They walked on the side of the road until they came to a one-story building with sliding glass doors. Malik could see through the glass windows and doors. Rugs of various styles, colors, sizes, and shapes were displayed. He followed the men into the building. Inside, there were rugs everywhere.

A boy of about eighteen walked up to them and the men greeted him warmly.

"Where is Sadiq?" the men asked the boy.

"He's upstairs with a visitor. Let me go and tell him you are here." The boy looked briefly at Malik and then turned around and left.

The men continued to talk while Malik looked around the shop. He had the money he'd taken from his house before he came here. There were so many rugs here. Since his house was empty, he might as well buy one or two... or maybe he would wait and buy some when they went to that camp. He doubted, though, that the trader would give him the information he needed about the location of the camp without him buying a rug or two from the store.

A middle-aged man and another man about Malik's age strode toward them, and the two men who had brought him here raised their voices in greeting.

"You are both here!" the man around Malik's age said as he reached Malik and his two companions. The older man walked out of the store and one of the two men said, "We want to buy new rugs and we brought someone else along with us who wants to buy rugs as well. I hope you will give us a discount since we brought more business for you."

The trader turned to Malik and gave him a bright smile. "Welcome," he said. He waved his hand around the store and said, "You can choose any rug you want. We have a wide variety here."

Malik was not particularly interested in buying a rug now, but he headed toward the long line of brightly colored rugs to his left while the trader and the two men followed. Malik looked from one rug to the other while the trader entered into a lively conversation with Malik's two companions. They bargained back and forth about the rugs the men had apparently picked out before now. They finally settled on a price and the trader called his teenage assistant and told him to get the rugs for the men.

When the boy brought the rugs wrapped up in plastic, the men turned to look at Malik and one of them asked, "We are through here. Should we wait for you or will you find your way?"

"I will find my way. Thank you both so much."

The men spoke with the trader for a minute more and then left the store.

"So, my friend," the trader faced Malik, "have you found a rug you like?"

Malik said to him, "Not yet. Maybe you can help me pick one."

The man nodded. "I can do that. What is your budget and how big would you like the rug to be?" He pointed at a rug hanging on the shelf. "This is our biggest size."

Malik said, "These rugs are very beautiful. Where do you buy them from? Those men I came with told me you get them from a camp somewhere in the desert."

The trader frowned deeply. "So, you don't want to buy a rug from me, eh! You want to cut out the middleman, is that it?"

Malik sighed and said, "I want to know exactly where the camp is because there is someone who lives there I am looking for. If you can point the camp out to me or take me there, I will buy at least five rugs from you."

"It's good you want to buy many rugs from me," the trader said. "But I cannot tell you the location of the camp. I am sorry. The people who live there trust me to keep the location of their camp to myself."

Leila had told him that the camp consisted of Christian women who had either fled or had been chased out of their towns and families because of their faith. They had lived away from the world for a long time without telling anyone where the camp was just in case hostile family members or people from the past came to harass the inhabitants of the camp, or worse. Malik had to think fast or he would lose this opportunity. He said, "Just as I told you, I know some of the women in the camp."

The man stared incredulously at him.

"There's a woman there named Zainah. She's my sister and her husband's name is Faizan." The man's eyes grew big and Malik added, "The name of the leader of the camp is Miriam," He remembered clearly the name of the woman Leila had told him acted as the head of the camp. "Lastly, the woman I love lives there. Her name is Leila. She is the one I am really looking for. We lost contact some time ago but I need to find her... and my sister as well."

The man put up his hand up and said, "Ah, why didn't you tell me all this before?" He gave Malik a huge smile. "I have to be careful so I don't lose my business with them by just giving out the location of their camp to anyone. They are quite secretive. However, since you are either related to or know half of the people in the camp, I will take you there myself." The man laughed at his supposedly witty words, and Malik mustered up a small smile.

"You will?"

"Yes."

"Thank you so much," Malik said, almost hugging the man. Joy filled his heart. He had expected the man to just give him directions to the camp, but taking him there was way better.

The man said, "I will be going there in a month, so..."

"A month!" Disappointment settled over Malik. Why had he even thought the man was going to take him there now?

The man knit his brows and said to Malik, "Yes, a month."

"Can't you take me there tomorrow?" Malik asked.

"I am sorry, but I can't." The man said to him. "Besides, the place we are talking about is far from here. It's about a two-day journey."

Malik did not want to wait for a month. He said to the man, "Can you give me directions to the camp so I can set out immediately?"

The man chuckled. "You will never find the camp. And I am not even sure I can give you directions, as there are really no landmarks on the way there. I can only point you to the nearest town and still that will be a day's journey. After that, you will be hopelessly lost."

"But a month is too long for me to wait."

The man shrugged. "That is when I am going. I'm sorry."

Malik sighed and then told himself to be still. He had been looking for Leila for some time now; waiting for a month would not kill him, nor would Leila suddenly vanish within that time. At least he had some hope of finding her now. He prayed in his heart to Leila's Jesus, asking that he would see Leila at the camp when they finally went there. There was a possibility that she'd left the camp.

He smiled in self-mockery. Since he'd begun his quest to find Leila, he had been praying a lot to Jesus. Considering the fact that he had not yet seen Leila, that was saying a lot of prayers to someone he wasn't completely sure was God. But his mind was open to the possibility now.

He looked at the trader and said, "Okay, I will wait for one month. It's not like I have a choice anyway."

"Good," the man said. "Now, look around the store and see which five rugs you want to pick out." The man grinned at him.

Malik chuckled. "Before I do, I need to know. Is there anywhere in this tiny town where I can stay for a month?"

"Yes," the man kept his grin. "You can stay here."

"Here?" Malik frowned and looked around the store.

"Yes, upstairs with my family. We have a spare room and there's no reason why you cannot use it."

Malik blinked. This was another miracle. Maybe this Leila's Jesus really did answer prayers. But he would still wait and see if his prayers had been fully answered when they went to the camp in a month. He thanked the man and then strode to the line of rugs he had been checking out earlier. "Are you ready to choose?" the man asked gleefully.

Well, I guess the accommodation is not so free after all, he thought. He pointed out the rugs he felt would work well with his small home. As he did, he told himself to contain his excitement. After all, he wasn't completely certain that Leila would still be at the camp. But if she was, he would be the happiest man in the world. He couldn't wait to see her beautiful face again. When she had come to visit him at his father's farm, he had not gotten to kiss her because she was still married. This time, he would kiss her the way he had been dreaming about for years, and then the agony of their breakup would be totally forgotten.

EIGHTEEN

Leila pressed her lips together as she listened to the-happy, mushy conversations around her. She was sitting in Faizan and Zainah's tent. Miriam was in the tent sitting beside Ishaq, Sherifat and Reza sat holding each other, Faizan's sisters and their husbands sat together, each couple either holding hands while they talked or cuddled up. Faizan and Zainah acted as translators since Faizan's sisters did not speak or understand Arabic or French, and Sherifat, Reza, and Abdul didn't speak English. Leila understood and spoke English, though she was more fluent in Arabic and French and felt more comfortable communicating in those languages.

This meeting was supposed to be an informal meeting for the couples who were about to get married, but she and Abdul were the only ones who weren't mooning over each other. And that was because they were clearly not in love the way every couple here were, even Miriam and Ishaq, though they tried to hide it.

She and Abdul were getting married tomorrow. So were Sherifat and Reza. The whole camp had been agog since the day everyone found out that there was a men's camp some distance away from theirs. Leila remembered that day clearly. It had been about a month ago.

Ishaq had appeared at the camp unannounced with Reza and Abdul. Unlike the time when Abdul and Reza had come to the camp at night, Ishaq had come with them in broad daylight, without hiding. He had asked to speak with Miriam.

Many of the women in the camp had stared curiously at the men. Once in a while, one or two men came to the camp from town, but they were usually the same men every time: traders and the driver who took Miriam to town. But that day, there were three men. Three good-looking men. What really caused a stir in the camp was when first Sherifat and then Leila had been called by Miriam to join them. Clearly many of the women had stood outside Miriam's tent listening to the conversation, because when Leila exited the tent with Sherifat, Miriam, and the men, the whole camp was already agog with news that there was going to be a wedding.

When they had been sent for by Miriam, Leila had immediately known what it was about. She had gone to Miriam's tent reluctantly, asking herself over and over again if she was sure she wanted to marry Abdul even though her heart still belonged to Malik.

She had entered the tent and found Abdul there with Ishaq and Reza. Sherifat was sitting next to Reza while Ishaq sat beside Miriam. Leila's guess was confirmed as she noticed Miriam and Ishaq stealing glances at each other. They both liked each other even though they tried to conceal their feelings.

Leila had taken a seat next to Sherifat rather than beside Abdul and listened as Ishaq narrated the reason why he had come. Abdul and Reza had told him about their intentions to marry her and Sherifat. Ishaq looked around the tent and said, "It has caused quite a stir in our camp." He rested his eyes on Miriam again. "The men at the camp don't know what to do with Reza and Abdul's desire to get married. Many of them are complaining, but many are also relieved. We haven't yet told them that there is a women's camp not far from ours, but I think most have already guessed."

From time to time, as Ishaq spoke, he had stopped mid-sentence while he gazed at Miriam, his eyes intently studying her face. Leila had sighed. Clearly Sherifat was enamored with Reza, and Miriam seemed taken with Ishaq, and he with her. She was only one who did not have a true connection with Abdul. She had looked at him and found him staring at her. From the expression on his face, she knew that he liked her and thought she was beautiful, but she wasn't sure that there was anything more there. She, on the other hand, felt absolutely nothing. However, attraction wasn't needed to marry anyone.

Ishaq spoke for a long time talking about what it would mean for the men at his camp to discover that there was truly a women's camp near.

Miriam said, "It's the same for our camp, except that I am sure there are women listening outside the tent and they now know there is a men's camp not too far from here. There are many of them who have been dreaming of having a family of their own, so I'll have to tell you right now that your camp will soon not be safe from the women here. I have control of them in some way, but not totally. They will do whatever they want and I cannot stop them." She smiled at him, clearly to let him know that it was not so serious, and he smiled back.

They began to discuss the marriage and Sherifat and Reza said they wanted to get married as soon as possible. "Why wait anyway in this desert?" they asked.

Abdul also said he wanted to marry Leila immediately.

"What do you think, Leila? Do you want to get married now?" Miriam asked her.

Leila thought about it for a short moment and then shrugged. "I may as well," she said. What did it really matter if she got married now or waited? It was not like she had other prospects. She wanted a family and she was running out of time. Now would be the best time to get married.

They had all talked at length about wedding plans and decided that the wedding would be held in the men's camp on the same day. Miriam and Ishaq would both wed them.

Sherifat had smiled excitedly. So had Reza. Abdul had beamed at her.

Leila could not bring herself to smile back. She still thought about Malik constantly.

When they had all exited Miriam's tent after that meeting, Leila remembered the women who had been listening outside the tent scrambling away. Miriam had smiled, shaking her head and looking at Ishaq. "I told you," she had said. "It won't be long before more of these kinds of connections are made and we have to plan more weddings."

Ishaq had looked longingly at Miriam, and Miriam, who usually always had something intelligent to say, did not utter a word.

After Ishaq, Reza, and Abdul left, Miriam had remained silent and retired to her tent with a thoughtful expression on her face. She was clearly befuddled. She had given herself over to staying single for the rest of her life and had not expected at this time in her life to fall for any man. Since there had been no men around for years, that had not been an issue. But now...

Leila had made her way to her tent, feeling down, but trying to encourage herself. When Sherifat came alongside her, Leila groaned. Sherifat was over the moon happy and kept chattering about Reza and their upcoming wedding. Leila entered her tent and Sherifat followed her in.

All the women in Leila's tent had settled their

eyes on her and on Sherifat. Leila knew that they would soon descend on her, but all she wanted was to be left alone.

Leila sighed wearily as they immediately stood up from where they were sitting in the corner of the tent and came to meet her and Sherifat. They sat on her sleeping rug and asked her and Sherifat a multitude of questions. Sherifat gleefully answered all their questions, and they grew more excited and animated as she told them about Reza and about the men's camp.

Leila wanted to scream at her and tell her to be quiet. She was not supposed to tell them about the men's camp, at least not now. Yet she was telling them everything, including the news about Leila and Abdul's plan to get married on the same day as she and Reza.

After that day, as Miriam had predicted, more women from the camp, full of curiosity, had found the men's camp, and then the men had begun to come to the women's camp. Some even came along with Faizan's brothers-in-law. Now both camps had regular visitors of both sexes.

Leila was not as against it as she had thought she would be. The men were dedicated Christians and treated the women here with respect. A few other love matches had been made already and more weddings would take place in the future. She found she was surprisingly pleased with that, which was unexpected considering she had thought she would be against the men and women falling in love with each other. Her heart still ached when she saw couples who were truly in love looking into each other's eyes at the camp, but it was a bittersweet ache. She was happy for them, but slightly envious.

Today, she sat looking at the couples in front of her. Their demonstrations of love toward each other was sweet but a little painful to watch.

"I'm not sure you've shown me your wedding

dress, Leila," Miriam said to her. "I did not know you had bought one."

Zainah answered before she could, "Leila is wearing something she already has."

"Oh, okay," Miriam said.

Leila did not say a word. She knew Abdul was looking at her, but she refused to look at him. She was going to wear one of the dresses that Dauda had bought her. It was a sequined dress, off-white, with long sleeves, and it had a scarf. The dress would have to do.

"I'm so excited about this wedding," Sienna, Faizan's youngest sister, said, and Faizan interpreted her words. She snuggled closer to her husband and gave a long sigh. "Isn't it just beautiful that we are here to experience all this?"

Audrey, the oldest sister, faced Leila and said, "Thank you so much for letting us also share your wedding day with us. It means so much to us to renew our wedding vows on the same day that marks our parents' fortieth anniversary." She turned to look at Sherifat and smiled. "Thank you, Sherifat."

Sherifat beamed and said, "It's a day of love, and I love the idea of a huge wedding. Besides, the more the merrier." She giggled and wove her fingers through Reza's.

Leila said nothing. She did not speak as the conversation continued. She felt like an outsider listening as everyone talked about the wedding day. She couldn't muster up the excitement that was all around her.

Isabella soon began to cry in Faizan's arms, and he turned to Zainah and said, "I guess she's hungry and needs her mama now. I wish I could feed her myself."

Zainah chuckled and took Isabella from Faizan. She stood up with the baby and excused herself. She went to another corner of the tent to breastfeed her baby. The meeting ended soon after, much to Leila's relief.

Everyone soon left the tent and Leila headed toward Zainah. She groaned inwardly when Abdul intercepted her.

"Can I speak to you?" he asked, looking intently at her.

She resisted the urge to roll her eyes and nodded. "Okay," she said to him. "Do you want to talk in my tent?"

He shrugged. "That's fine."

They both walked out of Faizan and Zainah's tent and walked briskly to Leila's. They sat together on her sleeping rug and, without thinking, Leila put a pillow in between them. She looked at Abdul as she did that. If he was offended in any way by her action, he did not show it.

At the other end of the tent, Halima and Binta were on their loom, weaving rugs for sale. Halima looked at her and gave her a coy smile. Binta winked at her. They were now somewhat used to the presence of men at the camp, especially Abdul, but their fascination with her relationship had still not faded.

Leila turned and faced Abdul once more. "So what do you want to talk about?" she asked. "Is it about the wedding?"

"Yes," he said. "It's about the wedding."

"What about it?" Leila asked off-handedly.

"Leila, tell me the truth. Do you really want to marry me?"

Leila blinked in surprise. For a long moment, she said nothing as she thought about what to say to him. Finally, she said, "I do want to marry you, but..."

"You have reservations, don't you?"

"Yes," she answered truthfully.

He said, "It's because you don't love me, isn't it?"

She gave a deep sigh. "I'm sorry, Abdul. I wish I did, but I don't."

He looked at her without speaking for a minute and then gave a sad smile. "I think you don't really want to marry me, Leila," he said in a sad voice. "I think you're forcing yourself to want to marry me, but that isn't right. Not for you and not for me."

Her heart raced as she realized where this conversation was going.

"If you don't want to marry me, especially because you don't love me, then you shouldn't. We shouldn't get married, Leila. I love you, but you don't love me."

Leila shook her head and looked him in the eye. "But what are we going to tell everyone, especially Miriam and Ishaq? Everyone has been planning for our wedding. They will be disappointed."

He shrugged. "Sherifat and Reza are still getting married, and Faizan's sisters and their husbands are renewing their vows. Nobody will really miss us and the food they have cooked will be consumed quickly, if I know the men at our camp. Everyone will get over it. I don't want you to feel guilty about not going forward with this marriage."

"I'm so sorry, Abdul. I wish things could be different."

Abdul nodded. "Me too." He lifted her fingers and kissed the backs of her hands, and then her forehead. Drawing back from her, he said, "I wish you all the best, Leila. I truly do."

Leila sighed, feeling deeply saddened. It was true that she did not love him and had been forcing herself to marry him, but she did like him and she cared about him. She said to him, "Before long, you will find someone who will truly love you the way you deserve to be loved."

"And I wish you the same," he said to her. He smiled again and stood up. She stood up as well and watched him leave the tent with his shoulders sagging.

After he left, she sat down on her rug again with her heart aching. She was probably going to remain single for the rest of her life. It had not been so bad when everyone around her was as single as she was. Even though it was painful then, now with all these love matches being made and wedding plans in place for the future, it was excruciating.

She stretched out on her sleeping rug and stared at the empty space in front of her. She felt numb and empty, but without a doubt she knew the right decision had been made. She was thankful to Abdul for stopping her from making a big mistake. There was no point marrying him when the thought brought her so much confusion and doubt. Most of all, it was unfair of her to marry him when she did not love him. Now he could meet and marry someone who would love him. Still, the thought of spending the rest of her life alone did not sit well with her.

"Oh, Lord," she prayed, "please help me to be happy, truly happy for everyone who is finding love and getting married in this camp. And most of all, please help me to forget about Malik and give me contentment, because that is what I crave."

She shut her eyes and sighed. She needed contentment more than anything else— contentment and acceptance, or she would not be able to go on.

She groaned as Malik's face appeared in her mind. "Oh Lord, I just asked that you help me forget about him. Why am I still thinking of him?"

A gentle but firm voice whispered in her heart. "Pray for him, daughter. Now!"

She blinked in surprise. Without a doubt, the voice belonged to the Lord, but why was he asking her to pray for Malik? "Lord, I am supposed to forget about him, not pray for him."

Again she heard the words, "Pray for him now!"

"But I don't know what to pray for," she said. "Okay... I guess it's for his salvation." She listened but heard nothing more.

She began to pray earnestly that the Lord would save him and give him peace and happiness. She also asked the Lord to be with him always and protect him wherever he was. "If he has found love again," she prayed reluctantly this time, "I ask that he will be forever happy with the woman he loves. Thank you for saving him."

After she finished praying for Malik, she sighed again, her heart heavy. Now that she had prayed for him, she would think about him constantly. "Thank you, Lord," she said, sulking and slightly put off. This was the last thing she needed right now, thinking and praying for Malik. Especially for him to live happily ever after with whoever he'd found.

You are being selfish, she thought. Even if you are never going to see him again, the least you can do is pray for his salvation.

She pressed her lips together. That was true. She had to let go of her selfish desire to be with him and start praying regularly for his salvation. It would be hard to keep him constantly and intentionally in her mind and thoughts again, but she had to do it. Because his salvation was much more important than their broken love and her wounded heart.

NINETEEN

Malik hugged Sadiq's two children and smiled at Sadiq's wife. "Thank you so much, Sana, for your hospitality." He smiled at the children again and said to them, "I will miss you."

He had stayed in this house for a month and the family had been very kind to him. Every day, he'd gone down to the store with Sadiq and watched the man sell his rugs. Once in a while, he helped Sadiq around the store and also helped with some of the daily house chores.

Every day he'd tried to stamp down his impatience. Sadiq and his wife, and even his little sons, had gone out of their way to make him comfortable in their home. The least he could do was show his constant appreciation. Still, he had counted the days before they could go to the women's camp to see Leila. Finally, that day had come. His heart raced, as though it would leap out of his chest at any moment.

Sadiq's wife smiled at him. "You have been such a good guest. It's been easy to have you in our home. I hope you find the love of your life and both of you live happily ever after," she said.

Malik beamed and thanked her.

After he had waved again to Sadiq's wife and children, he carried his suitcase down the stairs while Sadiq followed him.

Sadiq gave instructions to his assistant, who would be in charge of the store while he was away. The plan was for him to drive to the camp with Malik, purchase the rugs he wanted to buy, and immediately head back to his house. The journey would be a long one, Sadiq had said. Malik knew he would be crazy with impatience during the trip. Every night since he'd come here, he'd dreamt of seeing Leila, holding her, kissing her.

Malik got into the black truck parked near the store. Before Sadiq got in, Malik brought out the ring he had bought for Leila to propose to her when he found her, looked at it, and then put it back in his pocket.

Sadiq got into the driver's seat and drove off immediately, and Malik took in a deep breath as the cool morning breeze blew on his face.

They chatted as they drove along the winding roads, through small towns and villages, and down deserted roads. Twice, they stopped at a roadside canteen to eat. By the time they got to the border, it was already nightfall. They crossed the border without any problems and continued their journey. Soon, Malik grew sleepy. He turned to Sadiq and said, "Aren't you feeling even a little sleepy, man?"

Sadiq smiled. "I've gotten used to driving this road to the camp without much sleep. I need to get there as soon as possible and then get back to my store and my family. I will sleep when I get home."

"Are you a superhero?" Malik laughed. "Because it takes special powers to drive as long as you do without sleeping."

"Well, I might get a little sleep on my way back. Sometimes I stop at a motel and sleep for an hour or two before continuing my journey, but on this leg of the journey, I won't sleep."

Malik stretched and yawned. "Well, I think I

will get some sleep. I'm a human being, unlike some people."

Sadiq grinned and then focused on the road fully.

Malik soon drifted off to sleep. And then he felt someone or something tug at his sleeve, and whisper, "Wake up!"

Terror filled his heart and he immediately woke up. His eyes widened in fear as he saw that they were heading for a cliff. He turned and saw Sadiq had fallen asleep at the wheel. They would go over the cliff in less than a minute.

Malik screamed, "Sadiq! Wake up!"

Sadiq instantly awoke and stepped on the brakes. The car tires screeched and the car finally came to a halt just before they went over the cliff.

Sadiq's mouth fell wide open as he stared with a look of horror at the cliff in front of them. "What happened?" he asked.

"What happened? You fell asleep!" Malik told him in a shaky voice. "We were about to go over that cliff."

Sadiq covered his face with his hands and shook his head. "We would have died, Malik, if you had not woken up just in time."

Malik frowned. "I would not even have woken up if something or someone had not tugged on my sleeve and told me to wake up. I actually knew something bad was about to happen before I opened my eyes." He clearly remembered the voice and the tug on his sleeve. It was all so strange.

"Well," Sadiq said, "whatever it was or whoever it was, we owe our lives to them. We are very lucky to be alive."

Malik shook his head slowly. "No, not lucky. Blessed."

"You are right," Sadiq said. "I should not have stayed up as late as I did yesterday. Anyway, I am glad you woke up and definitely glad you came along with me on this trip." He started the car again, reversed it, and they drove onto the road once more.

All through the rest of the journey to the camp, Malik stayed awake. He thought about the voice that had woken him up and how they would have been killed if not for it. Somehow he knew someone had been praying for him.

After driving for a long time, they entered a vast desert. All around them was nothing, absolutely nothing, except for sand—lots of sand. They drove for hours, and Malik grew increasingly tired and frustrated. "When are we going to get there?" he asked sullenly.

"Be patient, my friend," Sadiq told him.

Sadiq faced the road again and continued to drive. Malik said to him, "You were right, Sadiq. I would never have found this place on my own."

"We are almost there," Sadiq said.

They continued driving for another hour, and Malik narrowed his eyes at Sadiq. "Why did you tell me we were almost there when we are still so far away?"

"Because we are almost there," Sadiq said. He pointed. "Look!"

Malik's heart raced as he saw what looked like a multitude of tents some distance away. He turned to Sadiq with his heart drumming, excitement running through him, and said, "I can't wait to see my Leila." He suddenly became nervous and added, "What if she doesn't want to see me?"

"Of course she will want to see you," Sadiq said.

"What if she doesn't love me anymore? What if she has met and fallen in love with someone else?"

"Firstly, you are worrying too much," Sadiq told him. "Also, this is a women's camp. In all the years I have been coming here, I haven't seen any man around apart from Faizan and the driver who takes Miriam to town... and I know that man is married."

Malik smiled at Sadiq, taking encouragement in his friend's words.

Sadiq turned briefly to him and smiled. "I am sure Leila still loves you and there is no man around anyway for her to fall in love with. You see that..." he suddenly stopped speaking as he parked in front of a tent. Frowning, he turned to Malik and said slowly, "The whole place is deserted. How come?"

Malik looked around. The place did look deserted.

Sadiq said, "Sometimes, I arrive here during their morning or evening prayers, but when I do, I hear the sound of their voices, praying or talking. And then, there are usually a few people around. Today, I can hear nothing and I see no one."

Malik's heart sank. Had the women moved camp?

Sadiq came out of the truck and Malik came out, too. Sadiq stood in front of the tent and called out, "Miriam, I am here!"

No one answered. He called out again, but still there was no answer. Finally, he said to Malik, "We need to go inside the tents to check." He went into a tent near them and Malik followed him. They looked around. Everything seemed intact. The tent was not empty. There were rugs and pillows and even clothes everywhere, but there was no one in the tent.

"This is so strange," Sadiq said. And then his eyes widened. "Maybe they have moved camp, but this time Miriam did not tell me."

Malik stared at him. "They have moved before?"

"Yes. They were in a different location until a few years ago when they moved for a reason I do not know. Miriam came to town and told me about it and then led me to their new location. I hope that isn't the case this time. That will be really bad for my business if they have moved without letting me know." Sadiq shut his eyes.

Malik shook his head. "No, it cannot be," he said. "I didn't come all this way only to…" He could not finish his sentence as a sob rose in his throat. He had been so excited about the prospect of seeing Leila again. What would he do if they had truly moved? No, they could not have moved. Not now.

He looked around the tent again and said to Sadiq, "There are clothes and personal items in this tent. I don't think they have moved."

"Let's go and check the other tents," Sadiq said.

They went from one tent to the other. Malik felt like a creep. There were only women in this camp and they were intruding into their private space. Still, it was strange that no one was here and yet all their things were intact. Nothing had been taken.

When they came out of yet another tent without seeing anyone, Sadiq said, "I cannot imagine that they would move to a different camp without taking their things with them."

Malik's ears suddenly perked up as he heard voices in the distance. He turned toward the direction of the voices and saw half a dozen women coming toward him.

Sadiq said, "Look at those women coming toward us."

"Yes, I can see them, Sadiq." Malik began to walk toward the women and Sadiq followed him. When they reached them, Sadiq greeted the women and they greeted him back. They turned to Malik, looking at him with shy smiles on their faces.

"You are from the men's camp? You did not attend the wedding?"

Malik raised his brows to ask them what wedding and what men's camp, but Sadiq beat him to it.

One of the women said, "There's a double wedding taking place in the new men's camp we discovered just a while ago." She sounded animated and excited. "Everybody is there. We just came to get some things from our tent before going back." The women hurried away before Sadiq and Malik could ask them where the men's camp was.

Malik followed them immediately and so did Sadiq. The women hurried into one of the tents and Malik and Sadiq stood outside, waiting for them to come out again. One of the women came out immediately and Malik said quickly to her, "Can you take us to that men's camp?"

She shrugged. "Okay." Her eyes studied Malik's and then moved up and down his body and back to his face. She smiled sweetly at him. "You're handsome," she said. "If you stay here, one of the girls will probably scoop you up."

Malik smiled in amusement and said to her, "Actually, I am looking for one of the women here in particular. Her name is Leila."

The woman tilted her head toward Malik and said, "Leila? She's definitely taken now. She and Abdul were one of the couples who got married today. Two couples did and three others are renewing their marriage vows."

Malik's head began to swim and his vision blurred. Leila was married and married today of all days? Just when he'd finally found her again, now she was married to someone else. He felt like weeping, like sitting on the desert sand and sobbing his heart out. How could this have happened? What awful luck he had. He had arrived here a day too late, right on the day when the love of his life was getting married to someone else.

He shut his eyes and Sadiq said, "Malik, are you alright? You look like you're about to pass out."

Malik opened his eyes again and tried to steady himself on his feet. The woman was looking at him strangely. She said, "Maybe you should come into our tent and sit down."

He shook his head. "No, I still want to see Leila."

Even if she was married to someone else now, he wanted to see her face. Just once. "Can you please take us to the men's camp?"

"Okay," the woman said in a small voice. She looked back into her tent and called out, "Let's go, girls! They will soon start serving the food. I'm hungry."

Malik felt like throwing up. Leila had gotten married. The fact that she'd gotten married was not the surprising thing, because Leila was beautiful and any man would be lucky to marry her. But what was surprising was that she'd gotten married on this day, when he'd finally found her. She had married someone other than him. And the most troubling thing was that she had probably fallen out of love with him and in love with this new man.

"I really think you should sit down," Sadiq said to him. "At least for a minute or two."

Malik shook his head vigorously. "No, I want to see Leila." He wanted to look her in the eye and see if she had truly fallen out of love with him or if she had just settled and married another man. It wasn't as if it was going to help. She was already married and there was nothing he could do about it. But still, he had to see her. He had come all this way to do so and he was not going back until he did.

The women soon came out of the tent. They walked in front, while Malik and Sadiq walked behind them. Malik's heart hurt as he pictured Leila's beautiful face. For the past month since Sadiq had told him he would take him to this camp, Malik had continuously pictured himself with Leila; pictured her saying yes when he asked her once more to marry him and pictured them getting married immediately. He had planned to tell her that he had decided to put his faith in Christ, especially as his prayers had been answered miraculously, but now everything seemed like a joke. Like someone was playing a cruel joke on him.

He tried not to think about Leila being with another man as he followed the women, but images of her wrapped in a stranger's arms haunted him. Soon, he began to think that going to Leila's wedding where she had married someone else was a really bad idea.

Maybe I should turn back. What was the point of putting himself through more agony by going to see her now with her new husband?

He turned and said to Sadiq, "I don't think I can bear to see her married to someone else," he said. "I want to go back."

"Are you sure?" Sadiq frowned.

"Yes, I am sure," Malik said. Now, he could hear faintly the sound of singing and laughter. "I need to go now," Malik said and turned around. He began to walk away, back to the women's camp; back to the truck.

"Wait, Malik!" Sadiq called out.

Malik stood still, waiting for Sadiq to catch up to him. When he did, Malik began to walk fast again. They made their way back to the truck parked in front of Miriam's tent. Sadiq said to Malik, "Will you be all right waiting for me here? I have to go and find Miriam."

Malik groaned. "I cannot bear to stay in this place a minute longer."

"Please. I will only be a minute. Let me just go and find Miriam." He walked away briskly before Malik could say anything more.

When he was just a dark figure on the horizon, Malik bent his head and closed his eyes. It had all gone wrong. With all his heart, he regretted the day he'd broken up with Leila. If only he could relive that day again, he would make a totally different decision.

"But you would not have come to truly know me."

Malik jerked his head up. Who had said that? Was he imagining things now? He was hearing voices these days, and the voice he'd just heard sounded like the one that had saved him and Sadiq from being killed on the way here. Was he hearing the voice of God?

He felt a little afraid and intrigued at the same time, and he told himself to calm down. All he wanted was for Sadiq to come back quickly so they could leave. The earlier he left this place, the better.

"Get out of the car, Malik, and look behind this tent."

Malik's eyes widened in fear. The voice again, even clearer now than the last time. Again, the voice said, "Remember what you promised you would do when you found her."

Malik's heart pounded with fear and curiosity. Should he obey this voice or just ignore it. He thought about it for only a second and decided to obey. The voice had saved him from death just the day before, after all.

He got out of the truck and walked behind Miriam's tent. And then his heart stopped. A woman was crouching behind the tent, crying softly. He walked slowly toward her, his emotions roiling. She had her back to him, but he would recognize her form anywhere, even if he couldn't see her face.

The nearer he got to her, the more he was sure it was Leila. But why would she be here, crying on her wedding day?

She apparently heard his footsteps and turned toward him. And then his mouth dropped open. It was truly her. "Leila!" he called out.

Her eyes widened in clear shock and she stared at him as though he were a ghost. She shut her eyes and opened them again. "Malik! Is it you? But how are you here?"

"Leila, oh Leila!"

"Malik!" she cried and raced toward him. She fell into his arms and sobbed. "I cannot believe you're here.".

His heart pounded as he held her close. With all his heart, he wanted to kiss her, but he knew he couldn't. He had not been able to when she came to Dogon to see him two years ago because she was still married to Dauda then. Now he still couldn't kiss her because she was married to someone else. Depression descended on him, but he quickly pushed it away. At least she was in his arms. He had dreamt of seeing her for so long and here she was.

She pulled away from him and stared at his face. She said softly, "What are you doing here?"

He reached out and wiped the tears from her eyes. "Why are you crying, Leila?"

She gazed at him with a look that tore at his heart. Her eyes held an unmistakable love for him as she said, "I was weeping because of you. Because I missed you so much." She touched his cheek. "And now here you are. I cannot believe it."

He felt too overwhelmed to speak, and then he said, "I wish I had come a day earlier. Now you're married."

Confusion crept into her features and she said, "I am not married, Malik. Who told you I was?"

His mouth fell open and he said, "A woman I saw when I came here told me your wedding was taking place at a camp not far from here."

Leila said, "I was supposed to get married today, but I couldn't do it. I am still in love with you. I couldn't marry someone else even though I thought I would never see you again." She searched his eyes and shook her head. "I still cannot believe you're here, Malik."

Malik felt excitement running through him. He said to her, "You're telling me you're not married, Leila?"

"No, Malik, I am not." And then, before he could say anything, she leaned in and gave him the sweetest kiss ever. His heart pounded as they kissed and then she drew back again. She said with a smile, "Would I kiss you if I were?"

He couldn't think properly after that kiss, nor could he speak. After a minute, he finally found his voice. "Wow! I have been dreaming of kissing you for so long." He gave her a huge smile, joy enveloping him. He winked at her and said, "I won't actually believe you are standing here before me until I have kissed you the way I have been dreaming of kissing you for years." He gently pulled her into his arms, and this time he kissed her passionately and deeply, savoring her lips while his heart felt like it would explode.

Finally, he pulled away and she said, "Are you convinced now?"

He nodded and then remembered the ring he had bought for her. He knelt in the sand, brought out the ring from his pocket, took her hand, and looked up at her. He said, "Leila, you're all that I ever wanted, the only woman I have ever loved."

She covered her mouth as she looked down at him with tears in her eyes. It was at the tip of his tongue to ask her to marry him when he suddenly remembered his promise—that he would give his life to Jesus if he found her. He now knew who had spoken to him some minutes ago and saved his life. It was her Jesus, and now, her Jesus would be his.

She started to weep softly as she looked at the ring and at his face, and then nodded even though he had not asked her yet.

"No, Leila, before I ask you to marry me, I know you want me to share your faith, and I want to do that now."

Her jaws dropped and she said, "Really Malik? You will give your heart to Jesus for me?"

"No, Leila, not for you. At least, not totally. For

me… and because I now know that your Jesus is real. I want Him to be mine as well."

She stared at him in confusion and he said, "It's a long story. I am ready to give my heart to him if you will pray for me."

Leila nodded eagerly. "There's nothing I would want more," she said.

He smiled, shut his eyes, and listened as Leila prayed for him. After that, she asked him to repeat the words of prayer after her, and he did. He prayed the words from his heart, and as he prayed, committing his life to the one who'd died for him, he felt his chest expand. Love like he had never known enveloped him and overwhelmed him. When he was through praying with Leila, he opened his eyes and knew he was forever changed.

Leila smiled at him and said, "How do you feel?"

He looked up at the sky, which seemed somehow bluer and brighter, and then looked at Leila's pretty face. "I feel brand new, Leila. Like a completely new person."

Leila chuckled. "Well, that's good, but I hope the Malik I love is still in there. The one who wanted to ask me to marry him."

He laughed and looked at the ring in his hand. "Yes, I guess he's still here." Malik said, "So, Leila, I'm asking you to marry me again. Will you be my wife?"

Leila squealed. "Yes, Malik. I will be your wife!"

Malik stood up and gathered her into his arms. He drew back and then kissed her. She pulled back and he groaned and reached for her again.

"No, Malik," she said, her voice filled with excitement. "I have an idea."

He raised his brows. "What is it?"

"I was supposed to get married today, so why don't I?"

Malik tilted his head and studied her face. "What do you mean?"

"I mean there is a wedding ceremony going on now. Let's go and get married, Malik. Now."

"Now?" he said.

"Yes, now! Do you want to marry me now?"

Malik smiled at her. "There's nothing I would want more."

She took his hand. "Then let's go before the wedding ceremony is over and everybody disperses. Miriam and Ishaq will wed us."

He walked away with her, his heart pounding with anticipation. Never in a million years could he have hoped for a better ending than what was happening now. Not only had he found Leila, but they would be getting married today. God had truly given him a miracle. A huge one.

Leila pulled her hand away from his, giggling. "I will race you there," she said, and began to run as fast as she could.

He went after her, laughing and racing toward his new future; a future he knew would be full of love and laughter. He couldn't wait to spend the rest of his life with the woman he'd fallen in love with the first time he saw her, and with the God he'd given his heart to moments ago.

TWENTY

Audrey stood in front of the makeshift altar in the men's camp, holding Ken's hand and smiling at him. Behind them was a crowd consisting of men and women from both camps. To her right was Trisha and Frank, and to her left, Sienna and Bryan. They all held hands, ready to renew their vows and make their parents proud on this day that their parents would have celebrated their fortieth anniversary. Sherifat and Reza had already been joined together by Ishaq and Miriam; now it was their turn. Not to be married again, of course, but to declare their enduring love to each other.

She could not stop smiling at Ken. He looked so handsome in his dress shirt and pants. She was thankful she had brought along the cream satin dress she was wearing now.

"You look beautiful, Audrey," Ken said, looking deep into her eyes, the expression on his face one of overwhelming joy.

"You look very handsome yourself," she said to him, and wove her fingers through his.

She looked at Sienna, Bryan, Trisha, and Frank. Sienna and Trisha had tears in their eyes, while Bryan and Frank looked at them with such love, just the way Ken was looking at her now. It actually felt like they were just getting married. Her heart was full. They had all come a long way with their spouses. A lot had happened over the years and yet the Lord had been kind to them and seen them through all their difficulties. She and her sisters had husbands who loved them dearly. She couldn't wait to renew her marriage vows with Ken.

Miriam asked them to repeat the vows after her. First, Sienna and Bryan repeated their marriage vows, and then Trisha and Frank did. Lastly, Audrey repeated the vows with tears running down her cheeks. After that, Ken began to say his vows, and she felt as though her heart would burst with joy. She would get to spend many more years with this precious man who was her husband. There was nothing better than that. They had come a long way, and in spite of the pain they shared at not being able to have a baby, they still held out hope that one day it would happen. Audrey only hoped that it was not too late.

After Ken said his vows, Ishaq smiled at her and Ken, and then at her sisters and their husbands. He announced, "I now declare you men and wives again." He looked at Ken, Frank, and Bryan and said, "You may kiss your brides."

The entire crowd in the large tent cheered and clapped. Ken gently took Audrey's face in his hands and kissed her. When he stepped back slightly from her, he wiped the tears from her eyes with his thumb and she grinned at him. "You've been the best husband any woman could ever ask for," she whispered.

He kissed the back of her hand and said, "And you are the best wife any man could ever hope for. Thank you for marrying me, Audrey."

Miriam told them to turn around to face the crowd, and then said, "Everyone, let's celebrate these couples who have made a vow before God to continue their marriages for years to come."

The crowd cheered again and Audrey swallowed a sob. She turned to look at Trisha and Sienna and saw that their faces were glowing with happiness. They started to walk out of the large tent, and Audrey smiled as the crowd cheered.

Suddenly, she stopped in her tracks when someone... no, two people ran into the tent, yelling, "We want to get married!"

The two yelling people came near, and Audrey saw it was Leila and another man who was not Abdul. Yesterday, Leila had told them all that she could not marry Abdul because she did not love him. Now she was here, screaming that she wanted to marry another man. Audrey was confused.

The crowd went berserk, and then, from the front of the crowd, Zainah stood up and screamed. "Malik! You're here!"

The man Zainah called Malik looked at her and his eyes grew round. He ran to her and hugged her tightly.

Audrey turned to Ken with a curious expression on her face. "What is going on?" she whispered.

He shook his head. "I have no idea."

Ishaq raised his hands to still the crowd. When all the noise finally died down, he said, "Can someone please tell me what is happening here?"

Zainah spoke up. "This man is my brother, Malik. He and Leila have loved each other for a long time but were separated due to unfortunate circumstances. This is not something that just suddenly happened. They belong together, these two."

Audrey's mouth fell wide open. This was so strange. She looked at Leila and saw she was brimming with joy. Audrey took a deep breath and smiled. Since they'd come to the camp, Leila had been moody, and she had never seen her smile. But now she was glowing and had the biggest smile on her face. She looked really happy and in love with the man beside her.

Leila and Zainah's brother went to the front of the crowd. They stood before Miriam and Ishaq.

Miriam said, "So this is the Malik you've been talking about for such a long time, Leila."

Leila nodded.

"Well then, I guess I have no problem marrying you both. Do you, Ishaq?"

Ishaq looked thoughtfully at both of them. Leila had broken up with Abdul, who was his friend. Audrey held her breath. She would not be surprised if he declined.

He didn't speak for a full minute, and then he finally said, "Okay, Miriam. If you think it's a good idea to marry them, then I have no problem with it. I guess we will have another wedding."

Audrey giggled and said to Ken, "Wow! This is unexpected, and yet so fitting to the end of this special occasion."

She found a seat with Ken near Faizan and Zainah. Faizan was holding baby Isabella, and Audrey immediately lifted the precious bundle from him. She kissed the baby's cheeks, took a deep breath, and rocked Isabella in her arms. This was what she and Ken had been praying for—a precious little baby. The Lord had not yet answered their prayers, but at least she was holding her little niece in this beautiful, exotic place. That would have to be enough for now.

As Miriam and Ishaq joined Leila and Malik together in holy matrimony, Audrey listened absent-mindedly, preoccupied with the baby in her arms. From time to time, she turned to smile at Ken. Whenever she did, he smiled back and whispered, "I love you, Audrey." She knew it was his way of encouraging her because he knew her so well. He knew that holding this baby would bring up a lot of emotions for her. She was happy and grateful for today, for being able to renew her vows to Ken and mark their parents' anniversary with her sisters and their husbands, but she also felt a little sad.

After the wedding vows had been said and Miriam had declared the couple man and wife, Audrey cheered with the crowd.

Everyone soon filed out of the tent after Leila, Malik, Sherifat, and Reza. Miriam had arranged for a photographer to come to the camp to take pictures. After the newly wedded couples had their photographs taken with well-wishers around them, Audrey and Ken had their pictures taken.

After that, the photographer took Sienna and Bryan's picture, and then Trisha and Frank's. The photographer took a picture of Faizan and Zainah holding their baby, and then they all stood together to take a joint family photograph. Audrey stood beside Ken, Sienna and Bryan stood to their right, and Trisha and Frank, their left.

"Where should we stand?" Faizan asked the photographer.

Audrey said, "You and Zainah and the baby can come and stand in front of Ken and I." she grinned. "Since we are the tallest couple here, you will not be blocking us."

"No, you're not!" Trisha said, laughing.

The photographer finally directed Zainah and Faizan to stand beside Trisha and Frank. The photograph was taken and Audrey said to Sienna, "I'm so glad we came here." She looked around her. "This is the perfect scenery to renew our vows and mark Mom and Dad's anniversary."

Sienna agreed.

They all went back into the big tent after all the photographs had been taken. Now huge, steaming pots of food sat in front of the tent. The makeshift altar had been removed and brightly colored rugs and pillows placed in front of the tent.

Some women came and led the couples to the front. Leila, Malik, Sherifat, and Reza were already seated on some of the rugs. Audrey, her sisters, and their husbands sat on the other rugs.

Audrey smiled brightly when Faizan came to the front of the tent and asked everyone to come in and be seated. He had not told her that he would be acting as the MC of the occasion, but just like every other thing that had happened so far, it was fitting for him to be just that.

Everyone soon came in and sat down, and Faizan said the prayers to open the reception. After that, he gave a moving speech of how the women in the camp had saved his life and had truly accepted him in spite of his past. He looked at Sherifat and Reza and said, "I haven't known you for too long, but the little I know of you I like very much. You are two very special young people, and I know you will live happily together, loving each other more and more every day."

He looked at Zainah and said to her, "My love, you are my everything—you and our precious daughter. We were not able to renew our vows today, especially because of Isabella, but we will soon. I promise you."

He continued to talk about Zainah, and her face glowed. After that, he talked about Leila and her new groom, Malik. He said, "I'm just meeting you, Malik, my brother-in-law, for the first time, but I have heard so much about you from your sister and your bride, Leila, and I like everything I have heard. I feel like I already know you. You are family now. Take care of Leila. She's precious."

He turned to Leila and said, "You finally have your dream, Leila. At last, you have a husband who loves you. I pray that you have many beautiful children and will live happily together forever."

The crowd cheered again.

Finally, he faced Audrey and Sienna and Trisha, and told the short version of how he'd met them. He talked about finding them and then losing them when he came here. Now, they were together again.

He said, "Apart from Zainah and my Isabella, you girls are the best thing that has ever happened to me."

Audrey felt tears swimming in her eyes when he said that.

He turned to Ken, Frank, and Bryan and said, "You men have been the best brothers-in-law anyone could ever hope for."

He looked at Audrey, smiling. "I have missed living with you, Audrey, and you, Ken. I've missed your frankness and honesty and how you know how to give the best advice without beating around the bush. I love you, Audrey."

Audrey mouthed, "I love you, too."

He turned to Sienna and said, "Sienna, I have missed your sweetness and gentle kindness. You're one of the nicest people I know. Trish, I've missed going to see you and my precious niece, Ruby, every day. I haven't met Molly yet, but I hope to one day. I love you all and I cannot imagine my life without any of you in it."

Audrey could hear Sienna sniffling beside her. Trisha was wiping the tears from her eyes with a handkerchief.

He continued to speak about the happy occasion and about the appearance of the men's camp being a blessing that the women did not know they needed. "And you men, you are beyond blessed to have these women. I think the Lord intended for each camp to be a blessing to the other. It's our Savior's dream for us to be one, and I am happy to see it happening today, even though I was skeptical in the beginning." He pointed at the crowd, mixed with men and women. "I hope there are more weddings like this in the future, because there is nothing greater to celebrate than love."

Audrey felt overcome with emotions once more and found herself smiling throughout Faizan's speech. She finally stopped crying after Faizan finished his moving speech. A dance group put together by some women and men came out to dance and sing a few minutes later. After that, some children also sang, and then another group came out and presented a recital.

People all around the tent randomly raised one lively tune after another, and soon people were dancing in front and all around the large tent. Audrey got up and danced with Ken even though she did not understand the lyrics of the songs.

Food and drinks were served some time later, and the dancing and singing continued into the night. Multiple lamps were placed all around the tent, giving the whole place a romantic glow. Finally, at about daybreak, everyone began to disperse.

Audrey yawned, feeling sleepy. She turned, giggled, and said to Ken, "Can you believe we partied all through the night? This was such fun."

He nodded. "I just wish it could go on."

Audrey chuckled. "Not me. I need to sleep now or I will collapse right here."

Sienna and Trisha, who were standing next to her, laughed out loud. "I need to sleep as well," Sienna said and stretched.

Audrey left the tent hand-in-hand with Sienna, Trisha, and Zainah, while the men walked behind them. After some time, Audrey turned and said, "What are the sleeping arrangements tonight? Do we have to go back to the women's camp again without our husbands?"

Zainah answered, "No, all that has been done away with. I think everyone who is married will be able to stay with their other halves. That was what Miriam told me yesterday."

"Yay!" Audrey raised her hands with a grin. "So I get to spend the night with Ken."

"I think from now on until you guys leave, you can stay with your husbands," Faizan said in an amused voice.

"So are we staying here or the women's camp?" Trisha asked.

"I think there are more tents set up at the women's camp," Zainah answered.

Audrey held out her hand to Ken and he took it. Sienna and Trisha moved to their husbands' sides, and Faizan wrapped an arm around Zainah while holding their daughter in the other. He leaned down and kissed Isabella's cheek.

They all happily made their way to the women's camp. Audrey could see from the joyful expressions on all their faces that their hearts were as full as hers. At the women's camp, they separated.

Audrey smiled. Zainah was right. More tents had been set up by the women. She looked back and saw Leila and Malik go into a tent. Sienna and Bryan entered another, and Trisha and Frank, yet another one. Audrey said to Ken, "Well, I guess that one is ours."

They went into the last tent and Audrey immediately sat on the large rug that had been laid there. "Oh... what a day!" she exclaimed. "I enjoyed the wedding, but I am so ready to crash." She stood up again and turned her back to Ken. He unzipped her dress and she stepped out of it. She slipped into her night dress and lay down on the intricately woven sleeping rug. Ken lay beside her. She was thankful for the multiple pillows that had been placed on the rug. Even though it was softer than an ordinary rug, she was not used to sleeping on anything but a soft bed. Ken drew her close and before long, she fell asleep.

Her eyes flew open as her stomach turned. She quickly got up and ran out to the back of the tent. There, she threw up everything she had eaten at the wedding. Wiping her mouth, she shut her eyes, and leaned on the tent pole, feeling nauseated.

Ken came outside. "Are you okay, Audrey?" he asked. "You threw up again."

"Yes, and I feel nauseated." Audrey covered up what she had thrown up with sand and then took a deep breath and tried to steady herself.

Ken put his hand on her forehead, frowning with worry. "Maybe we can find a way to get to a clinic near here."

"No, I'm feeling better now," Audrey said. She took another deep breath and smiled to reassure Ken she was much better.

"Are you sure, Audrey?"

"Yes," she said. "Besides, how are we going to get to a clinic?"

They made their way back to the tent. Just before they entered, Bisma, the midwife Zainah had introduced her to yesterday, walked by and turned to Audrey. "How far along are you, anyway?" she asked in fluent English.

Audrey frowned. "What do you mean?"

The midwife looked taken aback. "You don't know that you're pregnant?"

Audrey stared at her. "What in the world are you talking about?"

The midwife came closer, put her hand on Audrey's belly, and patted it lightly. She looked up at Audrey and said, "You are pregnant. You did not know?"

Audrey's jaw dropped and her heart began to beat fast. She said, "No, I did not know. Are you sure I am pregnant?"

"I have been a midwife for a long time. I know when a woman is pregnant. I guess it makes sense you don't yet." The woman touched Audrey's belly again. "You've been here for some time, but it seems as though you are about two months' pregnant. Have you been feeling tired or sick? Are your breasts tender? Have you bled?"

Audrey stared at the woman in disbelief. Was she really pregnant? Suddenly, a wave of excitement crashed over her... and then she shook her head and told herself not to get too excited. She could not afford to get overly excited like the last time she thought she was pregnant, only to have her hopes severely crushed. She would not allow that to happen again.

Ken said to the woman, "You're sure she's pregnant?"

"I am," the woman answered. "However, if you want to be a hundred percent sure, you can go to the clinic in Blima. There's a small clinic there where you can check to see if you are truly expecting a baby."

"But how are we supposed to get to the clinic?" Ken asked.

The midwife said, "The trader who came yesterday, he is still here. He waited for the wedding ceremony, but he will be leaving this morning. I think he's still around, but he was loading his truck with rugs in front of Miriam's tent when I passed by..."

Without waiting for the woman to finish her sentence, Ken took Audrey's hand and they ran in the direction of Miriam's tent while Audrey prayed that the trader was still there.

The man was getting into the truck when Audrey and Ken rounded the tent. They called to him, but he did not hear. The truck began to move and Ken and Audrey ran faster, shouting for the man to stop. Some women who were coming in their direction waved their hands to stop the driver. The truck came to a halt, and Audrey breathed a huge sigh of relief.

They ran up to the truck panting, and Ken said to the trader, "Is there any way you can take us to the nearest town?" He turned to Audrey. "Blima... that's what the woman called it."

"Yes. We need to go to the clinic there."

The man looked at them and said, "Okay, get in."

"Thank God," Audrey said as she got into the back of the truck beside Ken.

The drive to Blima took a long time, and Audrey was surprised at how far away the town was. Throughout the journey, she talked to Ken about the possibility of them being pregnant. She kept smiling while telling herself not to get too excited. If she was not really pregnant, she would be devastated.

"I hope we are," Ken said. "But I'm afraid to believe too much so that my hopes are not dashed."

Audrey bit her lip. She just wanted them to get to the clinic so she could find out if she was or not.

Finally, about three hours later, they drove into the small town and the trader graciously took them to the clinic. They thanked him, but Audrey didn't know how they would find their way back to the women's camp. Cautiously, Audrey said to the man as she and Ken got out of the truck, "Can we ask you for a favor?" she asked.

The man smiled. "I already know what it is you want to ask me. You were one of the couples who renewed their vows yesterday, weren't you?"

They both nodded.

"You are such a beautiful couple," the man said. "Don't worry. I will wait here and then take you both back to the camp. I might have to spend another night there, though."

"You would do that for us?" asked Audrey.

The man nodded.

"Thank you so much,"

Ken thanked the man profusely and then walked into the tiny clinic hand-in-hand with Audrey.

The clinic was old, but it was very clean and looked functional enough. They entered the reception area and the receptionist, a young woman with braids, told them in broken English to sit down at a bench in the corner of the clinic.

Audrey grasped Ken's hand and took deep breaths. "I'm so nervous," she said to Ken.

"I am too," Ken told her.

The reception area was empty except for them. Audrey glanced at the clock on the wall. The time was almost one in the afternoon. Nurses passed by them, and Audrey tapped her foot impatiently. Finally, the receptionist told them to go into the office on their left.

They both stood up and entered the office, Audrey's heart drumming. The office was small, and a young, clean-shaven doctor looked up from his files and smiled at them. He told them to sit down and asked why they were here.

They told him about their suspicions that Audrey might be pregnant and he told them they would run a simple blood test now to determine if she was. After drawing some blood from her, he nodded and told Audrey and Ken that the test would take some time to be ready. They could wait at the reception area or go home and come back again.

"No, we will wait," Audrey and Ken said in unison.

"Okay," the doctor said.

Audrey and Ken left the office again and once more sat in the reception area. They both held hands while Audrey nervously waited for the test results to be ready. "Lord, please let me be pregnant," Audrey whispered over and over again. If she wasn't, she didn't know what she would do.

An hour passed, and then another, and Audrey began to worry that the trader would leave. "What is delaying the results?" she asked angrily. "They're supposed to be ready by now." She frowned. "That trader will probably be gone by now. If he is, how are we going to get back to the camp?"

Ken put his hand on her shoulder and said, "Let me go and check. If he's still there, I will beg him to be patient with us."

Audrey wanted to tell Ken that she needed him to stay with her, but they would be stranded here if that trader left. Ken had to go.

After Ken left, Audrey looked over at the receptionist. She wanted to scream and ask why the test results weren't ready, but she restrained herself.

Finally, a nurse came to her, "The doctor is ready to see you now."

Audrey's heart raced and she stood up. "Oh Lord. Where is Ken?" she strained her neck to look out the door. "Please bring him now."

The nurse stared curiously at her, and Audrey said, "Please, just hold on a minute. My husband will soon be here."

Ken, where are you? She groaned and then sighed in relief when Ken entered the reception area. He walked toward her, smiling.

"He is still waiting," Ken said to her. "He was coming back from wherever he'd gone to eat when I walked out. He thought we were ready to go, but I begged him to give us just another half-hour."

"Thank God," Audrey said. "The doctor is ready to see us now, Ken."

They both went into the doctor's office together and sat in front of the man. Audrey grabbed Ken's hand again and squeezed it. She looked up at the doctor, eager to hear what he was going to say, but at the same time, full of fear. When he smiled brightly, she shut her eyes and relief unlike anything she had ever known overwhelmed her.

She opened her eyes again and the doctor said, "You are pregnant."

Audrey turned to Ken and hugged him tightly, joy flooding her heart.

Ken squeezed her and kissed her hair. He whispered in her ear, "We are truly pregnant, Audrey!" His voice was choked with emotion and tears stung Audrey's eyes.

The doctor told them they were about two and a half months pregnant and then told Audrey she had to start prenatal classes immediately. He wrote out the prescription for prenatal vitamins for her, congratulated her and Ken, and sent them on their way.

Audrey felt like skipping as she and Ken walked out of the clinic to the waiting truck. "I cannot wait to tell my sisters," she said happily. She suddenly couldn't contain her joy and screamed. "Ken, can you believe it? We are finally pregnant!"

Ken hugged her again and they walked to the truck and got in. They thanked the trader for waiting for them, and then held each other tightly as the man started the truck.

Audrey rested her head on Ken's shoulder as he put his hand around her waist. She sighed in contentment. In less than a week's time, they would go back to the United States, and then they would share their news with Esther. She would be overjoyed because she had been asking for a sibling for some time now.

Audrey sighed happily. She couldn't wait to start a new life with a new addition to their family. God had already blessed them with so much, now He had blessed them once more with what they had been praying over for such a long time. If there was anything like a perfect life, she had it, and she was extremely grateful.

TWENTY-ONE

Trisha opened her front door and reached out to hug Lauren. "Come in, Lauren," she said, smiling.

Lauren came into Trisha's living room and sat on the sofa.

Trisha sat next to her and said excitedly, "So tell me, Lauren. How did your date with Mark go?"

Lauren shrugged. "It went okay. He's a really nice guy."

Trisha nodded. "Okay, I know he's a nice guy. I set you up, remember? I want to know the actual details of the date. What exactly happened? Where did you go?"

Lauren sighed and said, "About that, Trisha. When Mark and I went to dinner after we left the cinema, we went to your husband's restaurant, and guess who I saw there?"

Trisha shut her eyes and then opened them again. "I'm so sorry, Lauren. I forgot to tell you that Nick came here to handle the day-to-day running of the restaurant while Frank and I travelled."

Lauren looked away and shrugged. "I just wish you had given me a heads up that Nick was in town. We would not have gone to your husband's restaurant if I had known."

"But I thought you had gotten over him, Lauren. It's been, what? Over two years since you last saw him?"

"I have gotten over him, Trisha," Lauren said. "It's just that when I saw him again, it brought back a lot of the feelings I had for him. But anyway, I have truly gotten over him. About Mark. I like him, but..."

"But you don't think he's your type, because he's a nice guy."

"It's not that." Lauren sighed.

Trisha chuckled. "I know you, Lauren. You still like bad boys." Trisha shook her head. "Stop looking at me like that. Nick has already left Rosefield, and, no, he hasn't changed."

Lauren sighed. "I guess I will continue to remain single, but that is a good thing. I'm learning to love being on my own."

Trisha said, "I know, Lauren. Two years ago, you were obsessed with being in a relationship. Now I think you are a much happier person. I like this new Lauren."

"I just got closer to the Lord and found out that I am enough with Him. He's all I need. If He brings someone special into my life, that's fine. But if He doesn't, then that's also great." She grinned. "Trisha, that doesn't mean you should stop setting me up. If you find someone you think I will get along with, then don't hesitate to let me know."

"That was why I set you up with Mark, wasn't it?"

"I know," Lauren said. "But I just wasn't feeling it with him."

"Fair enough," Trisha put a hand on Lauren's shoulder. "You don't have to settle if that isn't what you want."

Lauren beamed and said, "And for your information, I don't really care if Nick has changed or not, or if he has left Rosefield..."

Trisha laughed. "Sure you don't."

Lauren laughed along with her and then changed the topic. She asked how the trip was and Trisha told her how much fun they'd all had and how fascinated she had been with the place. "I want to go back there soon," she said.

"You said it's just a vast desert and tents?"

"Yes, and a lot happened while we were there." Trisha told her about the men's camp and how the women discovered there were men staying near them, and the love connections that were made, and about the weddings and their vow renewals.

Lauren giggled. "Maybe I should go to that desert and find me a man," she said. "Imagine those women who had no hope of ever getting married suddenly having a full camp of Christian men move close to them. Life is just not fair."

Trisha laughed. "You have men everywhere in Rosefield, Lauren. You're just looking for a particular type of man."

"Well, like I said, Jesus is the only man in my life now, and He's enough." She searched Trisha's eyes and asked, "How about Faizan? How is he doing?"

Trisha gave her a small smile. "He's doing very well. He's very happy and his wife gave birth to a beautiful baby girl on the very day we arrived."

"What?" Lauren said. "She gave birth right on the day you got there?"

"Yes, she did. It was glorious!"

For a short moment, Lauren had a faraway look on her face, and then she gave Trisha a big smile. "One day, the Lord will give me my own family, too. But if he doesn't, at least I'll still be an aunt to Ruby and Molly. I hope you don't mind if I share them with you. When we're old and grey, I'll still come and visit and play with their children."

Trisha laughed. "I don't mind… but that is only because I think by then you will have yours."

Lauren's face lit up. "From your lips to God's

ears, Trisha," she said smiling.

*****

Sienna looked back for the final time at the house they had lived in for years in Lima. Ethan had been born and had grown up here. She would miss this place terribly. Most of all, she would miss the children and staff at the orphanage. Still, she couldn't wait to finally get back to Rosefield; back to the town she had grown up in, and, most importantly, back to her sisters.

Her dream was that Ethan and the baby that was in her belly now would grow up with their cousins and aunts. Now that would finally come true. She was giddy with excitement, but somewhat somber at the same time.

Bryan came to stand beside her with Ethan in his arms. He said, "Are you ready to go, Sienna?" He gave her a big smile.

She nodded. "Yes, I am."

Bryan locked the door and walked toward the taxi that would take them to the airport. Sienna pulled her suitcase behind her and stopped beside the taxi. After the driver had gotten their things into the trunk of the cab, she got into the backseat. Bryan buckled Ethan into his car seat and got in beside him.

They got to the airport about twenty minutes later to check in for their flight. After that, they went through security and settled down at the departure lounge. Ethan began to fuss, and Sienna handed him his favorite toy. She sighed in relief when he stopped fussing, and then placed her hand on her belly as she felt her baby kick.

Bryan turned to her and said, "Are you okay, sweetie?"

"Yes." She nodded. "I felt the baby kick again."

Bryan grinned and bent his head to kiss her belly. He said to her, "Maybe he or she will be a dancer. I won't be surprised since she was conceived on the night we did all that dancing at the women's camp in Africa."

Sienna smiled, remembering that night clearly. They'd had a beautiful ceremony where they'd renewed their vows and then had fun at the reception. She grinned at Bryan. "We had way too much fun that night, and now, here we are, with another child on the way."

Bryan looked down at Ethan and ruffled his hair. He said to their son, "Soon, you will be a big brother."

Ethan said, "I am big and strong!"

Sienna laughed. "Yes, you are, and you will need all that strength to take care of your brother or sister." They had refused to find out the gender of their baby, as they wanted to be surprised.

Ethan gave her a sweet smile and then focused on his toy train again.

An announcement came over the speaker saying that their flight would be delayed. People around them grumbled, and Sienna turned to Bryan and smiled. "Well, at least we will get to spend a bit more time in Peru before we finally leave for the United States. I will miss this country, though. I think I would like to come back and visit in the future."

"I know you already miss the children at the orphanage," Bryan said.

Sienna ran her fingers through his hair and said, "Yes, I do already miss them. After we have this baby, though, I will have my hands full with two kids. That will be like a full-time ministry."

They chatted about the memorable times they'd had in Lima and their eagerness to finally go back home. With Trisha and Audrey's help, they had already purchased a four-bedroom house in Rosefield. She couldn't wait to settle in with Bryan and Ethan and start planning the nursery for their coming baby. She said to Ethan, "You will have so much fun growing up with your cousins."

Ethan, who had his eyes closed, briefly opened them and then shut his eyes again, and Sienna smiled in amusement. She looked up when the same voice that had announced their flight would be delayed announced that it was time for them to board their flight to Boise. Everyone around them stood up. Bryan lifted Ethan into his arms and carried his hand luggage in his left hand.

Sienna stood up and they boarded their flight together.

After they had buckled their seatbelts with Ethan sitting on Bryan's lap, Sienna took a deep breath and said, "America, here we come!"

Throughout the long flight back to the States, Sienna chatted with Bryan while trying to soothe Ethan. From time to time, Bryan carried him until he grew restless again and wanted to roam the aisles of the airplane. Sienna grabbed him whenever he tried to do so and forced him to sit down on her lap again.

After their second meal, Sienna dozed off. She dreamt about Rosefield and her sisters. Her eyes suddenly flew open when she felt a tap on her shoulder. Bryan was smiling at her. Ethan was in his arms, struggling to escape.

"We have landed, Sienna," Bryan said.

She lifted her brows, surprised. "We're already in the United States?"

"Yep!"

She beamed, excited. Soon, she would see her sisters again.

The short plane ride from Boise to Rosefield was uneventful, except that her excitement grew once they landed. At the airport, after she and Bryan had collected their luggage, they made their way to arrivals. She saw Audrey and Trisha waiting for them from a distance. Dropping the bag she was holding, she flew to her sisters with her arms open wide, and they fell into each other's arms.

Audrey stepped back slightly and beamed. "Welcome back, little sister."

Trisha grinned and hugged Sienna again. "I am so glad you are finally back home where you belong."

Bryan and Ethan finally caught up and Audrey and Trisha gave Bryan a big hug. Audrey lifted Ethan into her arms and said to him, "You are such a big boy now."

He had a confused look on his face as he pointed at Audrey's belly, which was now huge, and then pointed at Sienna's as well. He said. "Baby in there and in there."

"Yes," Sienna smiled at him. "Two babies, Ethan. You're about to be an older brother and also get another cousin."

Trisha giggled and shook her head. "No, not two babies. Three."

Sienna covered her mouth with her hand and said, "Oh, Trisha! You're pregnant. I didn't know." She reached out and hugged her sister. "Congratulations, dear."

Trisha laughed; her face radiant. "I wanted to surprise you," she said.

Sienna wrapped her arms around Audrey and Trisha. "So, three sisters are pregnant at the same time. How cool is that?"

"Pretty cool," Audrey said. She put her hand on her belly and smiled. "I can't wait for this boy to come." She looked at Sienna and Trisha. "And for your babies to be born as well. Our children will not lack for playmates, I'm telling you."

"Wasn't that always our dream as kids?" Sienna said. "For all our children to grow up together and be as close as we are."

"Yes," Trisha said, smiling. "Remember we had that silly dream when we were children that we would all be pregnant at the same time."

"Yes, I remember that," Sienna chuckled. "We gave up that silly dream when we grew up. But here we are now! Our silly, childish dream came true after all. God does have a sense of humor."

"He does," Audrey said. "He's blessed us with so much and we have the greatest blessing now."

Sienna turned to look at Bryan and smiled. "Yes, we do." God had truly given her the greatest blessings anyone could ever have; a husband whom she loved dearly, a precious child, and another on the way. She said, "We've been blessed with so much love and abundance."

"What do you girls think about starting a foundation of some sort in honor of Mom and Dad?" Audrey asked.

"That's a great idea," Trisha answered.

"Yes," Sienna said. "I would love to go back to the women's camp soon and maybe help them out with whatever they need."

"I would love that, too," Trisha said.

They put their arms around each other again and made their way out of the airport. Bryan walked in front of them with Ethan.

"So, what shall we call the foundation?"

"How about The Sisters of Rosefield?" Sienna suggested.

"Umm... I don't know," Audrey answered. "Maybe, but we will think of more names when we get home."

"Whose home?" Sienna asked, smiling.

Audrey shrugged. "What does it matter? We are sisters. My home is your home, yours is mine." She looked at Trisha and smiled. "Yours too, Trish."

Trisha shook her head and said, "Umm... I don't know. Frank will not be super comfortable with you two living at our house. He will probably grow tired and throw you out within days."

Sienna and Audrey laughed.

They all reached Trisha's car and Sienna got into the back seat. Trisha entered the driver's seat and Audrey got into the passenger's seat beside her.

Sienna turned to look at her sisters, her heart beating with excitement. She could see on their faces how excited they were. They were all finally together again, as it should be.

Bryan and Ethan got into the back seat with her, and she put her arm around them. She looked at her husband and son, and then at her sisters in the front seat. And then a huge smile broke out on her face. She couldn't stop smiling as they drove to Trisha's, thrilled beyond words that she was about to start another chapter of her life with the people who meant the most to her, in the town that she loved.

A LOOK AT:
A PLACE CALLED DESTINY
(THE DESTINY SERIES BOOK 1)

Intrigue, romance and the love of god – author of The Sisters of Rosefield, Emma Easter, introduces a new set of flawed and loveable characters in the destiny series.

Twenty-five-year-old Rachel, nearing the end of her pregnancy, makes an urgent dash to flee her polygamist husband Mike Caldwell and his embittered first spouse Olivia. Pregnant with her first child, a product of her troubled forced spiritual union with Mike, Rachel knows if she doesn't escape her unholy relationship both her and her child will never be free.

She has been unable to accept this way of life and feels it is not right for her to act as a barrier to Mike and Olivia and the sanctity of their marriage. Her escape plan fails, due to Fallow Creek, the polygamy commune she lives in, employing a security detail of young men who guard against escape.

With help from the unmarried pastor Keith Thorn, of nearby town Destiny, they are reminded that with faith, love and trust in God's plan they can achieve anything.

Coming June 2020

ABOUT THE AUTHOR

Like the characters in her stories, Emma Easter juggles a range of identities.

In the low-income community where she works, Easter is known as a family medicine physician who treats patients of all ages and backgrounds.

College friends see her as an accomplished musician, having studied and mastered five classical instruments—but behind closed doors, she's just as comfortable rocking an air guitar to Creed. And when she isn't giving her heart, soul, and sanity to her three young children she's indulging in her most secret identity of all: meeting new characters, crafting fresh plots, and exploring every corner of her imagination.

Across all these different roles, one cohesive thread has tied everything together: her faith and love of Jesus Christ.

Find more great titles by Emma Easter and Christian Kindle News at https://christiankindle-news.com/our-authors/emma-easter/